LEGACY AT LIBERTY LAKE

Cheryl Devenney

ISBN: 0692929223
ISBN 13: 9780692929223

"<u>Legacy at Liberty Lake</u>" is dedicated to the memory of my brother, Tom. It was he who read my screenplay version many years ago, and said, "Cher, you ought to write a book about this." Well Tom, it took a while, but I finally did. I just wish you were here to read it.

This novel is the culmination of a lifetime spent listening to my parents' many stories of growing up Italian, in central New York. They are tales of hardship, courage, determination, discrimination, pride, and love. They are the fabric of my life which built my character, and sense of who I am. I always say, my father gave me my dreams, and my mother gave me the strength to see them through whether or not I achieve them. For that I am eternally grateful.

CHAPTER ONE

Amanda Carter pulled her Lexus next to her daughter's Mustang in the tree-lined driveway of their Southern California, home. The upscale neighborhood was one of a handful of lively beach cities within commuting distance of San Diego, and the house was walking distance from shops and eateries. The location and the sought-after school district had been the deciding factors when Amanda decided to move. As an advertising executive for a top agency, and a single mom, she put everything she had into succeeding in both roles.

When she walked into the great room, there was no sign of her daughter, Carly, so she looked out the French doors toward the pool. Instead of Carly, she spotted two open beer cans on the table, still wet with condensation. Following the sound of the music that blared from the second floor, she climbed the stairs to Carly's room and pushed open the door.

"Carly!" she exclaimed with disgust. Her seventeen-year-old daughter was half-undressed, her face in her naked boyfriend's bulging crotch.

"Oh, shit," Carly mumbled as both teens jumped into action, grabbing for clothes and dressing as fast as they could. Carly didn't know if she was more worried that her mother had caught her, or that Ryan would be mad and not want to see her anymore.

Amanda paced around the house until the boy scurried out, then walked back into Carly's room, seething. "What were you thinking?" she shouted.

"That you wouldn't be home for three more hours."

"So this is how you spend your days," Amanda said, jabbing her finger at the bed. "No wonder the towels didn't get washed and folded yesterday, and your room is a sty."

"It's summer vacation. I want to have fun."

"By having sex in this house?"

Carly pulled the covers over the rumpled bed. "Would you rather we did it in the car, or a motel?"

"I'd *rather* you didn't do it at all."

Carly sprawled on the bed. "But you're the one who made sure I started taking the pill and got the HPV shot."

"That's when you were dating Jason. This Ryan kid is a loser."

"I like him."

"Those surfer types party too hard and treat women like crap."

"I can handle it."

"You're seventeen years old. Too—"

"Eighteen in a month," Carly reminded her.

"Too young to have to handle it. You're grounded, and your car doesn't leave the driveway for three weeks." She took a deep breath. "That should free you up to clean your room and do the chores I give you."

It hadn't always been easy for Amanda to raise Carly alone, but Carly was a good kid. She usually maintained a B average in school, and she always hung out with a decent group of kids—that is, until she started dating Ryan. She didn't win any scholarships, but she had a flair for fashion design and had always planned to pursue that. Luckily, her college fund would be enough to send her to a prominent school of design in San Diego, thanks to her father, Michael Carvelli.

Eighteen years before, when Michael had found out about Amanda's pregnancy, he'd asked her to marry him. But Amanda, not ready for marriage, had thanked him and sent him on his way, asking for no support from him, financial or otherwise. Yet, within two months of Carly's birth, a one-hundred-dollar check began arriving every month from him. He assured her that he would not seek any parental rights. He just needed to send the money because it was the right thing to do.

That's when she set up the college fund. She had received a check from him every month without fail until, without explanation, they had stopped a few months before. She found out why when she got a call from Michael's Aunt Maria in New York. Maria had just learned about Carly from Michael's will, four months after his death. He had passed away at the age of forty-one from a congenital heart condition that had not been previously diagnosed.

Apparently no one in the family had known about Carly, and they were now very concerned about her health. Aunt Maria told Amanda that Michael's doctor recommended that any of Michael's offspring be tested for the same defect. Amanda wasted no time in sending Carly for the test. Luckily, she passed with flying colors. Relieved to hear the test results, Aunt Maria then asked if Amanda would allow Carly to fly to upstate New York to meet her and the rest of Michael's relatives at a family reunion taking place in a few weeks. Carly showed no interest in going, and Amanda accepted her decision.

Over the next week, Carly was tempted more than once to violate her grounding, but she had screwed up big time by getting caught and knew better than to push it. Her mom checked the odometer on the Mustang daily and called the house phone randomly throughout the day to make sure she didn't stray. At least her best friend, Krystal, could come over, and Carly still had her cell phone. But she hated not seeing Ryan and feared he would drop her for the next pretty girl who came along.

Less than two weeks into her restriction period, she and her mom were sitting at a table in her favorite Chinese restaurant. The outing didn't surprise Carly, because she knew her mother could never stay mad at her for long. Finally, they could talk about something besides her screwing up, and have some fun again. And they did, until her mother dropped a bombshell on her at the end of their meal.

"You know, I've been thinking . . . I think you should go visit your father's family in New York for their reunion."

Carly almost choked on her almond cookie. *Oh my God.*

"Why? Why are you doing this? You told me I didn't have to go." She sat back and folded her arms. "I've been really good the last couple of weeks. Done everything you said."

"Yes, you have. It's not that. I just think it's something you should do right now."

Carly lost it, and shouted, "I know you, Mom!" When the people next to them looked over at her, she lowered her voice a tad. "You want to get me away from Ryan."

"Well, that's true, but I also think you should go so they can meet you. I'm sure it'll make them feel better after losing your dad."

"But I don't want to go there," Carly whined. "I won't know anybody."

"You'll get to know them. I'm sure they're very nice people. After all"—her mom smiled—"they raised your father, and he was a great guy."

"If he was so great, why didn't you marry him?"

Her mom pursed her lips. "We've been down this road before."

Carly knew that tone and changed the subject. "But I'll miss my friends."

"You'll have your phone and tablet."

Carly became anxious. "But what about Ryan?"

"Well, you know how I feel about him, but if he really cares about you, he'll wait."

Carly couldn't deny that. "But my birthday is coming up. I don't want to be gone for my birthday."

"You'll be back two days before," Amanda assured her, "in plenty of time to start design school in September."

"Mom, I told you I'm not ready to do that yet. I want to go to junior college with Krystal and the others."

Amanda sighed deeply, but said nothing.

Carly thought she'd better let that go for another time and get back to the issue. "But I'll miss you," she whined again.

Her mother smiled. "I'll miss you, too, but it's actually a good time for you to go, because I have a business trip coming up at the same time."

"Well, if that's all it is"—Carly perked up—"I could stay at Krystal's while you're gone."

Amanda handed the signed check to the server and turned back to her daughter. "You're going to New York, Carly."

The day before Carly's departure, a suitcase and toiletries covered her bed as she flung articles of clothing around the room. So far the only thing in the suitcase was Carly's stuffed teddy bear that she'd had since childhood and took everywhere she went.

"I don't even know what kind of clothes the kids wear up there in farm country," Carly yelled down the stairs. They had learned that Aunt Maria lived on a dairy farm in central New York about two hundred miles north of New York City.

Her mom walked into the room. "I'm sure your clothes will fit in fine, and if you need something else, you can always buy it there."

"Are you sure they even have stores there?"

"Don't be ridiculous."

Carly tossed some denim shorts into one of the suitcases. "Well, whatever clothes I take are going to end up smelling like cows."

⚊⚊⚊

Carly had to stop in Chicago en route to Albany Airport, the closest one to Kingsburg, and about sixty miles away. She and her mother traveled often. They had flown to Hawaii, but never east of Colorado. She liked the chance this trip gave her to fly alone. That is, until she had to change planes in Chicago. The place had tons of gates spread over what seemed liked miles, and if not for airport assistance people, she probably would've missed her connection.

When she finally reached the correct gate, she boarded a much smaller jet than the 757 she flew in on from San Diego. Now, after settling into her seat, with earbuds in place and a smooth takeoff, her eyelids grew heavy. She had had to get up before dawn that morning to make the 7:30 flight that with her Chicago stop would get her into New York about five P.M. She dozed for a while, and about an hour and a half later, she watched from her window seat as the plane taxied into the gate. In comparison to San Diego and Chicago, this airport had small town written all over it.

Tired of sitting and anxious to stretch her legs, she yanked off her seat belt and stood up as soon as the seat belt sign went off. It had been a really long day of being tied to a chair, and she couldn't wait to get off the plane. But being in the second row from the rear, all she could do was inch along behind the rest of the passengers. As she reached the door, she panicked and her stomach did a flip. *I don't want to get off this plane.*

At the end of the walkway, she saw an older woman with dark hair sprinkled with gray, smiling from ear to ear and waving Carly toward her. She had to be Aunt Maria. As Carly neared her, Aunt Maria reached out, wrapped her arms around her, and gave her a quick squeeze. Backing off, she said, "I'm Aunt Maria, and this is my granddaughter, Christina." She motioned toward a pretty, young college-aged woman next to her.

The girls exchanged cheek-to-cheek air kisses, and Christina said, "It's so nice to meet you."

Carly smiled. "You, too."

"So how was your flight?" Aunt Maria asked.

"Good, thank you."

They stood in an awkward silence until Aunt Maria jumped in with, "Well, let's get you down to the baggage area."

Christina left Carly and Aunt Maria at the baggage claim while she went to fetch the car. The two made small talk about flying and vacations to fill the time. Aunt Maria seemed very nice, and Carly could tell she was trying her best to keep the conversation going, but frankly, Carly didn't know what to say since she really didn't want to be there, and she didn't have the energy to pretend that she did. Luckily, Carly's bag was one of the first ones to come down the luggage chute, so she snatched it, and they walked outside to meet up with Christina.

As soon as the automatic doors slid open, she could've sworn she had entered the sauna at their fitness club at home. By the time Carly loaded her bag into the trunk of Aunt Maria's midsize Chrysler and hopped into the backseat, she felt like she needed a shower.

They left the airport and drove toward the highway, but before they could get on the on-ramp, they had to pass through a set of tollgates, where Christina leaned out of the window and took a card from an automated vending machine. Finding this curious, Carly asked, "What's that card for?"

"Well, the New York State Thruway is a toll road, and the card tells the attendants how much to charge us when we exit."

They traveled west for a while on a two-lane road with very little traffic. Soon Carly noticed that they hadn't passed through towns like on the freeways at home, but she began to notice the recurrence of rest stops with restaurants and gas stations.

The farther away they got from Albany, the more trees lined the road, until she could see nothing out her window but a sea of green. She'd never known that many trees existed. She began to wonder if they would ever see civilization again.

In the meantime, she found out that Christina was a senior at Columbia University in New York City, majoring in business. She planned to get her MBA and get a job in the city.

Aunt Maria changed the subject. "Everyone is going to be so happy to see you. My sister Theresa, your grandmother, would have come to the airport, but Michael's death really put a strain on her, and she needed to keep her doctor appointment today." Aunt Maria continued, "And Sandra, her daughter, is a real estate agent and had to settle a sale with the lawyer today."

"Oh, well that's OK." Carly didn't know what else to say, but she was more concerned about checking the text message that had lit up on her phone. It was her mother, so she replied immediately, *"I'm here, & bored already. Want 2 come home."*

"Has your mother told you much about your father?" Christina turned her head toward Carly in the back seat.

"Just how they met, and that he was a great guy."

"But she wouldn't marry him," Christina probed.

"No, she wanted to finish school and have a career." Carly couldn't bring herself to tell these women that her mother didn't love their beloved relative.

"It's a shame you never got to meet him," Aunt Maria said, but put a more upbeat spin on it, saying, "Well, you're here with us now."

Carly gave her the biggest grin she could muster and changed the subject. "So is it always this hot here? I wasn't sure what clothes to bring."

They finally got to the Kingsburg exit, and made their way down the off-ramp.

"Well, this is it," Christina said, as they drove through a residential section. "Looks a lot different than home, huh?" Christina had mentioned earlier that she had been to Los Angeles once, on a trip with her high school class.

Carly couldn't get over how beat up everything looked. She had seen some tacky places around some neighborhoods at home, occasionally en route to somewhere else, but some of these homes looked dilapidated. They turned onto what appeared to be the main street. The brick buildings gave the place class, but the businesses were second rate. Clothing and shoe stores stood in between restaurants, a drug store took up one corner and a bank another. They passed a post office, a shoe repair shop, and a video game store. She searched for a familiar sign or logo, but couldn't spot any. Even the gas station names were foreign to her.

"Who's that statue of?" Carly pointed out the window.

"A soldier who died in the war. Some of the Revolutionary War was fought around here."

"Oh, I remember learning about George Washington, and stuff."

"You know, a long time ago this area was really active with lots of factories and businesses," Aunt Maria said. "It's a shame really. They all moved to other countries where the labor is cheaper."

"Yeah," Christina said, "that's why you pretty much have to move to bigger cities after college to get a job."

Carly counted only four stoplights before they passed through the entire downtown and reached the other side of town, where she caught sight of a McDonald's on the corner. It brought a smile to her lips, and a growl to her stomach. She sure could use a cheeseburger right about now, but she didn't want to be rude and ask to stop. Besides, Aunt Maria had told her she had food waiting for her at home.

They turned onto another road, and the houses became sparse. Soon fields replaced lawns between them. She hadn't ever been to a real farm, but she knew one when she saw it. Finally, Christina pulled up a private road that led to Aunt Maria's house.

"Ah, home sweet home," Aunt Maria said, getting out of the car.

Carly caught a knowing glance from Christina, before she opened the back door to follow her aunt. Carly could sense that Christina understood her predicament, and she knew she had an ally. No sooner had she stepped out of the car than a collie-type dog jumped up on her and ran his wet nose along her arm.

"Whoa," she said, bracing herself from falling backward.

"Buster, get down." Aunt Maria pulled the dog off Carly. "Sorry about that. He loves company."

"That's OK," Carly said. "I like dogs."

She looked up and couldn't miss the red barn and silo, much as she had pictured they would be. But except for Buster, the only other animals she saw were a couple of tabby cats roaming around the yard.

Christina pulled Carly's bag out of the trunk. "Let's get inside. We left my mom and dad here with my grandpa, so that the food would be all ready when we got home."

"You've got to be starving," Aunt Maria chimed in.

Christina's mom, Aunt Charlotte, met them at the door. She was a pudgy woman of about fifty, and Carly could see the family re-semblance. Aunt Charlotte yelled into the other room, and her husband, Walter, came out with Aunt Maria's husband, Joey, a man in his mid-seventies who walked with a limp. Uncle Walter didn't quite fit in with the others, who had predominantly dark hair and olive skin. Obviously, Christina took after him. And now, having met her father's aunt and cousin, she knew where she herself had gotten her dark eyes.

With the introductions over, her attention turned to the scrumptious aroma that wafted throughout the quaint old farm-house. Luckily for her growling stomach, her hosts wasted no time setting out the meal of baked pasta, meatballs, homemade pizza, and green salad on the spacious antique dining room table. Unlike any pizza she'd ever had, this pizza may have even been better than her favorite take-out at home.

Though completely stuffed, she managed to finish off the over-sized piece of chocolate cake they put in front of her. She jumped up to take her plate to the kitchen, but Aunt Charlotte stopped her.

"That can wait. Sit down and relax a while first. We're dying to get to hear more about you."

Carly knew they meant well, but despite the family's welcoming demeanor, all of their questions still felt like an inquisition, with her as the suspect. They wanted to know all about her childhood, her school, and her plans for college.

"So how do you like living in California?" Aunt Maria innocently asked.

Didn't they get that it was her home, and she'd never known anything different? "Oh, I love it," she said with a smile.

At least an hour had passed before the clock on the dining room wall mercifully chimed nine o'clock, and everyone took it as their cue to get up and take the dishes into the kitchen. With so much light still in the sky, she hadn't realized the time. It never stayed light this late at home. Of course, her watch read only six o'clock. Mom would just be getting home from work. And even though Carly was still on Encinitas time, it had been a really long day, and it felt more like nine to her. Luckily, the group effort made quick work of the kitchen clean-up, and soon afterward Christina's family said good night and left.

"Well, I'm sure you'd like to go to your room, and get ready for bed," Aunt Maria said. "It's upstairs, so you'll have your privacy. Uncle Joey and I sleep down here."

Aunt Maria led her up a staircase that creaked with every step to a bedroom in a loft, where she spotted her suitcase, brought up by Uncle Walter earlier.

"You'll find plenty of towels in the bathroom next door," Aunt Maria said, then pointed to the one small window. "I opened the window this morning to air the room out, and you can close it if you like, but it might be a little stuffy up here during the night."

"Thank you." Carly nodded, and looked around the room. "I'll be fine."

When her aunt shut the door behind her, Carly stood there in some kind of freaky time warp. The room looked like something she'd seen in an old black-and-white movie, with a brass bed and doilies on the dresser. The thick air engulfed her, so she opened the window wider. As she walked to the dresser, the floorboards mimicked the sound of the stairs. *Too spooky.* Standing in front of the massive dresser and its round mirror, she picked up an old-fashioned hairbrush from a matching set that included a mirror and comb. It had the softest bristles she'd ever felt. No way could she get this thing through her thick hair.

She took some ragged books off a small bookcase and thumbed through a few titles she'd never heard of. What was she doing here? Only this morning she was in her room, surrounded by her own stuff. She hated this creepy room, being with people she barely knew, and this whole place.

She opened her suitcase and fingered the familiar contents, stopping at her teddy bear. She took it out, pulled back the white chenille spread, and placed the toy animal up against the pillow. She donned her pjs, and with cell phone in hand, she lay down next to the stuffed bear and texted her thoughts to Krystal. When Krystal failed to respond immediately to her text, she curled up with teddy and fell asleep plotting her early return home.

⊷ ⊶

Carly rolled over, awakened by the ping of raindrops hitting the porch roof below her bedroom window. It took her a few minutes to orient herself and realize that it was actually raining. *Rain in August? Almost never at home.* But she wasn't home. She sighed and checked her cell phone for the local time. Ten o'clock. Aunt Maria had let her sleep.

Before getting here, she had imagined getting up at the crack of dawn to help with farming chores. But she had found out last night that they'd sold the herd and stopped farming a few years ago. The only livestock left were some goats and the pets she'd seen yesterday.

Krystal had answered Carly's text from last night, so she took a few minutes to text her back. She didn't wait for a response. No way would Krystal be up at seven A.M. Having decided that she would have no trouble convincing her mom to let her leave ahead of schedule, she resigned herself to staying the remainder of the week to satisfy the family. So she went into the bathroom to shower and get ready to meet her grandmother.

The trip through downtown and out to the other end of town took about fifteen minutes. As Aunt Maria pulled into the driveway, Carly saw two women surrounded by flowerpots on the sizable porch. When her grandmother wrapped her arms around her and wouldn't let go, Carly could barely breathe. It was as if her grandma didn't want to release Carly for fear that if she did, she would lose her son again.

"This is a miracle!" Grandma stood to look at Carly. "Let me see you. You're just beautiful. And so like your father."

"Thank you." Carly smiled, at a loss for anything else to say.

Grandma hesitated then said, "Please, come in." She led her from the entryway into a great room. Though in an older residential area, this house had obviously undergone a recent remodel, completely transformed to reflect current decorating trends.

"This is a nice house," Carly said in earnest.

"Yes, it's lovely, but I can't take credit for it."

At that moment, Sandra, Grandma's daughter, entered from the kitchen.

"So you're Carly." Sandra grabbed Carly's arms, and leaned in to plant a kiss on her cheek. "It's nice to meet you."

"Carly, this is your Aunt Sandra. My daughter, and your father's older sister. This is her house."

"Hello, it's nice to meet you, too," Carly replied.

A teen walked into the room, and Sandra added, "This is my daughter, and your first cousin, Brooke."

Carly sized Brooke up—about her age, but trying to look older. The girl had way too much make-up on.

The girls exchanged hello's with wary glances. Then Carly resumed her place as the center of attention, answering her Grandma's questions politely, but with little enthusiasm. Two days of recapping her childhood, and reciting her favorite subjects in school was more than she could take.

She longed for some real conversation with her friends and wondered what Ryan was doing today, or more importantly, what girl he was doing it with. Her mother had been right; he was out to get whatever he could from girls. But Carly didn't care. The fact that he chose her made her special and the envy of her girlfriends. Up until now, her only boyfriend had been Jason, a neighbor kid she'd known since middle school. Carly made up her mind while Grandma went on incessantly about Michael's childhood that she would call Ryan that night.

Aunt Sandra served hamburgers for lunch with some delicious cookies, called half moons, from the local bakery. When they finished, the adults cleaned up, leaving Carly and Brooke alone to get acquainted.

Brooke toyed with her cell phone and pretty much ignored Carly, so Carly checked for messages on her phone.

When a couple of minutes passed without a peep from Brooke, Carly spoke. "So what's there to do around here for fun?"

Brooke finished the last few words of a text message and looked up. "Mostly hang out. We have a couple of coffee shops on Main Street during the day, and at night there's always the bowling alley."

"Yeah, I guess you don't have an ocean to go to the beach."

"No, but we have a lake close by, and a bunch of us go out there a couple of times a week, whenever we can get a car. If not, we usually hang out by the pool in our yard."

Carly looked surprised. "You don't have a car?"

"Naw," Brooke said. "Do you?"

Carly's phone chirped, and she looked to see who'd sent her a text. "Yeah, it's a red Mustang." Carly then responded to Krystal's text.

"So you never knew about Uncle Michael until now?" Brooke said with disbelief.

"I knew some things, but not a lot."

"Didn't you wonder?"

"Not really. Mom was all I needed."

"Uncle Michael didn't bother to tell anyone, you know," Brooke said in a sing-song voice.

"I can tell I came as a pretty big shock."

"My mom almost went through the roof when she found out," Brooke shared. "But I wasn't surprised. We never saw much of Uncle Michael."

"Why not?"

"He lived with some woman in New York City. As far as I know, he never married or had any other kids." Brooke smiled. "At least none of them have come out of the woodwork yet."

Carly got the inference, but said nothing.

Grandma broke the silence when she joined them in the family room. "Have you told Carly that you're a finalist in the Miss County beauty pageant?" she asked Brooke.

"No," Brooke said without looking up.

Grandma turned to Carly as Brooke sank deeper into her seat on the sofa. "Well, she is. They'll announce the winner at the County Fair in two weeks."

"No kidding?" Carly said, trying to contain her amusement. "Will it be near here?"

"Yes, the fair grounds are just on the other side of town," Grandma said.

"Well, congratulations," Carly said to Brooke. "Too bad I'll be gone by then." But what she really meant was "How nerdy can you get? Thank goodness I'll be gone by then."

━═╬ ╬═━

When Aunt Maria told Carly to get ready to go to the mall the next day, she was relieved. Finally, something else to do besides relive her childhood. She had no idea they had a mall around this place. Grandma had given her one hundred dollars, and she imagined going off on her own without having to talk to anyone.

To her surprise, Aunt Maria had suggested that Brooke and her friends take Carly shopping, and so she found herself getting picked up by Brooke in Sandra's Nissan. They made two stops for Brooke's girlfriends, Kelly and Lauren, who proceeded to bombard Carly with questions about her life in California.

"Do you surf every day?"

"Almost," Carly lied. In fact, she only surfed once in a while, and she sucked at it. She spent most of her time tanning and strolling along the beach trying to be noticed.

"I'll bet your boyfriend Ryan surfs every day," Kelly said. "Do you have a picture of him?"

"Oh yeah, he does," she lied again, and scrolled to his picture in her phone. She couldn't admit to these girls that Ryan was more a wannabe surfer than anything else. If she had told them the truth, it would have been a letdown for them and jeopardize her newly acquired celebrity status.

"He's adorable." Lauren swooned over his picture. "You must miss him a lot."

"Like crazy."

"I'll bet he's dying back there without you, too," Kelly said.

"He's called every day since I've been here," Carly continued to lie. She didn't want to admit, especially to herself, that he hadn't responded to her last two texts.

"Will you give it a break with all the questions, guys?" Brooke pulled into the mall parking lot. "You didn't even mention my new haircut. Besides, we're here to shop, not talk about Carly's life in California."

Whoa, Carly thought, *what a bitch.* At that same moment, she looked out the window, and got a glimpse of the mall, which consisted of a few stores sandwiched in between a JC Penney and a Sears. *Oh brother. This shopping spree should take all of forty-five minutes. Oh my God. What am I doing here? Maybe if I really sob to Mom on the phone tonight, she'll let me go home tomorrow.*

"Don't you remember?" Amanda reminded Carly on the phone that night. "I'm leaving for Phoenix tomorrow, and I won't be back until next Wednesday."

"Well, will you change my reservation to Wednesday?"

"I'm sorry, sweetie. I figured you were going to be gone, so I made plans to visit Lana in Santa Barbara. I need a little vacation, too, and she was free."

"Believe me, this is no vacation for me. I'm miserable," Carly whined.

"Are you getting enough to eat?"

"There's always tons of food around here. Their Italian stuff is much better than that place by our house, and there's this great bakery in town. I'm going to gain ten pounds, I know it." Carly also knew her mother wouldn't like that. Amanda stayed trim and fit, and expected Carly to do the same.

"Oh. Well, do you have to sleep on the living room couch?"

"No. I have the whole second floor to myself."

Amanda kept going. "Are you out of money?"

"No, I still have what you gave me, because Grandma gave me a hundred dollars to take to the mall."

Amanda laughed. "Maybe I should come up there. It sounds pretty great to me."

"Ha, ha," Carly mocked. "You don't understand."

"Look, I know it's tough being without your friends in a strange place, but it's not forever. You can put up with it for a week and a half."

⊨⊦ ⊣⊨

Because the conversation with her mother hadn't gone as planned, Carly didn't want to go downstairs to breakfast that morning. All she had to look forward to was helping out with Brooke's eighteenth birthday/family reunion they were putting on tomorrow. It was bad enough she had to go to it, let alone act like she cared.

Today would be spent preparing someplace they all referred to as 'the camp.' Aunt Maria had a church meeting to attend, so Uncle Joey drove Carly to Sandra's house, and she rode with Sandra and Grandma from there. Carly remembered Brooke talking about a nearby lake, so when they had driven a few miles out of town and the green fields of the countryside took over the landscape, Carly wasn't surprised to see the water.

Sandra turned onto a road lined with tall trees that ran parallel with a sparkling lake. "This is Liberty Lake. Named for a Revolutionary War battle won by the American colonies nearby."

Another turn took them down a long driveway that came to a dead end at a garage that backed up to a house. The three got out of the car and walked around to the front of the sprawling log cabin–style house, its porch large enough for four rocking chairs and two deck tables. From where she stood, she saw several Adirondack chairs gracing the lawn beside the water, less than one hundred feet away. A wooden dock stretched out from the shore into the lake, where a mid-sized ski boat was tethered. When she looked off to the right, she saw two matching bungalows sitting across the driveway, along with what looked like a utility shed.

"This is your camp?" Carly asked with surprise. She had definitely not pictured anything like this. She figured it would be a campsite near the lake. She couldn't help but be impressed.

"Yes, it is. All three acres of it," Sandra answered, then corrected herself. "Well, not only mine. It belongs to the whole family. We all take turns using it, and we share the expenses." Sandra walked up the steps to unlock the front door. "Come on inside."

Carly followed her and Grandma into a great room anchored by a massive brick fireplace that stretched up to the ceiling. Leather sofas and chairs were arranged in front of it. An oak pool table took up one corner of the room and a big-screen TV another.

Sandra put her purse on the long wooden farmhouse table in the dining room. Carly hopped up onto one of the counter-height bar stools and leaned on the granite counter top, which separated the great room from the state-of-the-art kitchen. This "camp" reminded her of many of her friends' beachfront homes. Sandra went outside while Grandma took Carly to the other side of the house, but she only had time to glance into the five bedrooms and three bathrooms before hearing Sandra yell to them from the car to help her carry in snack food and decorations.

Once inside, Sandra wasted no time before giving her orders to dust, straighten, and rearrange furniture to accommodate the large crowd expected to attend the party. Carly, who rarely had heavy housework to do at home since their housekeeper came every week, balked at first. But she soon saw that Sandra was working right alongside her and Grandma. So Carly did her best to pitch in, despite her resentment at having to do this much work for dumb old Brooke, who she disliked more every day.

"Well, Carly, now it's time to put on your bathing suit and take a swim," Grandma said, after they'd finished the work and had eaten the deli sandwiches they'd brought with them.

"I'm ready," Carly said while digging into her duffle bag. "I worked up a sweat this morning. It sure isn't as cool by the lake as it is by our beach."

"Aunt Sandra's going into town to pick up some more stuff for the party, so go change in one of the bedrooms, and I'll meet you down by the lake."

Carly took her bag into a large room in the front of the house, with a four-poster mahogany bed and matching dresser. A lovely window seat overlooked the lake, so she walked over and sat for a moment to get a better look at the glistening water that awaited her. Then she jumped up, changed quickly, and grabbed her towel. Before leaving, she stopped in front of the dresser mirror to pull her hair back into a ponytail.

She glanced down and spotted an antique frame with an old brown-tinted picture of a young woman with long hair pulled back into a knot at the nape of her neck. Even though Aunt Maria and Sandra had similar types of pictures around their houses, this one caught and held her attention. For one thing, it was larger than most, and for another thing, it seemed so familiar to her. She couldn't imagine where she'd seen this woman before. It must be a family resemblance to her newly found relatives. But still the woman's eyes and expression seized Carly. The face of the woman in the picture was the same one she saw in the dresser mirror.

Outside, Carly ran past Grandma, who sprawled on a chaise lounge near the dock, and dove into the water. When she came up for air, she rubbed the water out of her eyes, and said, "Grandma, who is the woman in the picture in the room with the window seat?"

Grandma smiled and said, "That's my mother. Your great-grandmother. Looks familiar, doesn't she?"

"I guess," Carly shrugged.

"You must've thought so, or you wouldn't have asked about her."

"Yeah, I noticed." Carly dipped under the water again.

"So have we," Grandma admitted when Carly resurfaced.

"You have?"

"The minute we saw you."

"How do you all feel about that?" Carly said.

"I think it made the others feel a little weird. Personally, it makes me very happy."

Carly scrunched her brow. "Happy? Why?"

"I suppose it has to do with your father. Somehow, it makes his death easier to take. It's like things have come full circle. He and his family live on through you."

Carly climbed onto the dock and sat down. "What was her name?"

"They called her Tina. It was really Constantina."

"When was that picture taken? How old was she?"

"She was about seventeen. Hmm, that would've made it 1930."

"Wow, that was a long time ago. It's freaky to look so much like someone from that long ago."

"Amazing, really," Grandma agreed.

"When did she die?"

"In 1987. She was seventy-five."

"She doesn't look very happy in the picture. She barely smiled," Carly noted.

"Well, times were very hard then. It was at the beginning of the Great Depression, and they were very poor."

"I learned about that in school."

Grandma nodded. "Mama had it even tougher than most because her mother died when Mama was eighteen, and she had to raise her two brothers and sister."

"Well, where was her father?" Carly asked.

"Oh, he was there."

"I guess he had to work," Carly said.

"When he could get it, but Mama worked, too."

"Like my mom."

"Yes, but I'll bet you went to day care and after-school care."

"Sure," Carly said. "Didn't your Mama's brothers and sisters?"

"Oh, no. There was no such thing."

"Then how did she do it?"

"Would you really like to know about your great-grandmother?"

"She looks so similar to me. I guess I'd like to know if she was anything like me."

"Grandma smiled. "Well, I'll tell you everything I know about her and you can decide for yourself . . ."

CHAPTER TWO

Intermittent boat horns and train whistles followed Angelo Benedetti and Tony Farina along the path that wound around the banks of the Mohawk River in Central New York State, an area known for an abundance of snow. But on this first summer-like day in June of 1932, the sun threatened to melt the patches of ice left on the path from the harsh winter and the thirteen-year-olds jumped at the chance to return after school to one of their favorite swimming spots. Clutching their rolled up towels, they kicked stones, sometimes at each other, as they cavorted toward the water.

Once within earshot of their friends, the shouting, splashing, and laughter caused them to hasten their pace until they spotted a clump of bushes and slipped behind them to change into swim trunks. Angelo finished first, stepped out, and walked toward the river's edge.

"Come on, Tony. Hurry up!" he called behind him. Then he yelled to a group of boys across the water, "What are you guys doin' way over there?"

One of the boys yelled back, "The water's warmer over here."

Tony came out tying his suit strings. "OK, let's go."

Angelo hesitated. "I don't know why they gotta swim way over there."

"Aw, come on. You want them to call us chicken again?"

Across town, Angelo's nineteen-year-old sister, Tina, finished the last stitch of the day at Irene's Dress Shop. She hung up her smock and stepped out onto a side street off North Main Street. She turned the corner just as a bus pulled away emitting a cloud of black diesel into her face. Kingsburg, a town of over ten thousand people, was in the midst of rush hour. The sidewalk bustled with activity as she made her way toward home, past stately brick department stores, hotels, banks, offices, and restaurants owned mostly by middle-to-upper-income residents. Normally a prosperous town, some of its storefronts now stood empty, victims of the 1929 Crash.

Tina walked with the poise of a model. The natural curl of her auburn hair conformed easily to the latest short hairstyles without any help from a permanent wave. She crossed over the railroad tracks, and the scenery changed to smaller businesses with names like Sarducci's Groceries, Gurnski's Hardware, Sicola's Bakery, Carmine's Shoe Repair, Giuseppe's Bar and Grill, and Eduardo's Restaurant—names that reflected the immigrant population on the south side of town.

When the sound of screeching saws pierced her ears, she knew she was close to home. Instinctively she hastened her steps while passing the furniture factory because the workers never failed to hang out of second-story windows to send lusty whistles of approval down to her. The smell of sawdust followed her past the familiar faces of neighbors wiping their brows as they watched their children splash around in metal tubs or play in the streets, some on the heels of an ice truck.

She walked into the backyard of her family's twin house, and smiled at Tony Farina's mother, picking tomatoes in her vegetable garden.

"Wow, Mrs. Farina, you have a lot of tomatoes this year."

Mrs. Farina, a native of Italy, spoke in broken English, "*Si*, we have good *ensalatas*."

"Mama used to make the best sauce from those tomatoes," Tina said, looking around the yard. "Have you seen Angelo or Carmen?" With her mother dead six months, and being the oldest, Tina was responsible for the whereabouts of Angelo, six-year-old Carmen, and seventeen-year-old Eva.

"No Carmen, but Angelo and Antonio, they run out of here a little while ago. I think they go swim to the river." She wiped her upper lip with a towel.

"Oh no, you let them go there?"

Mrs. Farina threw her hands up. "Where else they gonna go?" She stepped back and took in Tina's bright pink dress. "You just make that dress?"

"Oh," Tina said, running her hand over the material, "you like it?"

"Oh, *si*. You make clothes like nobody I know."

Tina gave her a broad smile. "I'm lucky Irene is my godmother. She gives me leftover material." She reached over a woodpile stacked beside a nearby shed, and carefully picked up four pieces of kindling. "Do you know if my father is home yet?"

"Dominic's been home and go again to Adolpho the barber."

Tina moved toward the back door. "Then I better get supper started before he gets back."

Mrs. Farina shook her finger at Tina, "You work too hard. All day long at that shop, then when you come home, more work."

Tina shrugged, shifted the wood in her arms, and opened the door. "See you later."

"*Buona sera*."

There was some truth to what Mrs. Farina said, but the physical work didn't bother Tina. It was the emotional drain of trying to hold her shattered family together after the sudden death of their loving wife and mother. The constant strain of dealing with siblings and a father who could not admit their grief weighed on her. But if the truth were known, she was guilty of the same thing. In her zeal to do what she believed her mother would've wanted, she put her own grief aside as she tended to her family's day-to-day needs, despite their often-disagreeable behavior.

After putting on slippers and an apron, she tidied up the living room—picked up the boys' clothes strewn about and emptied her father's pipe tray. She looked around the house and sighed. It saddened her that no matter how hard she tried, she couldn't recapture the essence of "home" that her mother's touch had brought to the now-hollow house.

Defeated by the futility of the situation, she shuffled into the kitchen, threw the kindling into the cast-iron stove, and lit it before going down to the cellar to get some potatoes and carrots out of the bins. When she came back up she heard Eva and Johnny Rossini on the back porch, so she glanced out the window.

"You were a lot of fun, Johnny," Eva said, batting her eyelashes.

Johnny grabbed her, pulled her to him, and rubbed his face on hers. "I'm even more fun at night. Meet me at the bowling alley later."

She wriggled out of his grasp and said, "I can't. I have to work the night shift tonight at the station diner. But I'll see you tomorrow."

"Yeah sure," he said with disgust, jumped off the porch, and took off down the street.

Eva straightened her clothes and her long dark-brown hair, went inside, and walked past Tina on her way to wash her hands and face in the sink.

"Wasn't that the Rossini kid?" Tina asked. "I haven't seen him around lately."

"That's because he's been in reform school for the past year."

"Swell." Tina shook her head. "Is there anyone you won't date?"

Eva took the dishtowel hanging on the hook next to the sink and wiped her face and hands. "Not if they're good looking and treat me nice. When's the last time you had a date?"

Tina nudged Eva's feet over, opened the cupboard door, and pulled out a pot. She had no intention of getting into this with her sister again. "Never mind. Help me with supper."

Throwing the towel down, Eva said, "Can't. I have to work the supper shift at the diner."

"I thought you were off tonight."

Eva grabbed a couple of pieces of the potatoes that Tina had cut up. "Lucy called in sick. Pa around?"

"No. He's—"

"Good," Eva interrupted. "Maybe I can get out of here before he gets home." She bit into a piece of potato. "Where's Carmie?"

"You were supposed to be keeping an eye on him," Tina called after Eva as she walked out of the kitchen toward the living room and the stairway. "Didn't he tell you where he was going?"

"Naw," Eva yelled from the stairs. "He never does, but he's always around here somewhere."

<hr/>

Along with the lakes, rivers, and canals, the railroad was essential to the industry of the town, and its tracks crisscrossed most of the south side. Because of this, the areas surrounding them became playgrounds for neighboring kids looking for ways to amuse themselves. But they also presented financial opportunity for the south side's poor kids, desperate for any treasure they could dredge up: coal nuggets.

A valuable commodity used for powering trains, heating, and cooking, coal could be found wherever the trains passed, but most often in the railroad yards. Older kids scaled the fence with no problem, but the little kids were forced to pick up the pieces scattered close enough to the fence for them to snatch.

"I can get this one. I know it," Carmen said as he lay down on his side and stuck his arm through the opening in the chain link. He stretched his fingers as far as they would go, grabbed the piece of coal, and slipped it through the fence.

"I got it," he shouted, as a nearby train whistle sounded. "Here, you take this piece." He handed it to his friend, Patsy. "It's five o'clock. I gotta go home."

Patsy took it, dropped it into his cloth sack, and said, "C'mon, I'll race ya to Sarducci's."

The boys entered Sarducci's Grocery on the run, barely missing a display of olive oil and slamming the screen door behind them. Grocery items lined the store, and the produce section surpassed any in town, but the boys went straight to the candy counter where they dumped their bags in front of Mr. Sarducci.

"Whoa, Carmenooch," Sarducci said in his broken English. "You knock my store down. What you want?"

"Look, we did pretty good today, huh, Mr. Sarducci?" a breathless Carmen beamed.

Sarducci shook his finger in Carmen's face and said in only a half-serious tone, "You kids. You going to end up in reform school. When they come after you"—he raised his palms toward the boys—"I don't know nothing."

"Aw, c'mon," Patsy pleaded. "Count it. We get lots of candy, right?"

Shaking his head, Sarducci adjusted his eyeglasses and started counting. "Let me see."

"Thanks, Mr. Sarducci," Carmen said with a laugh. "And when they come after us, we won't say we know nothin' about you neither."

Sarducci grinned. "Thank you very much." He finished counting, and reported, "Five pieces. You each get five pieces. What you want?"

With noses pressed against the candy case, Patsy started, "I want two root beer barrels and a—" A huge commotion from outside interrupted him.

"Hey," Mr. Sarducci exclaimed, "what's that out there? All the noise."

The three ran to the door. Outside, a group of boys wearing wet bathing suits walked behind the fire ambulance. Carmen yelled, "It's the fire wagon!"

Sarducci made the sign of the cross. "Oh, *Madonna mia,* not another one."

"Let's go follow it!" Patsy flung open the door, and the boys darted out to join the procession.

As Tina's potatoes bubbled in the pot, she took the opportunity to sit at the kitchen table for a minute and flip through the *Vogue* magazine she had bought the day before. Dominic, a man of forty-two, well-tanned and muscular from his years of working in various jobs for the railroad, came through the back door with his brown speckled dog following him. He washed his hands in the sink and sat down opposite her at the table.

"Where are your brothers?"

"I don't know, Pa." She tried to change the subject. "Uh, you really got sunburned today."

"I don't complain." He spoke with better command of the English language than Mrs. Farina. "Today I made enough money for groceries . . . and you spend it on those fancy magazines."

"It was my money, and I have to keep up with the designs so I'll be ready when I go to New York."

"I told you forget about that. You stay right here until you get married."

"But I don't want to get married. I want to . . ."

Dominic dismissed her with a wave of his hand and opened his newspaper. She sighed, and got up and went to the stove to tend to the potatoes.

Within minutes, sounds from the street brought them to their feet. Tina ran out to the front porch, where she immediately saw the fire wagon and the neighbors trailing it toward their house.

"Pa! Oh my God. Pa!"

Dominic stepped out onto the porch. "What's a matt—"

The sight of the truck pulling up in front of their house answered his question. Tina, already at the curb with Mrs. Farina, watched a fireman lift a blanketed body out of the back and walk toward them. Clutching each other and praying in silence, the women held their breath as the man carrying his precious cargo passed Tina and stopped in front of Mrs. Farina.

"I'm sorry, ma'am, but that river is rough, and the boy swam out a little too far."

Mrs. Farina swooned and fell into Tina's trembling arms. "Oh no, Antonio!"

***

A few days later, the Benedettis readied themselves for Tony's funeral. Tina donned a simple black shirtwaist dress and went into the boys' bedroom to help Carmen get ready. She assumed that Angelo had dressed and gone ahead of them, but she hadn't seen Eva all morning. *Where did she take off to now?*

"Come on, Carmen," Tina pleaded while trying to comb his hair, "help me a little.

He squirmed. "You're hurting me."

"Well, stay still. And you behave in church this morning. Remember to say some prayers for Tony. That he'll be happy with God in heaven."

"OK. Is Tony going to see Mama in heaven?"

Tina hesitated, then answered. "Yes, I guess he will."

Before she had time to ponder more over the possibility of that, Eva walked through the doorway. "What time is the funeral?"

"Nine. You're going to be late. Where have you been?"

Eva leaned on the chest of drawers. "I told Peter I'd meet him this morning, cuz I couldn't see him last night."

"What in the world do you do on a date this early in the morning?"

"I'll never tell," Eva said, and sauntered out of the room.

The entire neighborhood mourned Tony's death and Mrs. Farina's sorrow, but none more than the Benedettis, whose family had known the Farinas in the old country. For the Benedettis, still grieving for Tina's mother, Luciana, this loss couldn't have come at a worse time.

A stoic Dominic answered a knock at the door. A young boy wearing a school band shirt and carrying drumsticks asked for Angelo.

"The band's supposed to meet at the school early, so we can march in the funeral procession. We're late, and Miss Snow's gonna have our hide."

The elementary school drum-and-bugle band was made up of boys chosen directly by Principal Abigail Snow. A stern, no-nonsense woman, she disciplined with a firm but loving hand. Early on in her tenure at the South Side School, Miss Snow recognized the difficulties that the recent immigrants of Kingsburg faced in their new country.

Motivated by her good heart and patriotism, she took it upon herself to help them acclimate to their new country by conducting English language and citizenship classes for them. She demanded that parents see to it that their kids attended school and expected the students to respect their elders and be in class. She showered praise on students when it was deserved and gave rewards for excellence. One reward she bestowed was a spot in her boys' band.

Dominic peered down at the boy with the drumsticks and tensed up. "I thought Angelo left already."

"I ain't seen him."

Dominic shook his head. "You go to school; I'll find him."

Dominic walked around the house calling Angelo's name but got no answer. He opened the cellar door, and lit a match. "Angelo?"

"Yeah?"

Dominic followed the voice halfway down the cellar stairs, peered underneath, and found Angelo huddled below them.

"Get up here. You're late. Miss Snow waits for you."

"Oh, do I have to go?"

"Come on!"

Angelo followed Dominic up the stairs with head down and deliberate steps. "It won't make no difference if I ain't there."

"Antonio was like a brother to you."

"He won't know," Angelo said, under his breath.

Dominic turned around and smacked him on the back of the head. "What's a matter with you? *Comare* Farina will wonder where you are. You go for her."

Most of the south side population turned out for the funeral. Shops closed, and schools excused the children so they could attend Tony Farina's mass at St. Paul's Roman Catholic Church. They walked from their nearby homes, summoned by church bells reverberating throughout the neighborhood. The bells called them to once again bury one of their youngsters. Tony's death marked the fifth drowning in the last three years.

The solemn crowd watched the hearse crawl toward the church from the Farina home, followed by the dirge of the band. Tony and Angelo had been in the band until they graduated to junior high school the previous year. Angelo's special invitation to take part in Tony's ceremony came as a personal request from Miss Snow. And it was out of respect for her, and for Mrs. Farina, that he marched behind Tony's casket to the beat of his drum, with head held high and tears trickling down his face.

⇒⇥ ⇤⇐

After the mass and burial, the mourners gathered at Mrs. Farina's house to offer emotional support and partake from a buffet that included pasta fagioli, fried peppers with potatoes, and endive stew, prepared by the neighbors. They took turns sitting next to Mrs. Farina to bemoan her tragedy as she sat on the couch in her parlor. When it came to Tina's turn, she opened her mouth to speak but burst into tears and ran into the kitchen, where some of the women were cleaning up. She headed straight for Irene Janson standing at the kitchen sink washing dishes.

"Oh, Irene, I want to be strong for Mrs. Farina, but every time I try to comfort her, I start crying."

Irene smiled, dried her hands on the towel at her waist, and pulled Tina to her. "It's all right." She patted Tina's shoulder. "There is no real comfort for her now."

Tina wiped her eyes with her hankie. "I try to imagine how she's feeling. I mean I know how I felt to lose Mama, but this was her son."

Irene touched the handkerchief in Tina's hand. "I remember when I sewed this for Luciana."

Tina squeezed the hankie tighter. "She always carried it with her,"

As Irene continued to console Tina, Dominic walked through the living room where Carmen was grabbing food and chasing around the table with Patsy. Dominic didn't say a word, but gestured to Carmen to sit in a nearby chair and stood watching until the boy complied. But when a friend approached Dominic to chat, Carmen darted for the table again. Instead of reprimanding Carmen, Dominic looked around and then went into the kitchen.

Tina and Irene jumped when Dominic yelled, "Tina, go take care of Carmen!"

Tina didn't hesitate but left immediately to find her little brother, dabbing her eyes with her hanky along the way.

Dominic turned to leave, but Irene touched his arm. "Dom, sit down." She pulled a chair out from under the table. "I'll get you a cup of coffee. I just made it."

"Thanks, Irene. How are you?"

"I'm good, but this is a sad day. How are you holding up?"

"I'm OK."

Irene put the coffee cup in front of him. "You were like a father to the boy . . . and it's so close after losing Luciana."

He waved her off. "That's in the past."

"Over fifteen years it's been since I lost Sam, but it seems like yesterday. I know what you feel."

"It's different for a woman. More natural."

"Natural?"

He pushed the coffee away. "The man, he's supposed to go first!"

Irene, of Polish descent, had been like a sister to Tina's mother. Her husband, Sam, a German man, had worked on the railroad with Dominic in the early days, after their arrival from their native countries. Irene and Sam had no children of their own but were godparents to Tina. After Sam was killed in a railroad accident nearly fifteen years before, Irene became Carmen's godmother. And when Luciana died, she became somewhat of a surrogate mother to all the Benedetti children.

Tina walked up to the table in the living room and grabbed Carmen's arm as he was about to lift a piece of fried bread dough coated with sugar off a plate.

"Carmie, that's enough. Why don't you go outside and play with Patsy?"

"Aw, can't I have just one more piece?"

She took a piece off the table and handed it to him. "Now go," she said, pushing his straight brown hair out of his eyes.

She turned around and saw a striking man in his twenties, his hair slicked down from a distinct part, looking at her. Dressed in a well-cut pinstripe suit in the latest style, his breast pocket lined with cigars, he looked out of place in the neighborhood.

He smiled at her. "I used to love weddings and funerals when I was a kid. All that food and everybody too busy dancing or crying to watch me."

She returned his dazzling grin with a guarded one. "I guess you didn't have an older sister."

"Only brothers. Did you know Tony very well?" He took a piece of fried dough off the table.

"All his life. I live next door."

"Sounds like you knew my cousin better than I did." He nibbled on the bread.

"I'm sorry. I should have offered my condolences to you. It's just that I haven't ever seen you around here."

"He's actually my third cousin or something. I'm paying respects for the family today."

"I'm sure Mrs. Farina appreciates you being here."

"So what's your name?"

"Tina. Tina Benedetti."

"Pretty name for a pretty girl."

"Thank you. It's really Constantina, but I hate that."

"Try Battista ."

Tina smiled. "Oh, really? You poor thing."

He shrugged. "It's not so bad. I only answer to Tommy. Besides, it got a smile out of you."

His remark forced her to smile again. "Tommy Capello, right?"

"You've heard of me?"

"It's a small town, Mr. Capello. Everybody knows . . ."

Before she could finish, they were interrupted by Miss Snow, standing behind Tommy.

"Hello, Tommaso."

He turned to her and stood up straight. "Hello, Miss Snow."

The principal looked over at Tina. "A terrible day for Tony's friends."

Tina threw her shoulders back and gave a faint smile. "Yes, it is, Miss Snow."

"Tommaso," Miss Snow said, "I want to offer you and your family my condolences. I know that Tony was your cousin."

"Thank you," he said, still standing at attention, but glancing down. "How are you doing today?"

She sighed. "It's always hard to lose one of my boys." She waited until he looked her in the eye. "He reminded me of you at that age."

Tommy tugged on his collar and wiped the moisture from his pencil-thin mustache. It occurred to Tina that Miss Snow wanted to talk to Tommy alone, so she excused herself and went to check on Carmen. Tommy couldn't hide his disappointment as he watched her walk away from him, before turning back to Miss Snow. "Uh, yes ma'am."

"Tina is a very pretty girl, isn't she?" Miss Snow said.

Tommy nodded, and Miss Snow continued, "Have you known her long?"

"I just met her now."

"Well, I'm sure you could tell that she's also a very nice girl."

Tommy wasted no time. As soon as his talk with Miss Snow ended, he wiped his sweaty forehead with the back of his hand and took off out the front door, hoping to see Tina on his way out.

Instead, on the path at the foot of the front porch, a small group of distraught men, fueled by liquor, waited for Tommy. When they saw he was in earshot, they bantered among themselves.

"Whatever happened to the pool the mayor was gonna build for us if he got elected?"

"Hell, that was only campaign talk."

"Yeah, that Tommy Capello," one sneered. "He'd say anything to get that guy in office."

Tommy stepped onto the path, and the men closed in on him.

"Here's the man to talk to right here."

"Yeah, Capello. We lost another kid waitin' for that pool your mayor was gonna build us."

Tommy stopped. "What are you talking about?"

"Listen to this, fellas. He forgot."

"Pretty short memory for such a young guy."

"The pool. The pool."

"You guys are drunk. Don't you have any respect for the dead?" Tommy had had enough, and pushed his way through their circle.

"You're the one who don't care. You and the *honorable* Mayor Steele."

Tommy turned to them as he opened the door to his roadster, and yelled back, "Go on home and sober up."

Drunk or not, the guys did not exaggerate Tommy's relationship with Mayor Steele and his south side constituency. Everyone knew that Tommy was out for number one. Growing up on one of the most notorious streets in town, as a kid he often found himself in trouble with the law for fighting and petty theft. He only skirted reform school because Miss Snow had intervened on his behalf.

Always a cute and charming boy, he was easy to like, but she had also seen a hint of promise in him that she refused to see squelched by his conduct and social standing. She had convinced the police to give him another chance after he had been caught stealing coins off the tops of empty milk bottles meant for the deliveryman.

They agreed, as long as she would personally take responsibility for his future behavior. At eleven, he couldn't believe that anyone, especially Miss Snow, would do something like that for the likes of him. Setting out to show her his gratitude, he made it through the tenth grade without another blemish on his record.

But after quitting school at the end of that year, he did anything he could to avoid the only honest jobs he was qualified for, which always involved manual labor. He preferred fast and easy money-making jobs like running illegal booze and strong-arm stuff. All of which led to him starting his own gambling and liquor business right under the nose of the corrupt local authorities.

He enjoyed his notoriety and showed no remorse for his chosen line of work to anyone in town, except Miss Snow. Knowing that he had angered and disappointed her, he avoided running into her at all costs. She on the other hand made a point to speak to him whenever the opportunity presented itself. Not surprisingly, he heard her voice in his head as he tried to sleep that night after his run-in with the angry men in front of the Farina house.

＝≼+ +≽＝

Tina had trouble falling asleep that night, too. The reality of Tony's death had struck her hard as she said good night to both of her brothers. *Mrs. Farina will never kiss Tony good night again.* The thought of Mrs. Farina's life without her son brought tears to Tina's eyes. She tried to sleep, but rest eluded her as she relived the funeral service and the rest of the day at the Farina's.

The only light moment in the day had been with Tommy Capello. He had come out of nowhere and actually made her smile through her tears. She hated what he was, and what he did for a living. It reinforced to the American people on the north side of town everything they perceived about the Italians. But despite her contempt for what he represented, she responded to his engaging personality and good looks. Determined to put him and his charms out of her mind, she drifted off to sleep.

She had only been asleep for about an hour when she awoke to Carmen crying. She grabbed her robe and tiptoed to his room, where she found him tossing and turning. "Mama, where are you? I can't see you. I can't see you."

Tina sat down next to him and bent over to touch his cheek with hers. "Carmie, wake up," she whispered in his ear.

Angelo turned around in his bed. "He's crying again? Every night I gotta hear him cry."

Tina looked over at him. "Go back to sleep, Angie," she whispered louder.

Now awake, Carmen sat up rubbing his eyes. "Tina, I can't find Mama."

"I know, honey. She's not here."

He threw his arms around her neck. "She's not in heaven either. I couldn't find her in heaven."

"Of course she's in heaven. You were dreaming. She's watching over us from there." Tina pushed him back down gently and kissed his forehead. "Now go to sleep."

After making sure that he was going to stay quiet, Tina tiptoed back out into the hall, where she looked into Eva's room and saw her sleeping soundly. She listened at Dominic's door, and hearing nothing, she went downstairs and found him passed out in a chair with an empty bottle of wine next to him.

CHAPTER THREE

The next morning Eva pounded on the bathroom door and yelled, "Hurry up, Angelo. I've got to get to work."

Tina pleaded with Carmen in the kitchen. "Please hurry up and finish your Ovaltine or you'll be late for school." No one mentioned Tony, and Tina wouldn't allow herself to think about him throughout her usual morning routine. After everyone was gone, she finished up the last of the dishes and left for work.

It wasn't until she walked by the black wreath on the Farina door that Tina let thoughts of Tony and his family swirl through her mind. Nothing would bring him back. She could only hope that his death would scare her brothers enough that they wouldn't go near the unsafe swimming holes.

But she knew that only a public pool would prevent them from treading those dangerous waters. There had been talk after the funeral that Tommy Capello could really have enough influence on the mayor to persuade him and the village to build a pool. She certainly didn't agree with his tactics, but if there was any chance that he could get them a pool, she was loath to admit that she might be able to overlook them this one time.

Now in front of the dress shop, Tina unlocked the door and picked up the day's newspaper. Inside, she turned on the lights and began opening bolts of fabric. Her project today would be to create an evening dress for the wife of a local businessman. She spread the rayon material on the cutting table and smiled as she touched it.

She loved her job because of the freedom she had to design dresses for her customers and herself, but she dreamed of the day that she could work in New York City and design her own clothing line. How would that happen any time soon though, what with her family's continued reliance on her? Until then, she felt lucky to be Irene's apprentice.

Tina looked up when Irene came in from her apartment in the back, carrying a moneybag. "How are you this morning?" Irene asked as she put the money into the cash drawer.

"Morning. I'm OK."

"It was a very nice funeral."

"I guess."

"Very sad, but good for Mrs. Farina to have all of her friends and family around her."

"I suppose you're right."

"You were talking to Tommy Capello. I didn't know you knew him.

"I don't. He just came up to me. He's Tony's cousin, you know."

"Oh." Irene smiled. "He's nice?"

"Actually he was. Considering . . ."

Irene kept her eyes down as she thumbed through some receipts and said with hope in her voice, "Maybe you'll go out with him."

Tina didn't hesitate. "No."

Irene looked directly at her and winked. "He's got lots of money, yes?"

"He's not my type."

"Yes, but . . ." Irene picked up the newspaper next to the cash register. "Did you see this article about Tony?

"No."

"Beginner at swimming makes foolhardy attempt to accompany companions across body of water. Nearly drowns friend who attempts rescue."

Tina reached for the paper in Irene's hand. "Let me see that." Tina took a moment to read the article. "This says that Tony's stupidity almost killed that north side kid. It doesn't say that they actually goaded him to do it by calling him a chicken."

"Is that what really happened?"

"Yes. Angelo told me that night that those kids knew he and Tony were afraid of swimming that far out but teased them into proving themselves."

"That's terrible. Poor Tony, he—" Irene was interrupted by the door opening.

It was Mrs. Upton, a regular customer.

"Hello, Irene," she said. "Can you show me some of your fancier dresses? It's my fifteenth anniversary, and my husband is taking me to the restaurant where he proposed to me." She winked. "I need a dress that will hide the pound I've gained for every year of our marriage."

"I understand. Let me show you a couple that might work for you."

When Irene had set up shop in Kingsburg many years before, she found it difficult to compete with the established shops owned by long-time residents. She worked for practically nothing in those days, catering to folks on the south side by doing mending and keeping abreast of the latest styles in order to create copies of expensive designer dresses using less costly fabric. Eventually her work began to be noticed by north side women with wealthy husbands who appreciated showing off their wives to other businessmen. But it wasn't until Tina joined her over a year ago that she began to offer original designs to the women looking for one-of-a-kind dresses.

After trying the dresses on, Mrs. Upton carried a blue one to the counter. "I think you're right about this one. I know Harry will like the color, too."

"Good." Irene rang up the sale.

Mrs. Upton picked up the newspaper on the counter and read the headline about Tony's drowning. "Can you believe it? Those kids do anything for amusement. And to think he almost killed the other boy with him. It's the parents. They have no control over them. They let them roam the streets until all hours of the night, too. You won't catch me in that part of town."

Tina looked up from her sewing and glared at Mrs. Upton. Irene saw it and looked at Mrs. Upton with a smile. "I hope the dress works for you, madam. It's one of our Tina's loveliest creations." She handed her the dress, and continued, "Come again soon."

Mrs. Upton glanced over at Tina and said, "Oh, yes. Thank you." Then she slithered out the door.

Irene stood there shaking her head. "She forgets who she's talking to. If my home was not in the back, I would be living 'in that part of town,' too."

⇥ ⇤

Two weeks had passed since Tony's funeral, and the Benedettis, though sad, moved forward with their lives. Once again, the young ones went back to school, and Dominic and Tina went to work as usual. On Friday night, the kids readied themselves to go out with friends. As they did so, Dom positioned himself in the kitchen with a whiskey bottle on the table next to him, and his pipe and pipe cleaners in hand. Everyone but Eva had left, and she spoke to Dominic as she passed by him on her way out the back door.

"I'm leaving now, Pa."

"*Aspetta un momento.*"

"Yeah, Pa?"

43

"When you get paid?"

"I told you a million times. I get paid on Monday."

"I got bills. I need your pay."

"I gave you this week's already."

"You did?"

"Yes."

"I don't remember."

Eva walked up to his chair, and pointed at the bottle of whiskey. "It's in there."

He raised his hand. "Watch your mouth."

With that, she opened her purse, took out two dollars, and handed it to him.

Later that night, Angelo sat crossed-legged with friends Vinny and Dumpy near the railroad tracks at a makeshift table lit by two votive candles. The spot, about a mile from the station, was hidden from view by trees and the remains of a caboose left to rust after a train wreck in the 1920s. No one usually bothered them when they went there to play cards and wait for the trains to speed by, spewing coal along the way.

They competed fiercely for the valuable nuggets and used them as poker chips while killing time in between trains.

"Hey, Angie, you won again. What's goin' on? You cheatin?" Dumpy said.

"I ain't gotta cheat."

Vinny pulled Angelo's baseball cap over his eyes, and smiled. "Yeah, well, you usually ain't this lucky."

Angelo took his hat off, and shook it out. "Hey, don't touch my hat."

"Big deal. You found it at the dump. How many people you think touched it before you?"

"That don't matter. It's a Yankees cap, and it's mine now."

"Oh, you and your Yankees." Vinny said. "They ain't so hot."

"No, only the best team in baseball. You watch. They can't lose with the Babe and Gehrig."

Dumpy changed the subject. "Hey, Ang, I hear your sister Eva's been goin' out with Johnny Rossini."

"And everybody else in town," Vinny added.

"What's it to ya?" Angelo snapped.

"I thought you could fix her up with me." Dumpy goaded, while groping the air with his hands and thrusting his pelvis in and out. "I'd like to get my hands on those big titties."

Angelo leaned over and grabbed Dumpy's shirt collar. "Shuddup about my sister, you shithead, or I'll beat your face in."

"Oh yeah, sure. Angie the tough guy. I ain't never seen you beat nobody yet," Vinny said.

Dumpy straightened his shirt and said, "Jeez, I was only jokin' anyways."

"Yeah well, nobody talks about my sister like that."

Vinny started dealing the cards. "Aw right. Shuddup and let's play cards."

Before they could finish a hand, the ground began to rumble. They dropped the cards and blew out the candles.

"Come on! Let's go!"

They scurried off to lie in wait in their usual positions behind an embankment that bordered the rails. They crouched there anticipating the whistle, but it never came. Instead, the train surprised them by slowing to a stop. They watched as two men stepped down from the front of the engine, and walked toward the back of the train near the boys' hiding place.

"Oh, crap. We're in trouble now."

"They're gonna have us arrested."

Angelo whispered. "Shuddup. Both of ya. They'll hear us."

They stayed as quiet and still as possible, considering they couldn't stop shaking. But they needn't have feared, because the men headed right for the freight car in front of them and stopped.

One of them slid the door open while the other held the lantern up to the opening and yelled into it.

The trio couldn't make out what he said, but within a minute two boys about their age climbed down from the car and stood with heads bowed while the engineer shook his finger at them. When the man finished his diatribe, he and his companion slammed the door shut and headed back to the front of the train, leaving the would-be passengers in the dark. The boys moved away from the tracks and closer to the embankment until the train pulled out.

The stowaways peered out into the darkness. "Where do you think we are?"

"We must still be in New York."

One of them spotted some lights in the distance and pointed. "Over there. That looks like something."

Angelo grew curious. He had heard about these "hobo kids" from his father's experience with them at work. "Jeez, I wonder where they came from."

Vinny jumped up. "Come on. Let's find out."

The threesome headed toward the stowaways but approached with caution.

"Hey. We saw what happened. Where'd you come from?" Angelo asked.

"Who wants to know?"

"I'm Angelo." He stuck out his hand, and one of them shook it. "These are my pals, Vinny and Dumpy."

"Dumpy?"

Dumpy shrugged. "It's really Joe."

Vinny laughed. "We call him Dumpy cuz he's the best at digging through garbage at the dump."

"You riding the rails, too?" one of the visitors asked.

"Naw, we live in town," Dumpy said. "We just hang around down here sometimes. What's your names?"

"Uh, my name's Billy," said one, and pointed to his friend. "This here's Henry."

"So where you fellas from?" Angelo asked.

Billy spoke first again. "Oklahoma."

"I'm from Tennessee," Henry said.

"Where youse headed?"

Billy shrugged. "Nowhere particular."

"Yeah, we pretty much just jump a car anywhere we can," added Henry.

"It don't much matter which way," Billy summed up. "We like to keep moving."

"Your family don't care?" Vinny said.

Billy shook his head. "Mine gave me twenty bucks and said find someplace else to live. We can't afford you since the new baby showed up."

"Jeez, that's rough." Dumpy said.

"Your family do that, too?" Angelo asked.

"Naw, I took off on my own. The old man probably didn't even notice till he felt like beatin' the crap out of someone, and couldn't find me."

"Anyways, it's better out here on the road." Billy added. "We do what we want when we want and get to see lots of places."

Henry rubbed his stomach. "Uh, you guys know where we could find some food?"

The three friends looked at each other, but Vinny was the only one to speak.

"We've got leftover spaghetti at my house. My ma wouldn't mind. You could probably sleep in the shanty out back tonight, too. Come on. Follow me."

Dumpy and Angelo parted ways with Vinny and his guests and headed toward their street. They walked in silence until Dumpy stopped and said, "Wait a minute. You hear somethin'?"

Angelo stopped and listened. When footsteps got closer, one of the cops slapped the palm of his other hand, and Angelo whispered. "It's a cop! Scatter!"

The boys took cover in different places and watched as the policemen, one tall and thin, the other short and stocky, walked down the alley looking from side to side. They closed in on Angelo and Dumpy. Dumpy tried to get away, but he tripped and fell almost at the feet of the tall cop.

The short one blocked the spot where Angelo hid and said, "Come on out of there, boy. You got nowhere to go."

Angelo came out from behind a garbage can and shuffled toward the short cop.

"OK, Benedetti, what'd you do with the stuff?"

"What stuff?"

"The stuff you took off the broad up on Hyde Street a little while ago."

"You're crazy," Angelo said. "I didn't take nothin' off nobody. I ain't even been up there for a week or so."

The short cop hesitated for a moment, then said to Dumpy, "How about you? Why'd you run away?"

"You was chasin' me."

The thin cop reached out and slapped him. "Don't be a smart-ass."

Still in the firm grip of the fat cop, Angelo said, "Look we didn't take nothin.' We just left the pool hall. We was in there all night, until about an hour ago. Go ask Sal. He'll tell ya."

The cops looked at each other.

Angelo squirmed in the cop's grasp. "You're hurtin' me."

The cop pushed him away and released him. "Go on. Get your asses out of here; they're greasing up the street."

⊷⧲⊶ ⊷⧳⊶

Tina and her best friend, Rosie, strolled home from the Main Street Movie Theater about eleven thirty. They had grown up together a few houses apart. Rosie's dark hair and plump figure wasn't the only way she differed from Tina. The two couldn't be more dissimilar in personality and their approach to life.

Tina wrapped her sweater tighter around her shoulders to ward off the now chilly air as they discussed the movie they had seen.

"I love Norma Shearer," Rosie said about the movie star. "I think this movie was even better than her Divorcee one."

"She sure doesn't have any problem jumping into bed with men."

"Well, who would, when one of them is Clark Gable?"

"Even when he's playing a mobster? That's not very appealing."

"Maybe not to you," Rosie said.

"And it is to you?"

"It's exciting. Not boring like most of the boys around here."

Tina smirked. "I'm sure Frankie would love to hear that."

"Oh, Frankie's all right, but I don't intend to lose it to him."

"Rosie!" Tina stopped and looked at her. "If your mother could hear you."

"She probably wouldn't get what I meant anyway. Her English stinks."

"Well, my mother would've killed me if she knew I'd 'lost it' to some guy before getting married. And yours would too." She paused and said, "Besides, we're Catholic!"

Rosie giggled. "Oh, Tina. You're just too good for words. I'm surprised you even go to the movies."

"I love the costumes. They're gorgeous," Tina said. "I'd give anything to be able to design a gown for Norma Shearer."

Deep in conversation, they didn't realize that they had taken the wrong way home until they found themselves approaching a men's lodge, one street over from their regular route. Tina noticed the group of guys standing in front of the club first and nudged Rosie to cross the street. But before they got to the other side, a couple of the young men stepped off the curb and blocked them from crossing.

"Hey, girlies, where ya goin'?" a guy with a red mustache said.

The other one chimed. "Why don't you come over here and talk to us?"

The women tried to dodge them, but the men stayed on them at every turn.

"You don't have to be afraid of us. We like pretty dago girls."

Rosie sneered, "Well we don't like you."

Tina glared at her with a look that said, *shut up, stupid.*

As Tina feared, it seemed to anger them. The redhead said, "That's a lousy thing to say when we're being so nice to you."

"We're only tryin' to be neighborly."

"Yeah, come over here and talk to us awhile." He pointed to the other guys on the street. "Meet some of our friends."

Tina tried to be diplomatic. "We can't. We've got to get home. Our families are expecting us any minute now."

The men pushed the women toward the group. "So what? Now come on over here." One of the guys reached for Tina, who tried to break away. But another one reached out and grabbed her and shoved her in between two buildings. She fought him as hard as she could.

"Hey, you're a wild one."

Another of the men reached for Rosie. "You don't have to fight like your friend. I don't want to hurt ya. I just want what you give those guinea boys."

Tina, still struggling with her assailant, bit him on the arm.

"You little bitch. You're pissin' me off now."

She braced herself for his slap, but he froze when a car roared up behind them and came to a screeching halt. With the sound of car doors slamming, he immediately let her go. But before he could turn around and run, someone grabbed him by the collar and threw him to the ground.

At the same time, someone else grabbed Rosie's attacker, and tossed him to the side. Both men attempted to bounce back up to charge their assailants, but within seconds one was punched in the stomach and the other in the face. The women stood trembling, with their backs to the fighting until someone touched Tina's shoulder and asked, "Are you OK?"

After some introductions, Tommy and his cousin Joe helped Tina into the passenger side of Tommy's roadster and Rosie into the rumble seat, where Joe joined her.

"How'd you two end up in front of that club?" Tommy said, after driving off.

"We went to the show tonight, and Rosie was talking so much afterward we didn't realize where we were until we were there."

Rosie straightened up. "I was talking so much?"

"Who was going on and on about Norma Shearer?" Tina said.

"Well, you were listening. If you're so much smarter, why weren't you paying more attention?"

Tommy interrupted their bickering. "Well, you both better be more careful."

"Boy, we were so lucky you were driving by," Rosie gushed. "Weren't we Tina?" She continued without waiting for an answer. "And you two already knew each other. Isn't that something?" She glared at the back of Tina's head. "Tina never mentioned it."

Tina turned around and glared right back. They continued the ride in silence.

"Here we are," Tommy said as he pulled up in front of Tina's house. "Where do you live, Rosie?"

"Two doors down. I can get out here, too."

Tommy gave his cousin a signal to walk Rosie home. They said goodnight, and Tommy took Tina's arm and they turned toward her door.

"Thanks for all your help," Tina said over the sound of a whistling train in the distance.

"Anytime. It's not every day I get to save a pretty girl from the bad guys."

"Really?" Tina said. "You look like you've had a lot of practice."

Tommy shrugged and gently touched her arm. "Are you sure you're all right?"

"Yes, I'm fine." They reached the door. "Well, good night."

"Uh . . . Maybe you could arrange it so you'd need my help again soon."

Tina smiled. "You're kidding, right?"

Tommy looked at his feet. "Yeah . . . look . . . I know that you work at Irene's shop during the day . . ."

"How do you know that?"

"It's a small town, remember?" He smiled and continued, "Anyway, how about I come by and take you to lunch on Monday?"

Tina cleared her throat. "No, thanks."

"Why not?"

"I'd rather not, that's all."

He squirmed. "Well, how about you call it a favor? After all, you owe me, right?"

Tina couldn't argue with that. "Since you put it that way. OK, pick me up at 12:30."

She was glad that everyone was asleep upstairs when she got home, because she needed to bathe. The warm water and soap calmed her skin, still prickling from her attackers' hands. She then went into the kitchen and made herself a bicarbonate of soda, hoping to relax her quivering stomach. She had tried to make light of the incident in front of the others, but now alone and in the dark, the tears gushed from her eyes.

Whistles, catcalls, and ethnic slurs were not uncommon in Kingsburg. She'd been the recipient of them or a witness to them all of her life, but this night had been different. She had feared for her well-being—so much so that the rage had risen up within her with every word and touch from her assailants. She had struck out without regard for the consequences and that surprised her because she didn't know that anger could spark such a violent response from her.

Unfortunately, despite her attempts to strike back, she had been helpless. She'd never say it out loud, but she thanked God that Tommy and his cousin had shown up when they did. So when he suggested she pay him back for the favor by having lunch, she couldn't refuse him. She agreed to go with him on Monday, but she would make it clear that it would be the only time.

⟞⊹ ⊹⟝

Tommy sprinted back to his car, feet barely touching the ground. He had talked her into seeing him again. He hated that he'd had to guilt her into it with the favor angle, but his elation outweighed his own guilt, and he focused on their next meeting.

He had a reputation around town. He'd worked hard to achieve it, but along with his connections and money came his ladies' man persona. He never denied that he enjoyed that part of it almost as much as the other, but this was the first time that it had failed him.

Tina was not like the other girls, though. He had known it within minutes of their meeting at the Farina house. She not only didn't seem impressed by him, she acted as if she didn't even like him. He rarely encountered that in the women he pursued. Maybe it was just her way of playing hard to get. *Yes, that must be it.*

Still high on his accomplishment, Tommy arrived home, jumped out of his car, headed toward his apartment behind his diner, and tossed his hat up in the air. But before he could catch it, a hand blocked his, deflecting the hat to the ground. His eyes followed the hand to its owner, who immediately formed a circle with four other guys around Tommy. Grabbing his arms, they pulled him to the dark side of the building and began an intervention of sorts. Tommy had only enough time to identify the group as the men who had accosted him the night of the funeral, before he felt a blow to his jaw.

When he could speak, he rubbed his jaw and said, "You guys again?"

"Yeah, and this time we ain't drunk," the apparent leader said.

"So, Tommy boy, our kids gonna have a pool this summer or not?"

Tommy wiped some blood tricking out the corner of his mouth. "Look, you gotta talk to the mayor about that."

"It wasn't the goddamn mayor who promised us a pool if we voted for him; it was you," said the leader.

"And you got what *you* wanted," another man added. "Your business is protected. *We* want what's comin' to us."

"What are you complaining about? You got those jobs you asked for at the foundry," Tommy reminded them.

"Hell, they needed workers up there anyways."

"Yeah, but you know they wouldn't have hired anybody from our district without inside help." Tommy relaxed a bit, thinking that maybe he'd appeased them with that, but it only incited the guy to grab his collar and pin him to the side of the house.

"Listen, that son of a bitch wants more than this one-horse town," the guy said. "He's heading for Albany, and governor. You got to keep your prick cleaner on that road."

"Yeah, he don't need any bad press," another guy chimed in."

The group backed off. "Look, we get the goddamn pool or the newspaper gets our story."

Tommy stood at his sink nursing his fat lip, barely noticing its sting. The screws put to him by those men hurt more. His ego had suffered a blow, and it made him mad. Usually it was him standing over some poor schlemiel, threatening to beat his head in if he didn't pay his debt. But he also knew in the back of his mind that the guys were right, and a shitload of guilt went along with that.

                                                    —⊰ ⊱—

The next morning, still a bit shaky from the previous night, Tina told Irene she couldn't work that day and stuck close to home, doing household chores. She took the laundry basket into the backyard, and began hanging the clothes to dry on the clothesline.

Eva called to her from the back door. "Hey, Tina, let me borrow your black chemise tonight."

When Tina told her no, Eva walked outside and grabbed a pear off the tree next to the clothesline.

"Why not?" She nibbled at the fruit. "You've got all those great clothes, but they're wasted. You never go anywhere."

"I do, too."

"Not with guys who would appreciate them. Come on. I've got somebody who'd love to see me in that dress tonight."

Tina didn't feel like arguing. "Oh, all right, but you owe me, and if you spill anything on it, you're paying for it."

"Thanks. I won't spill anything." Eva changed the subject. "Rosie's telling the whole town that Tommy Capello saved your lives last night."

"Well, our honor, anyway."

"Did those scummy guys at the Men's Club actually touch you?"

"I'm trying to forget about it, OK?"

"I beg your pardon." Eva acted insulted. "So tell me what it's like to ride in a roadster."

"Like a roadster, I guess."

"It's the flashiest automobile on the south side, and you didn't even notice?"

Tina handed Eva some clothespins from the pouch around her waist. "I hate to think about where he got the money to buy it."

Eva dropped the pear and grabbed a wet shirt out of the basket to hang. "So don't worry about it. You don't know how to have a good time. You should do what I do."

"You mean go out with every hoodlum that asks you?" Tina said.

"Why not?"

Tina turned to Eva with indignation. "I'd like to keep my reputation, thank you. I don't want yours."

Eva waved her off. "I don't care what the people in this town think of me. Let 'em think what they want with their dirty ol' minds. The boys know I don't give in to them. I just play them along." She shrugs. "So they tell stories to each other. I don't care. It's a game."

Tina picked up the basket. "And that's a good time?"

"You bet," Eva said, following Tina into the house with the clothespins. "I get some nice meals, free movies, and . . . lots of attention. Nothing like being around here."

⇒⇐ ⇒⇐

Tommy took Tina for lunch on Monday to a popular bar and grill outside of town. The place was known for its great food, and the smells emanating from the kitchen made her hungry the minute they walked inside. She'd only been there a couple of times before, because without a car of their own, her family rarely ventured farther than they could walk. Bus rides were reserved for trips to the nearest big city to tend to important business.

The owner, a friend of Tommy's, met them at the door and sat them at a private table in the back. Tina tried to act nonchalant despite the fact that the special treatment impressed her. They lunched on fish fry, one of the house specialties, and made small talk until Tommy commented on the style of her clothes.

Tina sat back in her chair and pushed her nearly empty plate away.

"What's the matter with my clothes?"

"Nothing. That's some hat you've got on. I never saw one like it."

Tina eyed Tommy up and down, taking in his two-tone shoes, plaid jacket, and paisley tie. "You're pretty flashy yourself."

He wasted no time explaining himself. "I like your clothes. They're just different than the other girls in town, that's all."

"That's the idea," Tina said. "They'll appreciate my work in New York City. Designers go there from Paris and everywhere. Haven't you ever heard of Elsa Schiaparelli or Coco Chanel?"

Tommy wiped his mouth with his napkin and smiled. "Any relation to Coco Cola?"

"She's a French designer who went to Hollywood to design costumes for the movies, and . . ." She could see a grin behind the hand in front of his mouth. "You think it's silly, don't you?"

Tommy straightened his expression and cleared his throat. "No."

Tina didn't believe him. "Well, let's see how much you laugh when I come back here famous and—"

"New York City's not like here, you know," he pointed out.

"I know that."

"It's loud and crazy. People rushing everywhere. Everything going so fast."

"Everyone knows that, but have you been there to see it?"

"Yeah."

"When?"

"When I was seventeen. I went down there for an amateur fight. I, uh, used to box. Anyways, that year I was the local champ and got to go down there to a state competition."

"Did you win?"

"Naw. I lasted six rounds. Had the guy dancing pretty good, but he got me with a left hook, and it was all over."

"Do you still box?"

"Not in the ring." Tommy smiled. "But my talent hasn't been wasted."

Tina shook her head, and gave him a disapproving look that caused him to change the subject.

"So how come you haven't gone yet?"

Tina started to respond but stopped while the waitress served them each a piece of chocolate cake. She couldn't resist taking a big forkful. "Mmm, this is so good."

"You were about to tell me why you haven't gone to New York."

"Well, I wanted to go when I graduated. Mama and I had it all planned." Tina put down her fork. "But then she died and . . ."

"Your family's lucky to have you." He picked at his cake with his fork.

"As much as I want to go, I would worry about them. Especially after what happened to Tony. It could've been Angelo or Carmen. They swim in those dangerous places, too."

Tommy shrugged. "That's where me and my friends swam every year, and most of us are still around."

"That doesn't mean things shouldn't be better now. Kingsburg needs a pool for the kids. I'll bet if the Mayor's neighbors complained about not having a pool, he'd build one."

"I don't know. Maybe," Tommy said, and finished his cake in two bites.

Tommy parked his car in front of Irene's shop, jumped out, and ran around to open the door on the passenger side for Tina.

"Thanks for lunch," she said, as she climbed out.

He grabbed her elbow. "I was hoping we could make it dinner next time."

Tina hesitated. "Well . . . I don't know."

"Oh, come on," he coaxed. "You didn't have such a bad time, did you?"

"No, it wasn't that. I have to cook dinner for the family."

"So, we'll go after you cook."

She tried to ignore the hopefulness in his eyes. "But I have to stay home with Carmen."

"You went to the movies the other night."

"That was because Irene took Carmen home with her. I usually have to be there."

He persisted. "I tell you what. Try to get out of doing that stuff some night, and we'll go out. You can always reach me at my diner."

"Sure. OK." She stepped toward the shop door. "I've got to get back to work. Thanks again for lunch."

"Constantina," Tommy called out.

She stopped and turned around.

"Pretty name for a pretty girl."

In spite of herself, Tina flashed him a smile as she pushed the door open and went inside.

CHAPTER FOUR

"Look, I was trying to get you elected. I told 'em what they wanted to hear." Tommy faced Mayor George Steele. He had called a meeting with the mayor and his assistant, Steven Anderson, at their usual spot in an abandoned barn outside of town. "How did I know these crazy people would remember about the pool?"

Tommy was already guilt-ridden by the guys at the funeral, but Tina's plea to him about a pool for the kids had clinched it. He had to do it for her. In fact, he couldn't think of anything he wouldn't do for her.

"There's no pool in my budget," Steele said without hesitation while shoving his pipe into his tobacco pouch.

"That's never stopped you from doing something you wanted before." Tommy tried to look as cool and calm as the mayor.

Steele lit his pipe. "I don't know what you're talking about."

Tommy knew better. "Don't give me that crap. I ain't one of your high-tone friends."

"I know perfectly well who I'm talking to, and you can tell your people to forget about the pool."

"Jesus, Mayor, to hear you talk, somebody'd get the impression that you don't think too highly of *my people.*"

Anderson, who had been standing off to the side, thrust himself between Tommy and his boss. "That's enough." He turned toward Steele. "George, how long are you going to listen to this small-time hood?"

Steele cleared his throat. "Are you finished, Capello?"

Tommy couldn't let it go at that. "Look, these guys mean business. They're ready to go to old man Hettinger with a story for his paper. A story like that could start the wrong people digging a little deeper into things they shouldn't know."

"And you really think I'm worried about Hettinger?" Steele put on his hat, and took a puff of his pipe. "Believe me, it would not be in his best interest to print that story, and he knows it."

Tommy had no comeback; he could only stand there speechless.

Anderson said, "We're done here," Steele turned on his heel, and Anderson followed him out.

Left behind, Tommy quickly unbuttoned his collar and wiped his face with his handkerchief. Then, with rage building, he grabbed a nearby pitchfork stuck in a bale of hay and threw it across the barn.

Miss Snow often enjoyed reading a good book on her favorite park bench. People passing by her never failed to show their courtesy with pleasant greetings, but they also respected her free time and didn't engage her in idle conversation. However, today she had more on her mind than reading, and the purpose of her visit to the park appeared in the form of Mayor Steele. He too removed his hat as he approached and wished her a good morning. But then she gestured for him to join her.

"What can I do for you?" he asked as he took a seat beside her. "Is the school short of funds?"

"We can always use more, but we're managing to maintain within our budget."

"Then why the summons to meet you?"

"I know that Tommy Capello has approached you about a swimming pool."

"Yes. Rather an extravagance right now, don't you think?"

"Not necessarily. It's hard to put the worth of one of our children in dollars and cents."

"We've had accidental drownings before."

"Precisely, and that's why I can't stand by any longer and watch another one of my children die needlessly."

"I'll tell you what I told Capello. There's no money allotted for a pool in the city coffers." Apparently planning to end their conversation, Steele stood up.

Miss Snow put her hand up as if to say, "I'm not done yet," and Steele resumed his seat. She fixed him with a stern stare and said, "I suggest you use some of the payoff money you've collected."

Steele's eyebrows rose almost to his hairline, and his face flushed. "How dare you—"

Again she raised her hand. "Don't forget, I taught school in this town when you were just a gleam in your father's eye. I've seen how you got to where you are, and I know where you want to go. You may be able to control Tommy because he depends on you for his livelihood, an arrangement that I don't condone. But I choose to overlook it because I prefer to devote all of my energy to my students."

A passerby tipped his hat to her, and she nodded to him. "But don't think for a minute, George, that I can be handled. We both know that I'm quite highly regarded in this community, and in Albany. I know a lot of people who know a lot of people—some that could make or break your career."

Miss Snow rose, and he took his cue from her to do the same. Facing him, she tapped him lightly near his breast pocket with her forefinger, and while looking him directly in the eye, instructed him as she would a disobedient student, "Build the pool, George."

Like everyone else in the neighborhood, Tina had heard the rumor spreading around that the town would build a pool. She wanted to believe it but decided that she would wait to celebrate when she saw the children frolicking in the safety of the crystal-clear water.

She stopped in Sarducci's on her way home from work a few days later to pick up some things for supper. Entering the back of the store, she turned to the bushel of oranges, ignoring the voices coming from the back room. When she heard Tommy's name, she edged closer to a basket of cantaloupes right outside the doorway. Grabbing a melon, she used the basket as a shield while she listened to their conversation.

"We should've threatened Steele a long time ago."

"Naw, it's because the time was right. He's getting ready to make a play for his friends in Albany."

"Capello knew it too, and he wanted us off his back."

"All he wants is to be left alone to run his business without . . ."

At that moment, Mr. Sarducci walked up to Tina, poised behind the cantaloupes. "You gonna buy that cantaloupe, or you gonna squeeze it to death?"

Tina and Rosie met for a picnic lunch at the park two weeks later to witness the pool groundbreaking ceremony nearby. Tina wanted to see the mayor stick the shovel into the ground with her own eyes. On the other hand, Rosie hoped to catch a glimpse of Tommy, whom she assumed would also be there. When she didn't see him anywhere around right away, she whined, "I was sure he'd be here. I didn't come here to listen to the mayor's old speech."

With nothing else to do but look around too, Tina watched as Steele posed for pictures and held court with reporters. She turned and spotted Tommy standing behind a group of people. But before she could tell Rosie, the voice of the Fire Marshall boomed from the podium, grabbing her attention.

"Good afternoon. I'm happy to see that so many of you are here to witness the groundbreaking for our much-needed pool in our fair town. And we have our own Mayor Steele to thank for it. So at this time, I'd like to ask the mayor himself to say a few words."

Steele replaced the fireman at the podium as reporters moved in closer with their notepads and cameras. "Thanks, Harry. I'm proud to be able to stand up here today and set in motion a dream that I've had for a long time . . ."

Rosie giggled over the mayor's words. "Yeah, ever since Tommy gave him a talking to."

"You mean, threatened him," Tina corrected her.

"Yeah, isn't he something?" Rosie waved coyly to Tommy across the way. "I honestly don't know why you don't like the guy. If he'd asked me out, I'd have gone in a minute."

Tina glanced his way and saw him tip his hat to them. "You know what he really cooks up in that diner of his, don't you?" Tina said with disdain.

Rosie smiled. "I think it's exciting. He's the closest thing this town's got to a gangster."

Tina didn't have time to respond to Rosie's silly comment. Their attention returned to Steele who thanked the Fire Department for giving up their refurbishing funds to build the pool, and introduced Steve Anderson. Tina had heard enough, so without waiting for the shovel to hit the dirt, she signaled to Rosie to leave.

The next few weeks crawled by. School had ended for the year, summer had officially begun, and the boys, though delighted, required more supervision. Carmen asked Tina every day when the pool would be ready, and in the meantime, she prayed that the kids would stay safe as they continued to swim at their usual places. One saving grace was that the builders had allowed the older boys in town to help out with the pool construction by hauling dirt and cleaning up.

Tina, though relieved that it would keep Angelo out of trouble, was surprised that he gave up his baseball time to work on the pool. He actually seemed to like it, and he boasted to everyone that he was "building the pool." Luckily, her father had started getting called in to work more frequently since summer weather lent itself to repair jobs on the railroad. Not only did it bring in much-needed money, it gave him less time to feel sorry for himself and take it out on Tina.

When not at Irene's shop, Tina tried to keep up with the ever-present household chores, which she found boring, and at times, backbreaking work. She knew other girls her age had married and had to keep house, but they had chosen that way of life. In her case, fate had cast her into this unwelcome role, and she still longed for the day that she could leave Kingsburg and begin the life she envisioned for herself.

Tired, and needing a change, she recalled Tommy's offer to take her to dinner. She could really go for a nice dinner at a fancy place with waiters at your beck and call. She had seen first-hand at their lunch that Tommy really knew how to show a girl a good time. But she still had trouble accepting his line of work and his tactics for getting what he wanted. So she reminded herself that she wouldn't fall victim to his charms and made sure that she kept her guard up when he met her outside of Irene's shop on her way into work one day.

"Hi there." Tommy blocked the doorway. "Got a minute?"

"Just one," Tina said.

"I'm still waiting to hear from you about that dinner you promised me."

"I don't remember that I promised," Tina said.

"Well, how about it, Constantina?"

She grinned at his use of her full name, and said, "I really can't say now, and I have to get to work."

"Well, I'm not giving up, you know?" He smiled broadly and leaned toward her. "I'll wait to hear from you."

Tina smiled, sighed, and said, "OK. I'll let you know." Even though she had no intention of doing so.

━┿ ┿━

As the completion of the pool neared, the town buzzed with excitement and anticipation. Miss Snow, who usually went to visit family for the summer, delayed her trip in order to attend the celebration. The kids could hardly be contained for the entire week before the opening.

Opening day activities began with a parade of marching bands, local merchants, religious leaders, and town officials, all led by Grand Marshal Mayor Steele, to the pool site, where a host of events were scheduled throughout the day. The mayor had instructed his staff to go all out to capitalize on the event. Steven Anderson wasted no time in obliging by using any and all of his contacts to attract politicians and celebrities to jump on the bandwagon. All of them sought positive publicity in a time when Americans had become disillusioned by President Hoover and his party's inability to save them from their financial woes.

Local entertainers performed, but the appearance of Tom Mix, a well-known cowboy movie star, gave the residents of Kingsburg something to talk about for years to come. Although the Mayor and Anderson got credit for it, it was purely a stroke of luck that Mr. Mix happened to be performing in a circus nearby. He had come to town with his horse to use the services of the blacksmith down the street from the Benedettis.

Excitement radiated throughout the house that morning, as everyone got ready for the day. In particular, Angelo beamed with nervous energy. "You know, we almost didn't make our deadline in time, cuz the concrete guy got there late the other day. We weren't sure the pool would even be dry today," he said, clearly having taken ownership of the pool construction.

Tina giggled. "Well, you kids did a great job. You should be proud of yourselves." She kissed him on the cheek.

Angelo promptly wiped the kiss away. "Cut it out, will ya?" he said, but his bold grin and crimson face gave him away.

Tina had assumed that Carmen and Patsy were already in place on the parade route, but instead she found them at the blacksmith's with the rest of the neighborhood kids. They had spotted the cowboy while on their way to see the parade that morning and planned to stay there and follow the entourage as it made its way to the pool site. Tina had never seen Carmen so happy. As she continued on up the street to meet her friends for the parade, she remembered the delight she'd seen on her brothers' faces that morning and couldn't help being thankful to whoever was responsible for the pool and the long-overdue pleasure it brought her family.

After the parade, the crowd made its way into the park, where local food vendors had set up carts with hot dogs, peanuts, cotton candy, and other carnival treats. The residents from both sides of the track mingled as Tom Mix demonstrated his rope tricks, guest speakers sang the Mayor's praises, and performers belted out the latest tunes. Tina and Rosie walked up to Irene as she had pulled Carmen to her for a hug.

"Carmen, sweetheart. How's my boy? All ready to swim today?" Irene took two nickels out of her purse and held them out to him. "Look, I've got something for you. Go buy yourself something to eat."

"Gee, thanks, Irene!" He snatched the nickels. "You're swell," he said, and ran off with Patsy.

"You're going to spoil him, Irene," Tina said with a smile.

"I hope so." Irene glanced at Rosie. "How are you, Rosie?"

"Good, thank you, Mrs. Janson."

"The Capello boy was looking for you, Tina."

"Oh yeah?" Tina said, using her best nonchalant voice. "Where is he?"

"He's over near the soft pretzel stand that he set up. You like pretzels, yes?" Irene hinted.

"Come on." Rosie tugged at Tina's arm. "Let's go say hi to him."

Tina let Rosie pull her toward Tommy but waited for Rosie to speak to him first. "Hi there, Tommy. I hear your pretzels are pretty good. Tina and I would like to split one," she said, handing him a nickel.

Tommy turned around, and ignoring Rosie, handed a pretzel to Tina.

"Thank you." Tina quickly broke a piece off and handed the rest to Rosie. "Rosie likes them better than I do."

"Well, enjoy." He finally looked at Rosie and said, "Say, I wonder if you could do me a favor, and take a couple of these to those two women over there?" He pointed to two gray-haired ladies sitting in the shade. "They're my aunts."

Rosie gave Tina a smirk, then turned back to Tommy and sighed. "Sure. Be happy to."

Tina took a step away to follow Rosie, but Tommy grabbed her arm and signaled to her to follow him away from the crowd.

"You never called me about that dinner." He sounded more disappointed than annoyed.

"I've been busy, I guess. Like you. I hear that you're the man to thank for all of this."

"You get some credit, too."

"Me?"

"You're the one who talked me into thinking the kids should have a pool."

Tina wasn't convinced. "So that's the only reason?"

"Well"—Tommy cleared his throat—"I was trying to impress you."

She felt her face flush, and all she could mutter was, "Oh."

"Rosie was pretty impressed," he said.

Tina laughed, and without thinking, said, "Rosie's in love with you."

Tommy didn't look amused. "I was hoping you would be."

"I'm not as easily impressed."

"I meant, be in love with me."

This time, she couldn't muster any comeback. And he must've misinterpreted her hesitancy, because he grabbed her quickly and pulled her to him. But she realized what he was doing, so she yanked herself out of his arms, and hurried away.

Although the children had loved the cowboy and enjoyed some of the other festivities, they remained eager for the ribbon-cutting ceremony that would signal the opening of the gates to the pool. So when the horn actually sounded to announce that the time had arrived, the kids wasted no time lining up at the gates. They waited through the mayor's speech, as well as Miss Snow's statement of gratitude and of course, more pictures, before they could let loose in a collective yell at the top of their young, but sturdy lungs.

Tina dragged into the house that night. She didn't know why, but she did know that she suffered more from emotional exhaustion than physical. It had been such an unusual day. In addition to all the festivities, Tommy Capello actually told her that he wished she loved him. Of course, she didn't love him. But why hadn't she minded the brief moment that his face had touched hers? She didn't know what to make of that.

⊨⊨ ⊨⊨

From that day forward, the pool was the most popular spot in town for its kids. The Benedetti boys and their friends were no exception and made sure that they arrived early enough to claim a portion of the pool for themselves. A bit shy at first, all of the town's youngsters took a few days to settle in and become comfortable with the new playground.

The afternoon of the fourth day, Angelo, Dumpy, and Carl led some others from their neighborhood to the pool, where they dropped their towels and yanked their pants off as fast as they could.

A north side kid yelled from across the pool. "Look out, here come the wops!"

Angelo and Dumpy looked at each other, and turned around to see where the voice had come from.

"Yeah, look at those crummy trunks of theirs." Another kid yelled, referring to their homemade swimsuits. "Where'd ya buy those?"

A third kid chimed in. "Go on back to your own side of town. You don't belong here."

"We got just as much right to be here as you. Maybe more, cuz we helped build it," Angelo said.

"Big deal. You dug and hauled some dirt," the first kid said with a laugh. "That's what dagos are good for."

With that, Angelo dove off the side into the pool, and landing right next to him, threw a punch into his nose. After recovering from the blow, the kid returned one to Angelo's chin. Within seconds, the water turned crimson, and their friends jumped in flailing their arms at each other.

A policeman rushed to the poolside. "All right, all right. All of you, break it up, and get out of there!"

The boys waded over to the steps and took turns climbing out.

"OK, who started this?"

"He did." The north side kids spoke in chorus, while pointing to Angelo.

"What's a matter with you, Benedetti? The mayor builds a nice pool for you and your friends, and you still got to make trouble."

"But, officer, these guys was calling us names." Carl pointed to their smart-aleck faces.

The officer smacked his nightstick into the palm of his hand. "You never heard of sticks and stones will break my bones—?"

"Yeah, but . . ."

The cop shook his head. "Proves what I've always said: 'You can take the grease ball out of the slums, but you can't take the slums out of the grease ball.' Now all you south side kids get out of here!"

Dominic had spoken to Mr. Sarducci about increasing Angelo's work hours until school started. Some days, the extra five hours a week kept him peddling produce around town until suppertime. When he did get off a little earlier, he wasted no time getting ready to meet his friends for the evening. This Saturday night, a dance was to be held in the church hall. And although he and his buddies didn't dance a lot, they couldn't miss an opportunity to flirt with the girls.

"Hey, Mr. Sarducci, Mrs. Donato was complainin' about the escarole again," Angelo told his boss when he returned to the store.

Mr. Sarducci waved him off. "Heh, it's not my produce; it's her cooking." He smiled and inspected Angelo's cart. "It looks like you did pretty good today, Angie. Here's a little something for you."

Angelo looked pleased with the quarter and shoved it into his pocket. "Thanks, Mr. Sarducci. See ya tomorrow."

When he arrived at home, he let the screen door slam behind him and ran right past Tina, working in the kitchen, on his way upstairs. Tina shook her head, but kept right on cutting up the carrots she had picked from the garden earlier. As she scooped them up to put them in the pot, Angelo yelled down, "Hey, Tina, where's my clean shirts? I can never find nothin' around here anymore."

Taking the pot to the sink, she yelled back, "They're in the basket down here in the back room."

She filled the pot with water while he flew down the stairs. She followed him into the back room, pulled a shirt out of the basket of laundry, and handed it to him.

He slipped his arms into the shirt. "Pa come in yet?"

"No," she answered, "but he told me to tell you that the vegetables need picking."

"Oh, all right, I'll do it tomorrow after mass."

"And"—Tina hesitated—"he left something for you to do down cellar."

"Now what?" Angelo walked over and opened the cellar door, with Tina on his heels.

At first, only the familiar mustiness combined with the stale smell of wine hit him as he walked down the stairs, but within seconds, he jumped at the sound of a chicken cackling and flapping its wings.

"What am I supposed to do with this?" he said, turning back to Tina in the doorway.

"Pa wants it for dinner."

Angelo's face dropped and turned white. "Why do I have to do it? It's his job."

Tina shrugged. "I guess he thinks you're old enough now. I'll be right back."

After she left him on the stairs, Angelo looked at the chicken, who seemed to be looking him straight in the eyes. Angelo glanced over at the ax hanging on the wall with dried blood on it, then back at the chicken. He continued slowly down the stairs, took off his clean shirt, picked up the ax as if he was afraid to touch it, and set up the chopping block on the workbench. Ax in hand, he took a deep breath and began to cluck, calling out, "Here chick, chick, chick. Here check, chick, chick." But the chicken walked away from him.

"Come on, chickie. This wasn't my idea. C'mere, chick, chick, chick."

Creeping closer to the bird, he lunged toward it but fell on his stomach when it jumped free. Angelo tried again with the same result, so he tried to block its way. But the chicken turned and went the other way. Angelo stopped, thought a minute, lowered the ax, and pretended to look at something behind him. Unfortunately, the chicken would have none of this game and was ready for Angelo when he lunged yet again.

"Damn it," he said. "C'mon. I don't want to be here all night!" He started chasing the bird around the room, prompting the bird to screech and take flight from one side to the other, feathers floating everywhere.

Upstairs, Tina heard the commotion and threw open the cellar door to see what was going on. She stood in silence as Angelo continued to chase the chicken. Then, much to his surprise, he caught it. He took a moment to catch his breath, and carefully took the chicken, fighting and scratching, to its guillotine.

Once Angelo was finally able to spread the bird's neck on the block, he squeezed his eyes shut, and quickly brought the ax down toward it. The chicken flinched and cackled as the ax missed it. Tina watched him do the same thing twice more, each time missing by about six inches, before she shook her head and walked down the stairs.

"Angie, go get cleaned up to go out. I'll take it to Sarducci's."

With a look of relief, Angelo let go of the chicken and replaced the ax on the wall.

"Come on," Tina said, laying a hand on his shoulder as she followed him up the stairs. "I'll put some mercurochrome on those scratches."

When Angelo got home that night a few minutes past his ten o'clock curfew, he found the back door locked so he went around to the front. The front door was locked as usual, but he could see Dominic through the window, sitting in his chair, smoking his pipe.

Angelo rapped on the front door and called out, "Hey, Pa, it's me, Angelo." When Dominic didn't respond, Angelo pounded on the door and called again, "Pa, come on."

Once again, no response, so Angelo went to the window and tapped on it. Dominic looked over at the window. He slowly snuffed out his pipe, got out of his chair, turned off the light, and headed up the stairs.

"Where are you going?" Angelo pounded on the door. "Let me in! Why are you doing this again?"

Obviously, Dominic had no intention of opening the door for him, so a defeated Angelo sat down on the porch steps mumbling and swearing under his breath. Then he darted from the house and ran down the street.

Inside, Tina came out of her room rubbing her eyes and met Dominic at the top of the stairs. "What was all that noise?" she said through a yawn. "Was that Angie's voice I heard?"

"The boy knows what time to come home," Dominic said on his way to his bedroom. "After that I lock the door."

"Where is he? You didn't let him in?" Tina panicked, flew down the stairs, and called out the door to the empty street.

The next morning, a groggy Tina poured Dominic a cup of coffee at the kitchen table. "Why are you so hard on Angie?" She put the pot back on the stove and sat down across from him. "I'm worried about him gone all night."

"He's OK. He takes care of himself."

"But he's only a . . ." Tina stood up when she heard Angelo slam the back door.

He walked into the kitchen on his way upstairs, and Tina grabbed his arm. "Angie, are you all right? Where have you been?"

He pulled his arm out of her grasp, and stood there. "Irene's," he said.

Dominic stirred his coffee, cleared his throat, and voiced his disapproval to Angelo without looking up, "Why did you go there?"

"I went to Carl's the last time."

"Are you hungry?" Tina said.

"I ate." Angelo moved toward the stairs, bumping into Eva on her way into the kitchen.

"What's he mad about?" Eva said as she opened the cupboard and took out a cup and saucer.

Ignoring Eva, Dominic got up and said, "I'm going to mass." And left without another word.

When Dominic was out of earshot, Eva looked in his direction and said, "Good morning to you, too." She dropped down into a chair with her coffee and shook her head. "God, I love this place."

Always the peacemaker, Tina sat down to explain, "He had a bad night."

"Oh yeah? How many bottles did he go through?"

"What do you care, anyway? I'll bet you don't even know that Angie didn't sleep here last night . . . since you barely made it home before dawn yourself."

"I've got a life of my own."

Eva doesn't care about anybody, but herself, Tina thought. "Pa locked him out again," she said."

"Yeah? Well, the door was open when I came home, and Pa was dead to the world."

Tina shook her head. Besides being exhausted from lack of sleep, she saw herself as the rope in the tug of war going on between her father, Eva, and Angelo. It took all of her strength to keep from snapping in half, and she feared for what would happen when she did. These were the times she really wished that her older brother, Luciano, had lived. Instead, he died as a toddler the year before she was born. If only he were here now to carry some of her responsibilities.

She would light a candle at church this morning to ask God for help with this burden.

But before meeting Rosie for the ten o'clock mass, she filled the largest pot they had with water, and put it on the stove. Then she took off the pot of tomato sauce that had been simmering all morning, and set the table for their usual twelve o'clock Sunday dinner.

After mass, Tina had to walk by Irene's shop on her way home, so she stopped in to check on some materials she needed for a dress she planned to work on the next day. She didn't want to disturb Irene, so she let herself into the shop. As she went through the drawers, Irene walked in from her apartment in the back.

"Tina, what are you doing here today?"

Tina turned. "Looking for this thread," She held out the spool. "I wanted to make sure I had it for Mrs. Shultz's dress."

"OK, but nobody should work on Sundays. You go with your friends, and enjoy your day off."

Tina had expected her to say that, and smiled. "All right, all right. I'm leaving."

"Before you go, come inside," Irene gestured toward her apartment. "I'll give you some of the blintzes I made."

Tina followed her in. "Maybe they'll make Angie feel better. Pa's still mad at him." She sighed and groaned. "How can I go to New York and leave those two alone? They'll kill each other."

Irene patted Tina's hand. "Please try to be patient with your father, and the time will come for you to go."

That afternoon, while Tina and Rosie socialized with their friends at the soda fountain, Dominic called upon his old friend, Irene. She had sent a message through Carmen that she wanted to talk to him.

"Oh, Dom, I'm glad you came." She opened the door wider for him. "Come on in and sit with me." She pointed to the couch. "I just poured myself some coffee. You'll have a cup with me?"

"OK. Thank you." Dominic took a seat on the couch, and Irene poured his coffee from a carafe on the coffee table.

"Irene, I'm sorry Angelo bothered you last night. He should not have come here."

"And why shouldn't he?"

Dominic answered with a shrug and took a sip of coffee.

"He needed to talk to somebody," she said. "He was very mad at you."

"Heh, that's the way it is. He don't listen to me. All the time he's gone."

"He's getting older."

"Carmen don't talk to me either. Now his sisters, he talks to them all the time."

"They miss Luciana. That's all."

"Six months, she been gone. That's enough time to cry!"

Tina and Rosie finished their sodas, said goodbye to their other friends, and walked out of the drugstore. Rosie turned toward their street saying, "Come on. I've got to get home. My cousins are coming over."

"No, wait"—Tina stopped—"I remember that I forgot something at the shop earlier. I meant to take some material home with me for a dress I'm working on. I'm going to sneak back before I go home."

"Sneak?"

"Irene will kill me if she sees me in there again. She hates me working on Sunday."

"Oh, OK." Rosie shrugged. "I'll see you later then."

Tina arrived at the shop and unlocked the door. She tiptoed across the room, so as not to alert Irene.

Back inside the apartment, Irene and Dominic continued their conversation.

Dominic's voice softened. "I'm sorry, Irene. You mean well, I know, but . . ."

"I just want to make it all right again for you." She touched his face. "For all of you," she added.

Taking her hand from his face, he kissed it. "You are such a sweet woman. Why have you never remarried after Sam?"

"All the men as good as Sam were already married."

He put her hand down. "But alone all these years . . ."

"I have the shop," she said. "It takes up so much of my time. And your children. I've always felt like they were my own."

Dominic nodded, and gave her an awkward hug. "Uh, again thank you for letting Angelo stay . . ."

Back in the shop, Tina had heard voices through the apartment door left ajar, and tiptoed closer to eavesdrop. Recognizing her father's voice, she peeked into the room.

"You don't have to thank me, Dominic. I did it out of love."

Tina smiled at the couple's expression of friendship, until Dominic pulled Irene to him with fierce abandon and kissed her on the lips. Tina stood in shock, fighting to suppress an audible reaction.

Inside, Dominic seemed to realize the line he had crossed and released Irene. But Irene's response was to draw him back toward her and say, "It's all right."

Tina lost all feeling in her body as she watched her father and her beloved friend undress with a sense of urgency that she had never experienced in her young life. She didn't want to see any more and covered her eyes until she could coax her feet to take her out of that place as fast as they would carry her.

The next morning, Tina was torn between never going back to Irene's again, and going there to confront her about what she had seen. In the end, she went to the shop and decided she wouldn't talk to Irene at all. She would work on Mrs. Shultz's dress in silence.

Irene unlocked the door as Tina had walked up to it. "You're here bright and early this morning," Irene said pulling up the window shade.

"I wanted to finish Mrs. Schultz's dress." Tina walked straight to her machine and began threading the bobbin.

"That one. She's in almost every day while we're making her dresses. She thinks if she stands over us, we'll do a better job. Who knows, maybe she's right." Irene began sorting material. "I'm expecting the shipment any day now with that material we ordered special for Mrs. Steele. Now there's a nice lady. With the mayor for a husband, you'd think she would be pushy, but she's so easy to work for."

Tina placed the material on the machine without responding.

Irene didn't seem to notice. "I hope you got a lot of rest yesterday, because we will probably be here late today. We've got a bridal party of eight coming in. The McDonald wedding is Saturday."

"OK." Tina wanted Irene to stop talking, but she didn't.

"Your father will have to cook dinner tonight. He's a good cook. He should cook more often." She stopped for a breath. "I remember when your mother was alive, when you were little, he would invite all the neighbors over and cook them enough food for an army."

Tina pursed her lips and reached for the scissors.

Irene barely missed a beat. "Everything, he'd cook. Luciana wouldn't have to lift a finger. He would do it all. He would say to her—"

Tina dropped the scissors on the table. "Stop it, Irene! How can you go on and on like that? As if nothing happened. Talking about my mother . . . just like you used to before . . . before . . ."

"Before what?"

"Before I saw you yesterday. You and Pa . . .

Irene swallowed hard. "What? What did you see?"

"I came back to get my material. I didn't want you to know, so I snuck in. When I heard Pa's voice, I looked in and . . ."

"What were we doing?"

"Oh, Irene, it's bad enough. Don't make me say it."

"Oh, Tina. I'm so sorry."

"How could you do that? How could you both do that . . . to my mother?"

"I love him," Irene whispered.

"Since when?"

"Since before you were born. Your father was so kind to me when my husband died. I think it was then that I fell in love with him."

"And all that time, mama thought you were a friend," Tina snapped.

"I was. She didn't know."

"So both of you were betraying her behind her back."

"It wasn't like that. Dominic didn't know either. Not until yesterday."

"So as soon as she's gone you moved—"

"It wasn't that way."

Tina would hear none of it. "It doesn't matter how it was. You did it, and I hate you!"

The words reverberated in Tina's ears, much like a slap, and to look at Irene's face, she might have actually struck the blow.

Irene slumped in her chair, put her head down, and rubbed her brow for several seconds. When she lifted her head, her eyes brimmed with tears, and her voice quivered. "You are young yet. You don't know how a woman feels."

Tina could not comprehend the depth of Irene's emotions and would not accept her excuses for what she believed to be Irene's betrayal of her mother. She lashed out at her, "Well, you want him? You've got him. You deserve each other. But don't think I'm going to be a bridesmaid in your wedding!"

CHAPTER FIVE

Angelo huddled in the darkness, clutching the belted pillowcase filled with all his valuables, waiting for the 4:00 A.M. freight to pass through the Kingsburg crossing. When it did, he slipped the knapsack around his neck and took off in chase toward a boxcar with one of the doors partially open. He had no problem catching up to it, but leaping onto the moving train proved to be harder. When he finally grabbed on, he fought to keep his balance atop the car and shimmied his way through the door.

Once inside, he crouched in the corner and waited for his eyes to adjust to the pitch-dark car, panting from fear as much as from the physical exertion. He sat without moving for several minutes, until the train made its way through the crossing and began to pick up speed. Only then did his breathing ease as he stretched out his legs. Now able to see better, he rummaged through his bag for a flask of water and took a gulp that tasted better than any he'd ever had.

He remained on guard, listening for any signs that he would be found, until the ambient light disappeared. He hugged his knees and relived the events that had led him here. His father's last rejection had been more than he could take. Eddie's and Henry's reasons for leaving home and their romantic tales of freedom on the rails wouldn't stop repeating in his ears. By Sunday afternoon, he had made up his mind to follow them.

With mostly darkness around him, he became aware of the rumbling wheels beneath the damp, hard wood floor. Although not nearly as comfortable as his bed at home, the rocking floor and the noise reminded him that with each revolution of the wheels, he was getting farther away from Kingsburg and his father. That made him smile. Before long, he lay back, and using his knapsack for a pillow, let the continuous rhythm of the car rock him to sleep.

<hr />

That same morning, Tina heard someone whistle from below her bedroom window. She looked out and saw Carmen's friend Patsy waiting with a rolled towel in his hand.

Downstairs, Carmen yelled, "Hey, Eva. I'm going swimming!"

Tina opened her door. "Wait, Carmie!" She ran down the stairs to find him in the kitchen.

Carmen looked confused. "Oh, where's Eva?"

"She had to work."

"Don't you have to work today?"

"No."

"OK, well, Patsy's waitin' for me." He turned toward the front door.

"Got your towel?"

"Yeah." He held it out. "Bye."

Tina grabbed his hand, pulled him to her, and gave him an extra-long hug. "Be careful, all right?"

He tried breaking away, but she waited until he answered before kissing his cheek and letting him go.

"OK, see ya." He wiped his cheek with the back of his hand and took off.

Tina hesitated and then went to the window to watch him and Patsy run down the street. When they disappeared from view, she went back up to her room to continue packing. She had decided that she couldn't stay in that house any longer. Not after what had happened yesterday. Her stomach became queasy just thinking about her father and Irene, let alone having to face them again.

Besides, her father wouldn't need her around anymore, now that he and Irene would probably marry. And wasn't this the opportunity she had prayed for, a chance to start her new life in New York City guilt-free? Still she hated leaving her brothers, and though she didn't want to admit it, she would probably miss Eva, too. So before leaving, Tina ironed their clothes and baked a cake. Then she wrote a note, apologizing for abandoning them.

Tina was glad to find the train station busy when she arrived. It would be easier to blend in with the crowd and not be seen by anyone she knew. She caught a glimpse Eva in the diner where she worked and took care to avoid her, finding a seat on the opposite side of the room. Confident that she would not be disturbed, she took out a pad and pencil and started sketching dresses.

Her concentration was broken when a policeman rushed into the waiting room. Out of breath, he went directly to the lunch counter and asked for Eva. When Eva stepped to the counter and the officer began talking, Tina couldn't make out what he was saying. But Eva became agitated, yanked her apron off, and hurried with the policeman out the door.

A vision of her father lying injured on the tracks sprang into her mind, and she ran up to the counter, identified herself, and asked a young waitress what the police had wanted with Eva.

"He said that Carmen was in trouble and that he would take her to him."

Oh God, not Carmen, she thought. "Did he say where?" she asked the young girl.

"I think he said at the lake." Tina turned to leave, and looked down at the suitcase in her hand. She couldn't run and take it with her. So she handed it to the girl and took off out the door.

Tina ran all the way to where the south end of Liberty Lake formed a cove. The lake bordered the north side where it was calm and well-suited for swimming and boating. The water at the south end was affected by a factory's back-up generator, which often caused whirlpools and other movements dangerous for swimmers. But it was close by, and the young kids liked to play there.

She followed the commotion as she neared the shoreline. She strained to find Eva, Angelo, or her father, but she couldn't spot them amid the maze of local and state police, firemen, onlookers, and children running around.

Finally, she came upon a neighbor. "Have you seen my family?" she asked, her voice urgent.

The woman pointed to Eva, talking with a fireman.

Tina ran to her. "Eva, what happened?"

Eva spun around. "Tina, where were you? I've been looking all over for you."

Tina didn't answer, but looked up at the fireman. "I'm Carmen's sister, too. Where is he?"

"His foot got caught on a clamp out there," he pointed to the water. "The clamp is attached to that pole he's hanging onto. One of our guys tried getting it off with his bare hands, but he couldn't do it, and I don't know how long your brother can hold on."

Tina tried hard to grasp the situation. "So what are you going to do?"

"I've called for help and more equipment."

"He's out there all by himself?" Tina broke away from them and ran closer to the water's edge. "Carmen, Carmen!" she screamed.

Out in the distance, Carmen grabbed the pole tighter with one hand and waved at them with the other.

She panicked. "Hang on with **both** hands, Carmen. Hang on tight!"

She immediately set out to find Patsy. When she found him, she grabbed his arm, pulling him toward her. "What were you two doing here?"

Patsy looked terrified, his eyes red and tear-filled. Sniffling, he said, "Uh, Carmen wanted to. We didn't have money for the pool, and we wanted to swim."

"Money?" Tina had no idea what he was talking about.

Before he could answer, Irene pulled up in her weathered station wagon and made her way to them. "What happened?" she asked.

Tina heard her, but still uncomfortable about the scene at Irene's yesterday, she only walked away.

Eva looked confused as she watched Tina leave, but she turned to Irene and cried, "Oh God, Irene. Carmen's stuck in the water."

"Stuck?"

"Somehow his foot got caught on a clamp in the water. They can't get it loose, and he has to hang onto that pole so he won't drown."

"How terrible!" Irene strained her neck to see him in the water. "Where's your father?"

"They sent somebody for him."

"And Angelo?"

"I don't know," Eva said. "He left before I got up this morning."

Irene shook her head and called out to Carmen. "Carmen, baby. Hold on tight." She turned around to wipe her tears and make the sign of the cross.

In the meantime, Tina had found out from Mrs. Farina and some other neighbors that the town had begun charging the children to swim in their new pool. That, of course, prevented most of the south side kids from getting past the gates. Somehow, Tina wasn't surprised. She knew a pool had been too good to be true.

She would be angry if worry about Carmen hadn't consumed all of her energy. Her neighbors tried to comfort her, and when she could take no more of their platitudes, she stormed up to the fireman. "Where are those men you called? I'm afraid he won't be able to hang on much longer."

He pointed to two men approaching them with ropes and life-saving rings. "Here come some of them now."

"Where's the boy?" one of them asked.

"Out there. The first thing we need to do is to take the rope and tie him to that pole. He can't hang on much longer by himself."

"OK."

"Were you able to get the helmets?" the fireman asked his associate.

"The Army Air Force has a couple of them available, but they're about twenty miles away at the base. They'll arrive on the one o'clock train."

Tina had already begun to blame herself for Carmen's plight, and she couldn't take standing around waiting and watching Carmen bob up and down in the water. "Can't you keep trying to work on the clamp until they get here?"

"Look, my guys can't stay under long enough to do what has to be done. We're doing the best we can."

Before Tina could respond, she heard a voice from behind her. "What the hell is going on here? Get my son out of there."

When she turned around, her father was in her face. "You know better than to let Carmen come here!"

She explained how the boys had ended up there but avoided saying that she had been at the train station when it happened. Dominic accepted her answer and looked to the fireman for the details of the situation. Tina and the others had no choice but to wait from the shore while the men secured Carmen to the pole.

With that accomplished, Carmen rubbed his eyes as one of the men handed him a canteen of water from inside the rowboat. The onlookers breathed a collective sigh of relief that Carmen no longer had to rely on his strength to keep afloat.

In the meantime, the divers had arrived. They made their way out to the scene with their helmets. Unfortunately, rain clouds seemed to have followed them from the army base and threatened to compromise the already challenging rescue. While they worked, a hush fell over the shore, as the Benedettis and their friends did the only thing they could: pray.

Angelo awoke when the force of the train stopping caused him to slide forward. He sat up and wiped his eyes with his sleeve. When the blurriness cleared, he remembered where he was, and he heard footsteps outside. Then the boxcar door flew open. The glare of the sun made him squint so much that he could barely make out the silhouette of a uniformed man with a billy club in his hand. Angelo could only tremble in the corner as the officer jumped into the car.

"Well, good mornin', sonny boy. Had a nice ride?"

"Uh-huh."

"Good," the guard said as he took Angelo's arm and pulled him up. "Let's go."

The guard jumped out first, waited for Angelo to do the same, and grabbed his arm again. Looking around, he pulled him over to the side of the car, and swung his club at Angelo's other arm. Angelo cried out and went down on his knees. Still writhing in pain, he felt the club on the side of his neck, and everything went black.

When Angelo came to, he rubbed his throbbing head and stood up. It took him a few minutes to get his balance. When he did, he looked down for his knapsack but didn't see it. He turned around and spotted it in a puddle by the tracks. Snatching it up, he emptied out the soggy contents. The flask was the only thing still intact, so he gulped down the rest of the water.

He had known that they might throw him off the train, but Billy and Henry hadn't said anything about getting beaten up worse than his father had ever done to him. His arm was bruised, and his head sported a lump, but the growl in his stomach is what got his attention. Down on the ground was the now-waterlogged food he'd brought with him. Knowing he'd have to find food elsewhere, his eyes followed the tracks for signs of life. Just a mile or so down, he saw a crossing where buildings and homes flanked the tracks, and he began to shuffle toward it.

He followed the bend in the tracks at the railroad crossing and looked up to see the skyline of a big city in the distance. He figured that there would be plenty of grocery stores where he might find free food. Mr. Sarducci always put his old produce and day-old bread outside his back door for neighbors to take if they wanted. With his spirits lifted, and anxious to get to the closest store, he threw his shoulders back, took a deep breath, and quickened his pace.

Having made his way into the city, he now stood at the foot of a towering building and looked up at the windows. When he had counted eleven stories, his head began to spin, and he listed backward. As he stepped off the curb at the corner, a taxi horn sounded a warning, causing him to sprint to the other side of the street as the cab narrowly missed him. He continued on, and after passing a few grocery stores with no back entrances, he gave up the idea of getting a handout. His stomach ached, and he began to panic. Until he came upon a delivery truck parked in front of a market.

"Need some help with those potatoes, mister?"

The man with a sack over his shoulder turned toward Angelo and gave him the once-over. "Sure. Grab one."

His pay for unloading the truck bought him a bowl of chili and a cup of coffee at a diner. After he finished eating and using their toilet, he walked outside. The sun had set, and he began to wonder where he would sleep. For lack of anything else, he found lodging in an alley near three other homeless fellows using cardboard and newspapers for a bed. The cold, hard ground offered no comforting rhythmic beat like the boxcar, and the stench from nearby garbage cans made him nauseous. Despite these things, and the incessant noise of the city, he finally drifted off.

He awoke to the nudge of a billy club on his back and heard the voice of a cop with an Irish brogue.

"You'll be needing to move on, kid."

Angelo opened his eyes. "What?"

"I said you can't stay here. It's against city ordinances."

Angelo sat up and looked around. His neighbors were nowhere to be seen.

"I didn't know, sir." He did know that he wanted no part of that billy club staring him in the face.

"Well, I'm here to tell you it's true. Where you from, son?"

"Kingsburg, sir."

"Ran away, huh?"

Angelo nodded.

The cop lifted his hat, and scratched his head. "Come on. Get up. Come with me."

Angelo had no choice but to follow him to jail.

Three blocks later, the cop stopped in front of a window sign that said FRIENDS MISSION—GOD IS HERE FOR YOU. EVERYONE WELCOME.

Angelo sighed with relief when the cop led him inside and spoke to a kind old woman at a desk. He turned to Angelo and said, "They'll fix you up. Now stay off the street and out of trouble, or I won't be so friendly the next time we meet."

Angelo thanked the cop and waited for directions from the old lady. He didn't know what to expect but figured it had to be better than a moving boxcar or the street, so he took the blanket and pillow she gave him and followed her into a dark room where he could barely make out the rows of cots lined up. She pointed to an empty one on the other side of the room, and he wound his way past arms and legs of snoring men to get to it.

He put the pillow on his cot and eased himself down. Then he curled up and pulled the blanket up to his nose. The snores and mumbling of the men had replaced the sounds of the city, and the stink of stale booze and body odor now reeked more than the garbage in the alley. He pictured Carmen in bed in their room and couldn't remember why he had always complained about having to sleep with him. Afraid to fall asleep, he fought to stay awake, but he lost the battle just before daybreak. The next he knew, someone was calling, "Soups on."

He stood in line with the others as a couple of women spooned out oatmeal and gave them biscuits. He poured himself some coffee and took his seat on the bench at the long table. All the seats faced the same way, so he was spared from having to face his disheveled fellow boarders, but he'd barely had a few bites before a minister stood before his "congregation" and started preaching the word of God.

Angelo, who'd been an altar boy for the past four years, laughed to himself at the sound of this man trying to convince him to find God. But his stomach couldn't hear a thing and welcomed the hot meal. After taking a warm shower, he walked out feeling like a new man and ready to move on. Having decided that he'd had enough of this city living, he set off to catch the next freight that he came upon.

━━┥╀ ╀┝━━

Sprinkles began to drop on the spectators, as the men finally emerged from the water, but no one moved from their place.

Everyone's eyes focused on the man lifting Carmen out of the water and into the motor boat.

Tina wiped her face, now wet with a mixture of rain and tears, and murmured, "Thank you, God."

She tried to get a glimpse of Carmen, but the diver had wrapped him in a blanket. When the boat arrived at the shore, the crowd ran toward it, and Tina had to fight her way through to get ahead of them. She finally caught up to Dominic, who had made his way to the water's edge with Dr. Channing, the local physician. Together they watched the men lay Carmen on the shore.

Channing immediately pulled instruments out of his black bag and examined him as Tina, Eva, and Irene watched over his shoulder. The cut on Carmen's foot encircled his entire ankle, so the doctor made quick work of bandaging it and turned to the family surrounding him.

"He seems fine, but take him home and put him to bed. He's had quite an ordeal, and he needs to rest." He handed Tina a jar. "Here is some salve. Be sure to apply it twice a day, and I will check on him in a couple of days."

Tina took the salve, and Dominic scooped Carmen up into his arms. "Come, Carmen."

"I'm hungry, Pa," Carmen whimpered.

"Good. We'll go home to eat."

They walked toward the fire wagon, where a fireman waited by its open door. Dominic put Carmen into the vehicle and got in behind him. Tina and the entourage of family, friends, and neighbors headed back to their homes. Irene attempted to talk to Tina, but Tina ignored her. Instead, she looked over at Eva.

"Go to Sarducci's to get Angelo."

Tina turned and walked off by herself, staring at the ground. She could hardly sort through the happenings of the last couple of days. The shock of Sunday afternoon at Irene's seemed so long ago, dwarfed by the fear of losing Carmen.

Now on the street, deep in thought, she heard her name. She looked up with tears in her eyes to see Tommy standing by his car. "Come on, let me give you a ride home."

Overwhelmed by the day's events, she stopped and held his gaze only long enough to reveal the hurt, anger, and contempt she felt for him and his accomplice, the mayor, before going on her way.

Tommy drove home with a lump in his throat. Tina's look had hit him harder than any punch he'd ever gotten in the ring as a boxer. He knew she blamed him for Carmen's ordeal because the neighborhood had given him credit for persuading the mayor to build the pool. Who knew that after his meeting with Steele there was a chance in hell the pool would happen? Maybe he had hit home with the campaign angle. At this point, he didn't care. After this close call today, he wanted nothing to do with the pool or the mayor.

But how to make Tina know he had been no part of the scheme to milk the kids for the cost of the pool? She could barely stand him before; now she hated him. None of his usual charm would smooth this over, and he saw no way to get into her good graces. But she was the best thing that had ever happened to him, and he couldn't give up.

Tina hesitated at the sight of her suitcase on the front porch when she arrived home. She'd forgotten all about it. After putting it away and disposing of the note she had left in her father's room, she went to Carmen's room, where her father had undressed his weary son. After tucking him into bed, she wasted no time before frying up some loose hamburger in onion and garlic and adding crushed tomatoes. It bubbled on the stove while Dominic went out to the vegetable garden to get the makings of a salad. Carmen hadn't eaten all day, and he needed the meat to rebuild his strength.

Tina looked up from the stove when she heard the screen door slam and called out, "Angelo?"

"No, it's me," Eva answered from the back room, and stepped into the kitchen. "He wasn't at Sarducci's because he wasn't supposed to work today, and Mr. Sarducci hasn't seen him since yesterday afternoon."

"Well, Pa was looking for him, and I can't believe he didn't show up at the lake today. Practically the whole town was there."

"You know that he and his dumb friends hitch a ride out of town to fish sometimes."

"That's true," Tina reasoned to herself. "You better go up to Carmen, and see if he's OK. Tell him I'll be up in a few minutes with his supper."

Tina could hear laughter from the hallway as she carried a tray to Carmen's room, and found Eva tickling him when she entered.

"Yeah, Carmie. We didn't think you wanted to come home," Eva laughed. "You seemed pretty *attached* to that lake."

Carmen shrieked and slapped the sheet. "Yeah, that's a good one."

"I don't think that's very funny," Tina said as she sat the tray in front of him. "After the day we spent, how can you joke about it?"

"Oh, Tina," Eva sighed. "You're such a drip."

Carmen shrieked again, this time with his mouth full. "Yeah, you drip like water."

Tina realized he was right, but tried not to smile. "I don't care. Make fun of me, but I want you to eat this whole plate, and then I'll read you a story before you go to sleep." She peered over at Eva. "Eva can do the dishes tonight."

Tina tried to sleep with an open ear, but when she Carmen resting comfortably, she drifted into a deep sleep. The sound of his voice calling her name awakened her. With eyes only half-open, she could barely see Eva sound asleep in the bed next to hers, before she made her way into his room.

"What's wrong, Carmie?"

"My foot hurts real bad," he cried.

She leaned over, touched his warm forehead, and whispered, "Angelo, are you awake?"

When he didn't answer, she got up and turned on the lamp. She looked over at Angelo's bed and saw that it had not been slept in. Her stomach sank. *Not again.*

She sighed, sat down next to Carmen, and tried to lift the bandage. "Let me see your foot, baby."

"Don't touch it," he begged.

"I won't. I just want to look."

"Ouch!" He began to cry. "You're hurting me."

"I'm sorry. I didn't even touch it."

"Yes, you did."

"I have to look under the bandage."

"No."

"Carmen, I have to."

"OK, but do it quick."

She lifted the gauze from the angry wound, and when the air hit it, Carmen jumped and yelled out. Dominic entered the room. "What's the matter?"

"Look at his foot, Pa."

Dominic took a look and said, "It hurts pretty bad, huh, Carmen?"

"Yeah, Pa. Real bad."

"I'm going to get the salve and more bandages," she told Carmen, rising to her feet and signaling for Dominic to follow her.

In the hallway, Tina whispered to Dominic, "Something's wrong. He's got a fever."

"If he's not better in the morning, you call the doctor."

"OK, Pa . . . Oh, and Pa." The tone of her voice dropped. "Angelo's not home. Did you know that?"

"No. Maybe he went to Irene's again."

"I'm sure she would've sent him home."

"He'll be home when he gets hungry."

Tina tossed and turned the rest of the night. Her worry alternated between Carmen's injury and Angelo's absence. No one had seen or heard from Angelo all day, and it frightened her. The previous morning at the train station seemed almost like a dream to her now, and she couldn't imagine not being there for her brothers when they needed her.

Finally realizing that she'd never be able to sleep, she got up. Her watch said six-thirty as she tiptoed out of her room and into Carmen's, where he laid there whimpering.

"Carmen, is your foot feeling worse?"

"Yeah," he groaned.

She bent over, touched his burning forehead, and ran out of the room.

Eva stirred has Tina approached her bed. "Eva, get up. I need you to go get Dr. Channing!"

"Right now? It's not even eight o'clock."

"Yes, now. Go around to his house entrance. It's Carmen's foot. It's badly infected, and he's got a fever. Hurry up."

As the doctor examined Carmen, Tina paced around the room biting her lip. When he finished, he called her and Eva aside. "I want to take him to the hospital."

"The hospital?" Eva said, as if she hadn't realized that was a possibility.

Tina hadn't been ready for that either. "Is that really necessary?"

"Yes. His fever is 104, and we've got to get it down. There are things we can do for him there that we can't do here."

"All right, I'll get him ready." Tina turned to Eva. "Go try to find Pa at work, and check with Dumpy and Vinny to see if they know where Angelo is. He's been gone too long."

"OK. I have to stop by the station too, because I'm supposed to work later. And I'll let Irene know."

The doctor explained to Carmen that he would be going to the hospital. Carmen wailed that he didn't want to go, and Tina tried to comfort him as she gathered a few of his things. But he didn't quiet down until Dr. Channing scooped him up in his arms.

"Come on, young man. Let's go make you feel better."

The doctor's confident tone helped calm her too as she closed up the house and joined them in the doctor's car.

At the hospital, the nurses whisked Carmen away, leaving Tina alone in the waiting room. She tried to sit still, but her inactivity caused her to think back to how, because of her preoccupation with her own problems the day before, the blame for Carmen's injury fell directly on her. She stood up and walked to the end of the hallway and stared at the sign on the exam room door. *Oh, why won't they let me in there?*

She wandered back to the waiting room at the same time Dominic arrived.

"Where is he?" Dominic asked her.

"They took him into a room a while ago, and I haven't heard anything since."

"What does Channing say?"

"That he could treat him better here."

At that moment, a young nurse's aide approached them. "Miss Benedetti?"

"Yes?"

"They sent me to take you to Carmen's room."

Tina got up to follow her, but hesitated and gestured for Dominic to come with them.

"This is my father," she told the aide.

The aide led the way until the sound of Carmen calling her name told Tina that the room was nearby. She hastened her steps and went in, but Dominic hung back at the doorway while she walked to the bed where Carmen lay shivering under icy cold towels.

"Carmie, I'm here." Tina stroked his forehead. "Pa's here, too."

"Tina, make them stop. I'm so cold."

Tina looked over to the nurse at the foot of the bed and watched her roll a towel floating in a tub of ice water through a wringer. When she finished she took the towel and laid it over Carmen, causing him to jump up and squeal, "It's too cold!"

"Now lie still, young man. We have to do this." The nurse eased him back down and gave Tina and Dominic a pleading glance for help. Tina looked over at a stoic Dominic, clutching his hat at the foot of the bed, and saw that he would be no help.

She turned toward the anxious boy. "Carmie, they have to do it. It won't be much longer." She tried to distract him. "Listen, you never told me about that movie you went to see with Irene. What was it about?"

"I don't know," he mumbled.

Dominic's eyes had glazed over, and he continued to stare in silence as Tina struggled to divert Carmen's attention. "Sure you do. Think."

"Uh"—Carmen swallowed hard—"It was about a guy whose horses got stolen by some bad guys, and he . . ."

With that, Dominic moving in slow motion placed his hat on his head and walked out the door.

Eva finally arrived at Carmen's room during afternoon visiting hours with a sandwich wrapped in waxed paper, and a canning jar of coffee for Tina. She hesitated to approach Carmen, as if frightened by the sight of the spirited little boy now drained of all his energy by fever and pain. She eased over to his bedside, did her best to cheer him, then took Tina aside in the doorway and whispered what she had learned about Angelo.

"He must've slipped out of the house right after Pa left for work, and headed for the tracks. Dumpy said he sounded serious and made him swear not to tell anyone."

"I can't believe this. What made him think he could get away with that? Pa's said plenty of times how kids get caught riding box-cars and get thrown off."

"I know, but Dumpy said they met some kids a couple of weeks ago who told him they'd made it all the way from Oklahoma or something, so I guess he figured he could do it too."

"And he was right." Tina rubbed her forehead. "This is terrible."

"What are we going to do? Should we tell Pa?"

"We have to. Have you seen him lately?"

"No. Hasn't he been here?"

"Yeah, for a few minutes late this morning, but he left."

Eva rolled her eyes. "Sounds like Pa."

"You better go home and see if he's there. Tell him that Carmen needs him. Oh, and you're going to have to tell him about Angelo."

"Do I have to do it?" She screeched. "He's going to yell at me."

Tina shushed her. "Eva, he has to know right away."

"Oh, all right." Eva prepared to leave, but stopped. "Irene came with me. She's waiting outside. I'll tell her to come in."

"No, wait," Tina said. "You stay here. I'll send her in, and I'll go use the toilet and wash my face."

"OK." Eva stepped back into the room, and picked up the sandwich and jar. "Here. You better take this and eat it in the lobby."

＝＋ ＋＝

Carmen spent a long day alternating between burning up and freezing cold. Finally, sheer exhaustion took over, and he fell asleep. Tina had sat in the chair next to him all day wondering why God hadn't chosen her instead of Carmen to suffer so. Why this innocent baby, when it should be her in that bed?

Relieved to see him finally resting, she folded her arms on the foot of the bed, placed her head on them, and slept herself. At eight o'clock, with some light still in the sky, the nurse tapped her gently and told her that visiting hours were over for the day, and she had to leave. After an unsuccessful attempt to persuade the nurse to let her stay, she kissed Carmen's cheek and made her way down the hallway.

Tina found Rosie reading a magazine in the lobby. "Hi," she said with a sigh.

Rosie tossed the magazine aside, jumped up, and wrapped her arms around Tina. "How is he?" she asked.

Tina savored the hug for a moment, then broke away. "Not good."

"I'm so sorry. I thought they would help him here."

Tina flopped into a chair. "They're doing everything they can, I guess. It's just not working."

"Are you here by yourself?"

"Yeah, now I am. My father was here for a few minutes this morning, and Eva and Irene came by for a little while this afternoon."

Rosie shook her head and sat next to her. "What would they all do without you?"

Tears moistened Tina's eyes. "Oh, Rosie, it's all my fault that Carmen got hurt."

"That's silly. It wasn't—"

"No, I wasn't around that morning after he left to go swimming, so I didn't find out that he didn't stay at the pool."

"Well, you had to go to work."

"But that's just it. I didn't go to work. I packed my suitcase and went to the train station to catch the 10 o'clock to New York City."

"You didn't tell me you were going to do that!"

"I know. I didn't tell anyone. I decided that I had to get away from everybody and do what I wanted to do." She began to sob. "And now Carmen's suffering, and Angelo's gone."

"Gone where?"

"He told Dumpy that he was going to hop a freight and get as far away from Kingsburg as he could. And now nobody has seen him for two days."

"It's not your fault he left."

"Yes, it is."

"How do you figure that?"

"I resented having to stay home and take of him, and Carmen, and Eva, and I wished so hard to be able to leave that I willed these things to happen."

Rosie smiled. "Boy, I always knew that you thought you were a little bit better than everybody else, but you don't really think you have that kind of power do you?"

Tina stopped sobbing and looked at Rosie with disbelief. "You think I act like I'm better than everybody else?"

Rosie handed her a handkerchief. "Sure. You always have. But your friends don't mind. You don't mean anything by it. You're only being you."

"I just think I should always do the very best I can to make things right for me and everyone I care about."

"I know. It's OK. But I'm trying to make you see that you alone are not responsible for everything that your brothers and sister do and everything that happens to them."

"But I feel like I let my mama down."

"You're your mama's child, too. She wanted you to be happy and healthy. And I knew her well enough to know that she'd hate you being so hard on yourself."

Rosie had her faults, but she was always there for Tina. So on their way home, she managed to convince her that she wasn't the only one responsible for her brothers and sister. Then she waited until Tina was safely inside before turning toward her own house.

With Carmen and Angelo gone, Tina wished that Eva was home. Instead, the silent darkness enveloped Tina as she walked into the house. Even after she turned on the kitchen light, the eerie stillness caused her to hesitate before going to the sink to get a drink of water.

When she finished, she went to the parlor and turned on the radio. The familiar croon of Bing Crosby broke the silence and helped to distract her. Where did Dominic go that was more important than being with his sick child? *Might he be with Irene? No, Irene would insist he go to be with Carmen.* Rosie's words had helped to fuel Tina's anger about Dominic's indifference to his family, so although she really wanted to take a bath, she hunkered down in the parlor and waited for him to come through the door.

The slam of the back screen door jolted Tina awake. Startled, it took her a moment to realize that she had drifted off on the couch. The radio station had long ago signed off, and all that remained was a low-level hum, allowing her to hear her father rustle about in the kitchen, opening and closing cupboard drawers and doors.

Tina got up and turned the dial off, and stepped into the kitchen as Dominic gave the dog, who had accompanied him in, a cracker.

"Good boy," he murmured to the animal while patting him on the head.

Tina spoke from behind him. "Hello, Pa."

Dominic looked back at her. "What are you doing up?"

"Waiting for you."

"What's a matter?" His words were slurred, which was unusual for him. Even though he could drink most of his friends under the table, he almost never showed it.

Tina edged closer to him. "We've got trouble, Pa."

"Eva told me about Angelo. He thinks it's better out there? Well, let him find out."

"But, Pa . . ."

"Is Carmen's fever gone?"

"No."

"Why not?"

"I don't know. It's not. Why did you leave today?"

"He asked for you, not me." Dominic pulled the cord on the kitchen light, the room went dark, and he staggered past her into the parlor.

She followed him in. "You could've helped."

"How?" He moved to the stairway, then stopped.

"To make him feel better."

Holding the rail, he started his ascent. "You made him feel better."

Tina stopped at the foot of the stairs and watched him go. "Pa, he needed both of us," she cried out. "He's so sick and in pain." She waited for his response, but he continued on up in silence.

"I couldn't make him better," she shouted. "Maybe if you'd been there, he'd . . ." Her voice trailed off at the sound of the bedroom door shutting behind him.

CHAPTER SIX

The sun peeked out over the hills as Tina walked at a fast clip toward the hospital on the north side of town. Luckily, she knew the woman volunteer stationed at the entrance and was able to talk her into letting her go up to Carmen's room. Before pushing the door open, she took a moment to breathe deeply, capture her courage, and force a smile.

"Good morning, sweetheart." She went to his bedside, where he lay unresponsive. She used every bit of cheerfulness she could muster. "Carmie? I told you I would be back first thing this morning."

She could barely understand him as he attempted to say hello, and a touch to his forehead told her he still had a fever. The nurse walked through the door, so Tina signaled for the woman to move to the opposite side of the room with her.

"How was he last night?" she whispered.

"He was fitful, and I couldn't get him to eat anything."

"When will the doctor be here?"

"Probably around eight-thirty."

Tina had prayed for an improvement, but instead Carmen was worse. *Now what will we do?* Her mind raced with morbid thoughts, and she fought back tears. She hated to admit they were as much for herself as for Carmen. The nurse began her routine with the water and the towels, and Tina prepared herself to hold Carmen still. She soon saw that it wouldn't be necessary; he no longer had the energy or the will to fight the procedure.

The process continued for the next two days. Eva, Dominic, and Irene took turns with Tina at Carmen's bedside, and Tina stopped at the church each day to light a candle. Discouraged because her prayers seemed to go unanswered, she ran out of Carmen's room more than once when she could not stop her tears from flowing.

Taking her turn one morning, she broke down. *Oh, Mama, I can't do this without you. And now I don't even have Irene,* she sobbed as she walked into the women's bathroom.

A sense of hopelessness consumed her as she stood alone in the tiny space. It had only been a matter of days since Angelo was home, Carmen was healthy, and Irene had been her friend. When she closed her eyes and splashed water on her face at the sink, she pictured the cleansing substance miraculously washing away the life-changing events of the past week. And she wished with all her heart that when she opened them, she would be back at the grand opening ceremony with Rosie and Irene, watching Carmen and Angelo brim with excitement over the new pool.

Within minutes, somewhat composed but still bleary-eyed and despondent, Tina set aside her emotions and shuffled back toward Carmen's room. Turning the corner, she noticed someone in front of his door and picked up her pace. As she approached, she thought she recognized the familiar figure but blinked twice to clear her vision.

When she was sure, she ran to him, wrapped her arms around him, and crushed the Yankees cap he held in front of him. "Angelo!"

Angelo smiled but struggled to speak. "Ugh," he said with a laugh, "I can't breathe."

Tina released him. "Oh, I'm sorry." She stood back to look him over. "How are you?"

"I'm OK. Where's Carmie? Mrs. Farina told me he was sick and that I should come here."

Tina explained Carmen's situation to Angelo, then brought him into the hospital room to say hello.

Angelo stopped inside the door and whispered, "What do I say?"

"Just talk to him like you always do. Only say something happy to make him feel good."

Angelo crept up to the bedside, where Carmen lay with eyes closed, agitated and fidgety. He stood there a minute before speaking. "Hey, Carmie. How ya doin', kid?"

Carmen's eyes fluttered at Angelo. "Angie?" he whispered.

"Yeah, it's me. Sorry I ain't been here sooner, but I was, uh . . . workin'."

"OK."

"Hey, uh, Mr. Sarducci's been askin' for ya. Guess he misses ya comin' around with the coal."

"Yeah?" Carmen croaked.

"Sure. He told me to tell you to hurry up and get better. He's gonna raise the price of coal as soon as you get back."

Carmen closed his eyes again and struggled to answer. "OK."

Angelo pressed his lips together before he spoke. "OK, I'll see ya later, kid. I, uh, gotta go to work."

Angelo looked up at Tina, and blinking back tears, he ran out of the room.

Tina followed him. "Angie, wait."

He stopped, and Tina went to him. "I know it's hard, but I know it made Carmen feel better."

Angelo wiped his nose with his sleeve. "I guess."

She changed the subject. "Angie, where did you go?"

Angelo recapped his trip for her, softening his run-ins with the police, and ultimately saying that he came home because he missed everyone.

"Even Pa?" She asked.

"I don't know. But I'm not afraid of him anymore."

With Angie now safely at home, Tina's burden had lessened somewhat, so she dozed off in the chair. Tommy, who had hesitated to visit a couple of days ago, couldn't stay away any longer. When he showed up and found Tina asleep, he went to get her a cup of coffee, then sat down to wait for her to awaken. Finally, she stirred, and he offered her the coffee. When she refused, he insisted, so she took a sip, and then another.

"Thank you. It's good."

Tommy could see the exhaustion on her face and the pain in her eyes. "How is he?"

She shook her head, and he placed his hand on hers. "What can I do?" he asked.

She shrugged. Feeling helpless, he took out his wallet and handed her several bills.

"I can't take that. Besides, it won't help Carmen."

They both looked up as Dominic entered the room. Rejected, Tommy put the money and the wallet back into his pocket.

"Oh, hello, Pa. Do you know Tommy Capello?"

"I know who he is," Dominic barked.

"Good to meet you, Mr. Benedetti." Tommy held out his hand, but Dominic ignored it. Tommy could tell he wasn't wanted, so he got up to leave. "Well, I'd better get going. Uh, you take care of yourself, Tina."

Tina looked up and into Tommy's eyes, and smiled. "Tommy, thanks for coming. Oh"—she held up the cup—"and for the coffee."

"My pleasure," he said, and turned to her father. "Goodbye, Mr. Benedetti."

Tommy was still in earshot when Dominic blurted out his opinion of Tommy. "Since when you friends with him? Big shot he is with his money and the pool . . ."

⊷⊷ ⊷⊶

Tommy drove to his diner and parked out front. He sat for a moment before moving, deep in thought. He couldn't get Dominic's remarks out of his head. *"Big shot he is with his money . . ." The old man has me pegged. I'm a fake, and he knows it.* Even though Tommy had more dough stashed in his house than Benedetti had probably ever seen in his life, it was dirty. The old man was no dummy. Dominic had probably had the same choices himself back in his day that Tommy had, and he'd chosen to stay on the up and up. Knowing that made Tommy feel like the bum he knew he was.

He got out of the car and walked down the street to St. Paul's Church. He entered through the sacristy, as he'd done as an altar boy. It took him back to the days when he would arrive ahead of the priest and other altar boys, to prepare for mass. Could he really have been that young and innocent?

He walked out onto the altar, made sure to genuflect, and sat down in the first pew of the empty church. After making the sign of the cross, he knelt down and said the "Our Father" and "Hail Mary" in his head. Then he did what he had come to do: ask God to make Carmen well and make Tina forgive and respect him, even though he doubted that God would listen to a guy like him.

Later that night, Angelo made his way through the park with a wagon full of fertilizer bags and crept to the fence surrounding the pool. He slung a bag over his shoulder and climbed halfway up. As he prepared to heave the sack up and over the fence, a man's voice called out, "Halt. You there, what do you think you're doing?"

Angelo dropped the bag, jumped down, and turned slowly toward the police officer.

"What is it you've got"—he got a whiff of the ripe fertilizer, and coughed—"Jesus! . . . in those bags?"

"Shit," Angelo said under his breath.

"What?"

Angelo sighed. "Manure. It's manure."

"That your idea of fun, Benedetti? Plugging up our pretty new pool with that shit?"

"Uh, no sir."

"Then why the hell were you doing it?"

"Steele's lucky I didn't plug him," Angelo mumbled.

"What did you say?"

"Nothin'."

"Wait a minute." The policeman stopped. "Benedetti, huh? You're the one with the brother who got hurt over to the lake."

"Yeah. You gonna take me in?"

The cop wiped his brow. "I should, but you'll stink up me and the station with that crap all over you. Besides, it's my dinner break. So consider yourself lucky, cart this manure back where it came from, and go on home."

That night, Tina said good night to Angelo before crawling into bed. Though her worry over Carmen never escaped her, Angelo's return helped to lighten her load. Tommy's visit had been interesting. He always seemed to show up whenever she needed someone. Even that dumb cup of coffee he had given her tasted better than most. Maybe the weight of the past week had worn her down. Whatever it was, the thought of him didn't seem to infuriate her nearly as much as it had a few days ago.

Tina arrived at the hospital the next day, and saw that Carmen had not improved. The nurse informed her that the doctor would be in later that morning, and he would like to talk to her father. Tina got a hold of Angelo and told him to find Dominic and Eva and get to the hospital as soon as possible. They all arrived before the doctor stepped through the door.

Dr. Channing led them into the hallway to give his report. "We haven't been able to stop the infection. We've used everything we have."

"What about another hospital?" Tina asked.

The doctor shook his head. "All the other hospitals nearby have the same resources."

Dominic, who had been standing off to the side, spoke up. "What are you saying?"

Channing hesitated. "I'm saying that going someplace else will cost a lot of money. And the only treatment I have is to amputate the foot."

"No!" Eva cried.

"I'm sorry." Channing turned back to Dominic. "We have to decide very soon."

"How long do we have?" Tina said.

"Well, the sooner the better, but no more than forty-eight hours. Dominic, I have some papers for you to sign."

"I'll sign no papers!"

"But, Pa, he just said that . . ." Angelo pleaded softly.

"I heard him!" Dominic spun around and strode away, leaving his family and the doctor dumbfounded.

A few minutes later, Tina stormed out of the hospital with Eva on her tail. "Where are you going?" Eva asked. "Why is everybody leaving?"

"We've got to do something," Tina declared as she led her sister toward the City Hall building.

At the front desk, Tina drew herself up to her full height. "We'd like to talk to Mayor Steele," she announced.

"I'm sorry. He's not in his office."

"We need to talk to him. It's an emergency."

"But I told you he's . . ."

"I have to talk to him now! My brother is going to lose his foot, or he may die, and the Mayor has to do something."

"Wait a moment." The woman got up. "I'll get his assistant."

Tina took a deep breath, and looked over at Eva. She was waving to her friend, Johnny Rossini, as he exited the probation office. When Steven Anderson appeared, Johnny skulked away.

"What's going on here?" Anderson demanded, towering above her. Though nervous and starting to regret her impulsiveness, Tina spoke clearly. "I'm Tina Benedetti. My brother Carmen is in the hospital, and he's going to lose his foot if we can't find another doctor to help him soon."

"That's a shame. But why do you think that Mayor Steele can help?"

His condescending tone fueled her anger. "He needs to pay for another doctor or hospital for Carmen, because it's his fault that Carmen got hurt."

"What are you talk—"

"Steele started charging the kids to swim," Tina said. "Carmen didn't have the money, so he went to the lake and got hurt."

Anderson dug in. "That was a financial decision. It doesn't make him responsible for your brother or any other kid . . ."

"Unless of course it was a kid from his neighborhood. He knew those kids could afford the pool, and he didn't care about the kids from our end." Surprising herself, she didn't try to censor her words. "In fact, he doesn't care about our neighborhoods at all. He thinks we're all tramps and thugs, but him not helping Carmen is criminal—and worse than we could ever be."

Anderson took Tina's arm, and pulled her toward the exit. "Now, that's enough. You need to leave."

Eva pushed herself between them and glared at Anderson. "You take your hands off her!" She put her arm around her sister's shoulders. "Come on, Tina. Let's go."

Frustrated and desperate, Tina knew what she had to do. So later that night, she walked into Tommy's empty diner and wandered around looking for signs of life. Seeing none, she looked down a hallway and spotted a door with light spilling out from under it. She tiptoed toward it and slowly turned the knob. The door opened, and she found herself at the top of a stairway to a cellar.

The smell of cigars and cigarettes hit her, and below she heard voices and the sound of dice rattling and slamming against a wall. She descended a couple of steps and saw several men playing cards and dice. Others stood at a bar, drinking. Her eyes searched the room, and she spotted Tommy sitting at an old desk, talking on the phone.

She caught the attention of the bartender, and he signaled to Tommy, pointing her out. Tommy's mouth dropped, the phone followed, and he made it to the stairway in a flash, where he hustled her up the stairs and into the diner.

"Tina, what are you doing here?"

"I need to talk to you."

He looked puzzled. "OK." He directed her to a booth. "Sit here."

She scooted into the booth, and he brought them each a cup of coffee. "How's your brother?" he asked as he slid into the bench across from her.

"That's why I'm here. Dr. Channing says he's done all he can for Carmen, and they're going to have to amputate his foot, or . . . or we'll lose him."

"Jesus."

"I went to Steele to beg him to get a specialist for him, but he was out of town, and his assistant said that Steele wasn't responsible for what happened, and he wouldn't help. Can you believe that?"

"Oh, yeah. That goddamn Steele. Maybe I ought to take care of him once and for all."

Tina placed her hand on his arm. "That won't help Carmen. But you've been around, and you have some money. Do you know of another hospital or doctor that could do something else for him?"

"I'm not sure."

Tina hated doing it, but she had no choice except to put herself at his mercy. "We can't afford anyone else, but Carmen needs help, and I don't know who else to go to . . ." Tears threatened. "I know I've been pretty miserable to you, but . . ."

"I'll pick you up in the morning. We'll go to Albany."

<hr />

Tommy bathed, shaved, and dressed faster than usual. He loved the idea of spending a whole day with Tina, even if it was under such bad circumstances. But he knew that it came with a risk. The doctor who had treated him after a prizefight while he was in Albany a couple of years ago might not remember him, or maybe he wouldn't or couldn't help Carmen. Tommy had to try, though, knowing that he'd never forgive himself for his part in Carmen's accident if the boy lost his foot.

The late August day was muggier than usual, and sweat dampened the shirt under his suit jacket as he walked up to Tina's front door. The thought of sitting next to her for an hour ride both ways to Albany didn't help either. What would they talk about? Would she talk at all? But she greeted him with a lovely smile and seemed to be in pleasant spirits as he showed her to his car. If just offering hope for Carmen made her this friendly, he really looked forward to the day when Carmen would fully recover.

Much to his relief, Dr. William Walker remembered him and agreed to examine Carmen the next day. Tommy and Tina would meet the eight A.M. train and take him to Carmen's bedside.

"Tommy, I can't thank you enough for doing this today," Tina said as Tommy helped her out of his car in front of Kingsburg Hospital.

"It wasn't that much," Tommy answered, relieved to be able to tell her that.

"But you offered to pay Dr. Walker for his time, and that won't be cheap."

Tommy shrugged. "It's OK."

Tina stared at the sidewalk. "Well, I want you to know that . . . whatever happens, I'll remember what you've done, and I'll always be grateful."

The station buzzed around them with early morning arrivals and departures. They had gotten there well ahead of the eight o'clock from Albany and had taken seats to wait in silence. In fact, they had hardly spoken that morning. There wasn't anything to say. The only important words would come from Dr. Walker after he examined Carmen.

So Tommy read the morning paper while Tina remembered the last time she'd sat in the station: the morning of Carmen's accident. She tried to wipe it out of her mind by counting the light fixtures hanging overhead, but she couldn't sit any longer and got up to pace back and forth in front of Tommy.

He looked up and watched her for a few moments, then folded his newspaper, tucked it under his arm, and stood up. "Come on. Let's get a cup of coffee."

Tina followed him into the diner, and they sat down at the counter. He ordered two coffees and two doughnuts and did his best to coax her to eat. But she only managed to take a bite of the dough-nut and a couple of sips of coffee before Walker's train arrived.

Dr. Walker and Dr. Channing walked into the waiting room to-gether after examining Carmen. "Well, Doc," Tommy said, "what can you do for him?"

Walker lit a cigarette and offered one to Channing, who de-clined it. They both sat down across from Tina, Dominic, and Tommy.

Dr. Walker's tone was somber. "Well, I don't have to tell you that you have a very sick boy in there. Ordinarily I would have the same prognosis as Dr. Channing, but recently I've become aware of a technique that might be appropriate here. It's unusual and not very appealing, but it has been found to work in some cases."

"What is it?" Tina said.

"The procedure uses common maggots to rid the area of infec-tion," Walker answered.

"Maggots?" Tina's eyes widened.

"What you talking, 'maggots'?" Dominic mumbled.

Walker took a drag off his cigarette. "I know it sounds absurd, but it really is medically sound. However, even with it I don't be-lieve we can save all of his toes. We'll have to remove the last two because the loss of circulation has caused them to turn gangre-nous. But once that is done, I feel that we will be able to attack the infection to save the rest of the foot."

Tina's hand flew to her mouth. "Oh my God."

Tommy could see the horror on her face. "Are you sure about this? Have you ever done this kind of thing before?"

"No, I haven't, but I have a colleague who has been successful with it."

Dominic looked over at Channing. "This is a crazy idea, no?"

"I admit that I had trouble with it at first. It's actually a method used for centuries. I didn't realize it was still considered acceptable practice, but I have faith in Dr. Walker, and my first and only concern is with Carmen's recovery. If this can increase his chances, than I have to agree."

A nurse approached Dr. Channing. "Doctor, you're needed in Emergency."

Channing rose and thanked the nurse, before turning back to Dominic. "I'll be available anytime you're ready to sign the release."

Tommy had made up his mind. "It sounds like we have no choice."

"What do you mean, 'we'?" Dominic growled. "This is not your decision."

"Pa!" Tina said.

"It's all right, Tina," Tommy said. "I'll wait outside."

Dr. Walker, who had watched in silence, spoke in earnest tones to Dominic. "I realize this is not easy to consider, but the sooner we start the procedure, the better it will be for the boy."

Dominic turned to walk away, but he stopped when Tina called out, "Wait! You can't just walk away. You were right. It's not Tommy's decision, or mine. They need your permission."

"I got to think about it."

"Think about what? There's no time," Tina pleaded. "You heard the doctor. He has to do something now."

When Dominic again turned to leave, her tone switched to anger. "Where are you going, Pa? Are you going to just let him die? Face this. You can't hide from us anymore. We're here. Mama's dead, but we're here, and we need you!"

Dominic made his way to the front doors, with Tina shouting close behind him. He hurried down the steps, and she stomped out after him. Tommy was waiting on the steps. She walked past him, headed for his car on the street, and got into the passenger side with a slam of the door. Tommy followed her and got in next to her.

"Are you all right?"

"Yes," she snapped and wiped her watery eyes.

"Well, where to?"

"Some place away from him."

They drove toward the outskirts of town. Tommy finally broke the silence.

"Are you going to tell me what happened?"

"There's nothing to tell. If Carmie loses his foot, it will be my father's fault."

"I thought he'd be happy we got Walker."

Tina shrugged with a wave of her hand.

➤⊰⊱➤

What a switch: Tina roaring mad at her father instead of him. He'd love to take advantage of the situation, but he knew the stakes were too high. The little kid's life was on the line, and it was killing Tina. It killed him too to see her suffer. Hell, he was lucky to be able to spend time with her, even if it was only to let her rant about her father. So he let her go on as long as she needed to.

When Tina ran out of steam, she curled up next to the door and sulked. They'd been driving for almost a half of an hour along Liberty Lake when Tommy slowed down to approach their destination. Oblivious to the passage of time or how far they had driven, Tina sat up and began to notice her surroundings as the car pulled up to a weathered house next to the lake.

"Where are we?" she asked through a yawn.

"This place belongs to a guy I know."

Tommy turned off the engine and got out, but Tina remained seated. He went around to her side, opened the door, and offered her his hand.

"Come on. I know where he keeps the key."

Tina hesitated and gave him a suspicious glare.

Tommy seemed to read her mind, and smiled. "When's the last time you went yachting?"

Her face relaxed a bit, and she took his hand, allowing him to help her out of the car. She smoothed her dress and followed him to a small shed, where he removed a loose plank and lifted a key out of its place. He unlocked the creaky door, pulled it open, and disappeared into the dank, musty darkness. "Tommy, what are you doing in there?" He didn't answer, but soon emerged dragging an old rowboat and a couple of oars behind him. Tina took a look at the so-called yacht and burst into laughter.

The gleaming water rippled softly over the oars as Tommy and Tina sat facing each other in the boat. Tina's mood had softened after a few minutes of gliding around the lake—so much so, that she had dropped her guard to answer Tommy's questions about her family and for her to inquire about his life.

"I wasn't a bad kid. None of us were. We were just tired of being hungry, and always lookin' for a way to scrounge up a few nickels. Being good didn't seem to pay off. We got blamed for everything bad that happened around town anyways."

Tina nodded. She knew he was right, and that things hadn't really changed much from when they were kids.

"So when we got restless enough, we looked for stuff to amuse ourselves or give pay-backs."

He hesitated, and his mischievous grin made her smile. "What are you thinking?" she asked.

"Oh, remembering one of those times."

"Tell me."

"Naw, you wouldn't appreciate it.

"Try me."

"Well, there was one cop that made more trouble for us than the others, so we worked out a plan to get back at him. He worked the night shift and ate at the Hyde Street Diner every day about eight o'clock. He'd park his car out front every time. We waited until the front parking space was full and he had to park a few doors down, by the alley. This night, five of us guys were standing by with a jack, a siphoning tube, and a gas can. While he was in the diner, we jacked up his car, took off all four tires and the hood ornament, and siphoned all the gas out of his tank."

"You didn't?" Tina said with surprise.

"Oh, yeah. And since it was my idea, I got to stick around while the others took off to hide the loot. So I got to see the stupid look on his face when he came out to get in his car. It was so great." Tommy grinned. "I'll never forget it."

She could see the cop's face in her mind and laughed.

Tommy loved the sound of her laugh and wished she would do it more. "They searched almost every house on the south side and some on the north side all night, but they never found the evidence or who did it. We'd hid the stuff down one of the guys' cellars, where we kept it for a couple of months. When we figured it had been forgotten, we sold it to a junk man for twenty-five bucks. Five bucks each. We thought we were really livin'. Probably the best day in my thirteen-year-old life."

Tina giggled. "That was terrific."

"So you don't mind that I was a juvenile delinquent?"

"I have two brothers. They can get into some real scrapes, but I'd never let anybody call them juvenile delinquents."

Tommy looked into her eyes. "I wish I'd had a sister like you . . ."

"You might feel differently if you talked to my brothers."

He smiled but continued to stare into her eyes.

Feeling self-conscious, she changed the subject. "Now tell me, how did you get into your uh . . . line of work?"

Tommy stopped rowing, put the oars down, and wiped his brow. "Well, I knew I wasn't going to crush stone all my life like my old man. Then about three years ago, this guy comes along and asks if I want to make some big bucks delivering booze to Schenectady. I did that a couple of times. He found out that I used to box, so after that, he set me up with another guy who needed somebody to do his collecting for him."

Tina winced. "Did you ever have to really hurt someone when you were collecting?"

Tommy shrugged. "I had to show 'em I meant business."

"What about what you do now?"

"It's good money."

"Doesn't it ever bother you that what you do is illegal?"

"Naw, if I didn't do it, somebody else would." He studied her face. "It bothers you though, don't it?"

She nodded. "I just think we should show people like Steele that we're capable of being more than hoodlums and tramps."

Tommy picked up the oars and Tina continued, "You're a very intelligent man. Why not use it to do something legitimate?"

He thought for a moment. "I guess it never occurred to me that I could." Then slowly pulling back the oars, he gave her a flirty grin. "So, you really think I'm smart?"

Engrossed in their conversation, they failed to notice the clouds that had rolled in above them, so the soft drizzle took them by surprise. Tommy wrapped his jacket around Tina and rowed them back to shore, where they dashed up to the cabin's porch for cover. Within a couple of minutes, the drizzle turned into a downpour that began to stream through the leaky porch roof.

"This key opens the house." Tommy turned the key in the lock, pushed the door open, and followed her inside.

They walked into the main room of the cabin and shook the water off themselves. Though it was still early, the dark gray skies provided little light, and Tommy fumbled around, found some candles, and lit them.

"We might as well stay here until the rain lets up." He pointed to a flowered couch with the stuffing popping out of it. "Make yourself comfortable."

She sat down and ran her fingers through her damp hair. Tommy gave a look of approval as he joined her on the couch. He took his wet jacket from her and removed a bunch of soggy cigars from the breast pocket before hanging it over a chair.

"Why do you always have those in your pocket? You never smoke them."

"How do you know I never smoke them?"

"Because I never smell them on you."

"You're right. I hand them out to people I meet. Makes me look like a big shot." He held a cigar out to her. "Have one?"

Tina took it. "I'd love one." Placing it between her two fingers, she put it to her lips, and simulated a puff.

"Hey, you look like you've had a lot of practice with that."

"Did I forget to tell you?"

"Yeah, you did. Anything else you'd like to confess?"

"Hmm. Did I mention that bank that Clyde and I robbed last month?"

"No, you didn't."

"Oh, well, it was a small one. Hardly worth talking about." She giggled, and he began to laugh.

Tina stopped suddenly, struck by a pang of guilt. "I've been having such a good time that I almost forgot about Carmen. I hope he's all right without me."

"Your sister is probably with him."

Tina knew better, and became sullen. "You don't know Eva."

Tommy leaned into her. "Come on, Constantina. I've only got you for a few more minutes. How about giving me another smile?"

She obliged, and keeping her face next to his she said, "You know, my mother was the only one who could get away with calling me that."

"I'm sorry. I won't do it anymore."

"That's OK. I don't mind. You've been so good to me . . . and Carmen."

"Is that why you like me now?"

She lowered her head and whispered, "I've always liked you."

Tommy took a moment to absorb what she had said. "No kiddin'?"

She looked up at him and shook her head. His pomade part had gotten mussed in the rain, and his naturally wavy hair had dried in curls. He hesitated, before he ever so lightly brushed his lips over hers. Seeing that she didn't mind, he did it again, lingering a moment longer. When he pulled back, she hadn't stirred but remained there, waiting for his next move. So he reached out, drew her to him, and kissed her solidly on the mouth. Tina surprised herself by not pulling away, and with the next kiss, she took his head in her hands and fell into his arms.

Tommy's kisses remained gentle but turned urgent as he began exploring her mouth with his tongue. She'd never allowed that from other boys, but now Tina went after his tongue with hers without thinking twice. From there, in one motion Tommy ran his lips down her neck to the lapels of her dress, and she shivered unexpectedly.

It brought her back to reality for a moment, making her realize what was happening. She had let her guard down, a wall really, that she had built to protect her pride and ambitions. Her common sense told her to yank herself out of his arms and retain her dignity. But his warm breath was telling her that he loved her, and an unfamiliar throbbing between her legs had a captivating effect on her. Tommy eased her gently down onto the couch and began caressing her breasts with his face, causing her to cradle his head in her arms and pull him closer to her.

Caught up in her fervor, he unbuttoned the top button of her dress. "You're so beautiful," he murmured, then nuzzled her exposed cleavage. When she did not resist, he took her hand, and led it to his crotch, rubbing it against the hard bulge in his pants. Unsure of her feelings at that moment, she left it there until the knot grew bigger.

"Tommy," she whispered.

He let go of her hand. "I'm sorry."

"No. It's OK."

"Are you sure?"

"Yes."

"You're not just doing this to get back at your old man, are you?"

Tina gave him a coy smile. "What old man?"

That was Tommy's cue to take her chin, kiss her lips, and lead her to the bedroom. There they sat on the bed, and he went to work unbuttoning the rest of her buttons. When his fingers proved to be too bulky to complete the job, she did it for him while he shed his own shirt as fast as he could. He gently slipped one of her bra straps off, then the other, kissing each shoulder. With one look at her breasts spilling out, he reached behind her and fumbled with the hook until he pulled back with the bra in his hand.

"Jeez" he said under his breath.

She was glad to know that he appreciated her attributes as much as she admired the ripples in his bare arms and his well-defined abdominal muscles. He seemed to have read her mind, because he wrapped those beefy arms around her naked torso, and his expansive chest fit perfectly against her ample breasts. How strange to have his damp skin on hers this sultry day. They fell back onto the bed together. He took one of her nipples into his mouth and sampled the other, as if trying to decide which tasted better.

Just as she was getting used to this lovely new sensation, he ran his hand down her body to that area between her legs that, now moist, continued to pulse. She heard herself let out a moan that grew more intense as his fingers drew circles around that magical spot until she felt an explosion there, and her whole body rushed up in delight.

She bolted up in surprise. Not sure what had happened to her. "Oh, Tommy!

"It's OK, baby."

With that, he removed his pants, revealing to her what had been struggling to stay put until that moment. Tina was startled, because even though she had seen her brothers' male parts, she hadn't expected the size and shape of Tommy's.

"Like this." He took her hand gently, wrapped it around his rigid, wet shaft, and moved it up and down. Once again, it grew harder from her touch.

He removed her panties, separated her legs, and eased himself on top of her. He licked her nipples, then kissed her hard before raising her hips and entering her. She jerked from the jolt of pain and let out a small squeal, so he stroked her face.

"I love you so much," he groaned.

"I . . . I love you, too."

"Does it still hurt?"

"No." She tightened her muscles around him and pulled him into her as far as she could.

"Oh, Tina," he moaned, and with only a few more thrusts, a shower erupted inside her.

CHAPTER SEVEN

Later that day, Dominic walked into the empty house, took his hat off, and hung it on the hook in the back room. When he did so, he spotted Carmen's cap hanging there, and he brushed over it. After washing up, he dragged himself upstairs. As he changed out of his overalls and boots, he caught sight of his wife's picture on the dresser, a ruby pendant adorning her dress. He opened the drawer below, pulled the ruby pendant out of a box, and fingered it. Gripping the pendant and looking at the picture, he squinted to hold back his tears. But, unable to stop them, he let loose a howl and began to sob.

Irene gripped her umbrella and dodged raindrops on her way to the hospital. She had closed the shop early after Eva told her what had happened that morning. She needed to see how Carmen was doing.

When she got to Carmen's room, she found Dominic sitting next to him as he slept.

"How is he?"

"Still burning up."

She went to Carmen and touched his face with the back of her hand, then looked at Dominic. "Can we talk a minute outside?"

Dominic followed her out into the hallway.

"Eva told me what they want to do. Dom, it doesn't sound like you have . . ."

"I told them 'OK.' They do it first thing in the morning."

She met his eyes. "I know it was a hard decision for you."

"I might have let him die," he said, with disgust.

"You would not."

His voice grew softer. "Luciana, she wanted him so much. The doctor said it was no good for her having him."

"After losing that baby boy the year before, she didn't care what the doctor said. Carmen was a part of you."

"And it was my fault . . . because of my baby, she was too weak. Too weak to fight the sickness."

"She never blamed you, Dom. She loved you and wanted to show it."

He took a deep breath and whispered, "Irene, that night. I shouldn't have—"

"No. I shouldn't have. You weren't free of Luciana. It was too soon."

He nodded. "Maybe. . . . maybe someday."

She touched his arm. "Come on. Let's go say good night to Carmen."

Tina sat in the chair of the cabin's bedroom, wearing nothing but Tommy's shirt, and watched him sleep. She kept reliving the afternoon's scenario in her mind's eye. Given the turn of events that morning, she never could've guessed that she would be sitting in that cabin, looking fondly at the man that she could barely stand a couple of months ago—especially having just done what they had done in that bed. But despite all her professed moral standards, making love to Tommy had seemed so natural, so right. Looking at him now, all of her misconceptions brought a smile to her face. *Wouldn't Rosie be surprised?*

She couldn't hear the rain anymore, so she looked at her watch. Seven o'clock. The days were getting shorter. It would be dark when they got home. She left the chair, sat down next to Tommy, and kissed him awake. He reached out and touched her arm, then grinned as if he'd realized it hadn't been a dream after all.

He tugged at her shirt. "Your latest design?"

She stood up, and twirled around. "Oh, yes. You like it?"

"Very much. You should wear it often."

She sat down again, and stared off into space.

"Are you OK with this?" He gestured toward the bed.

"Mmm-hmm."

"I thought maybe, uh, you were sorry we—"

"No, I'm not." She had surprised herself with her answer, and grew quiet.

He sat up and kissed her. "Thinking about Carmen?"

"No. Something Irene said."

Tommy and Tina drove back to Kingsburg that starless night with very little conversation. He pulled the car up in front of the hospital but left the engine running. She looked up toward Carmen's room on the second floor of the building. How strange that nothing here had changed since she'd left this morning, when during the same time, her life had been transformed forever.

"Are you sure you don't want me to come in with you?"

"Yes. I'll stay as long as they'll let me. You go on home."

He turned to face her and stroked her hair. "You're exhausted."

"I'm all right."

"Promise me you'll get some sleep tonight."

She nodded, and he leaned over and caught her lips with his.

"Thank you for rescuing me again." She smiled. "Even if it was from myself."

He winked and said, "My pleasure."

"You always seem to be there when I need you."

He took her hand and kissed it. "I'd do anything for you, ya know."

Tina walked into Carmen's room but stopped short when she saw Dominic sitting in the chair next to the bed, asleep. She noticed a sign at the foot of the bed that said, NPO, 0700 SURGERY. Tina looked at Dominic again, breathed a sigh of relief, and spoke a silent prayer of thanks. Dominic stirred, so she went over and placed her hand on his shoulder. When he stroked it, and pressed it fast against his cheek, she suddenly became a child again, confident that her father would make everything all right.

⊷⊷ ⊷⊷

Despite the previous night's optimism, the next morning brought the typical surgery-day anxiety. Would Carmen be strong enough to withstand the operation, and would it be successful? The family gathered in the waiting room with Irene and Rosie. Within a few minutes Tommy arrived, said hello to everyone, and took a seat across from Tina, greeting her with a nod and a knowing expression. A momentary flush came over Tina. Was she blushing on the outside?

Tina shuddered with the realization of being there with everyone after yesterday afternoon with him. Would Rosie notice any difference in her? Tina had stood in front of the mirror longer than usual that morning, trying to spot something in her face, her eyes, or even the way she walked or held herself. She couldn't see anything, despite the fact that a transformation had taken place inside her. Oh, she was still the same person, but now it felt like she was herself, with something extra. She wished she could tell her family and friends about it, but of course she couldn't. It was a secret, one that she could only share with Tommy.

Carmen had been in surgery for nearly an hour when she and Tommy went to get some coffee. It gave them a chance to rub up against each other while in line at the cafeteria and steal a kiss in the corner of the hallway.

"Tina, it's murder sitting in that room with you and not being able to touch you."

"I know . . ."

"We've got to try to get together."

"I'll be back here most of the night after the procedure. Maybe you can come by."

"I wish I could, but I've got . . . uh, some business to take care of tonight."

"OK. Tomorrow then."

They each brought back an extra cup. Tommy handed his to Dominic, who accepted it graciously, and Tina's was for Irene. After handing her the cup, Tina sat down next to her.

"I'm so glad you're here today," Tina whispered. "I don't know what we'd do without you."

Irene took Tina's hand. "Where else would I be?"

"Irene, I'm so sorry for the way I reacted, and for those things I said. You were right. I didn't know . . ."

"It's OK." Irene squeezed Tina's hand.

Tommy caught sight of Miss Snow first, and he stood up immediately as she strode into the waiting room. One by one, they each spotted her and got to their feet. She went to Dominic and offered her hand. "I just found out about Carmen when I got back from vacation. I'm so sorry. How is he?"

Dominic shook her hand. "He's having an operation to take off two of his toes."

"Oh, dear. How did this happen?"

Tina jumped in. "When they started charging the kids to use the pool, Carmen and his friend went back to their usual swimming place, and that's where he hurt his foot."

Tina explained about the day of his rescue, and the doctor's treatment. Miss Snow's concern turned to anger. "This is unacceptable."

"I know. I even went to the mayor to plead with him for medical help for Carmen, and he refused to do anything."

Miss Snow thought for a moment. "Tommy, will you please escort me to the cafeteria for some coffee?"

"I can go get it for you."

"That's all right. I'll go with you."

They walked toward the cafeteria, but Miss Snow stopped before arriving there. "Tommy, what do you know about this pool charge?"

"All I know is Steele decided he wanted more money and put a sign out front of the pool. When I asked him about it, he told me it was none of my business, that he was the mayor, and if I wanted to keep doin' what I was doin', I should keep my mouth shut." Tommy squinted back the pain. "Now look what happened to Tina's kid brother. Miss Snow, I'm sorry I ever told him to build the pool."

Miss Snow touched his sleeve. "It's OK, Tommy. It's not your fault. Go on back to Tina and her family. I've got something I have to do."

When Tommy returned to the waiting room, Dominic was pacing, Tina was flipping through a magazine, and Angelo was waking up, having dozed off in the chair. "How much longer is it going to be?" he whined.

Tina looked up at the clock on the wall. "Not much, I hope."

"Here comes the doctor," Eva said.

Everyone jumped up and formed a semicircle around Dr. Walker, who rubbed the back of his neck and stretched his shoulders.

"Well, it's done, and it went well. But he's pretty weak, so we're watching him carefully."

The group gave a collective sigh.

"Can I, uh, I mean, can we see him?" Tina asked.

"He'll be under the anesthesia for a while. I suggest you use this time to go home and rest. It will be this evening before we can perform the second procedure."

Dominic extended his hand to Dr. Walker. "Thank you very much, sir."

The family returned to the hospital that night to await Carmen's maggot procedure. They spent another anxious two hours before hearing that Carmen had gotten through it fine. Now all there was left to do was to wait to see if the infection had been eliminated, and for him to heal. Eva and Angelo left after saying good night to Carmen, but Dominic and Tina remained by his bedside, watching him closely and mopping his brow.

Later, with both Carmen and Dominic sleeping, Tina heard an ambulance arrive. She wandered over to the open window to look through the blinds down to the emergency door. She watched as a man jumped out of the front seat of the ambulance and ran to the back to open the door. Another fireman emerged from inside and the two of them lifted a stretcher out while a hospital orderly ran out with a gurney.

"Come on, guys. Get him onto here," the orderly shouted.

The firemen lifted the man off the stretcher, but the patient began to slip. "Be careful! This is the mayor, goddammit, and somebody worked him over pretty good."

Oh my God, Tina thought. "Pa, look. It's the mayor."

Before he could react, Carmen stirred, and they both went to his side. "How do you feel?" Dominic asked.

"Pa?" Carmen said with surprise. "My foot hurts."

"I'll tell the nurse," Tina said.

"I gotta pee."

Tina reached for the urinal, but Dominic took it from her. "Go home," he said.

"That's OK. I'll stay."

She hesitated until Dominic pulled the bedsheets back. "I said go home, Tina."

Tina knew that her father meant business, so she kissed them both and left father and son together. She walked home at a quick pace, her mind working almost as fast, thinking about Steele's beating. She hated the man and had trouble manufacturing any sympathy for him. He had a lot of enemies, but which one would've gone to those lengths to show it? The answer to that frightened her.

⊶ ⊷

The next morning, thinking that Dominic had left for work, Tina had a surprise when she walked into the hospital and heard voices inside Carmen's room. She stopped outside his door and peeked in.

"Come on, Pa. More. I'm really hungry."

"You better slow down." He gave him another spoonful of gelatin. "You gonna get a stomachache."

"I don't care."

"I care. Then I got a listen to you cry, 'Ooh, my stomach.'"

"When can I go home?"

"I don't know. The doctor will tell us."

"I can't wait to go find out if Mr. Sarducci really raised the price for the coal."

With that, Tina walked in, grinning from ear to ear.

The doctor had told them that Carmen would have to remain in the hospital a few more days, to keep his foot free from infection. But the news of his recovery put the whole family, along with Irene, in a celebratory mood—so much so, that Dominic stopped at Sarducci's on his way home to buy the ingredients for one of his special meals.

Now, they all sat in mouth-watering anticipation as Dominic carried the manicotti, braciole, sausage, and chicken cacciatori to the table. They all filled their dishes, and Irene offered a special blessing.

"Bless us, O Lord, for these thy gifts which we are about to receive from thy bounty." She fought back tears. ". . . and thank you for giving us back our Carmen."

"Now *mangia*," Dominic ordered.

Tina loved seeing her father, Angelo, and Eva happy and getting along. And it was good that Irene could join them. But the moment turned bittersweet when she looked over at the empty chair next to her father where her mother always sat.

"You haven't lost your touch in the kitchen, Dominic," Irene pointed out before taking another forkful of chicken.

They all enjoyed the best meal that they had had in a while. When finished, Eva gathered some other dishes with hers and took them to the sink. Tina followed right behind her with the leftovers.

"I'm late for a date," Eva said to Tina.

"Oh, who's the guy?"

"Johnny Rossini."

Tina nodded, and Eva continued, "He's been waiting patiently the whole time Carmen was sick. It's the least I can do. Besides, he really has been trying to stay out of trouble."

Tina looked her in the eye and smiled. "Well, that's good. I'm glad."

"You're kidding, right?"

"No. Go on out, and have a good time tonight."

Irene dried the last dish and put it into the cupboard. "I'll say goodnight and go home now, Tina," she said, taking off her damp apron. "You should get some rest."

Tina wiped off the sink and hung the dish towel on the hook above it. "I'm going up to the hospital to say good night to Carmen."

"Oh, Tina, you've got to be exhausted. Carmen will probably be asleep when you get there."

"That's OK. I want to go anyway." Tina did want to see Carmen, but she didn't mention that she had planned to have Tommy meet her there afterward. She would've liked to invite him over for dinner, but she wasn't ready to let everyone know about them yet. It had all happened so fast, and she needed time to get used to the idea herself.

Besides, even though her father had warmed up to Tommy because of his help with Carmen, she couldn't be sure how he would react to the possibility of having him as a son-in-law. Wow, that was the first time she had thought about that herself. Again, it was too much to think about right now, even though she couldn't imagine how she could reconcile having gone to bed with him if they didn't eventually marry. Before she could continue that train of thought, there was a knock at the door.

Tina went to answer it, with Irene right behind her, carrying her handbag. When Tina pulled the door open, she saw two uniforms.

"Yes? What's wrong, officers?"

"We're looking for Angelo Benedetti."

"He here?" his partner asked.

"Why do you want him?" This wasn't the first time the police had come looking for Angelo, but she was surprised that he could've done anything the last couple of days. He'd been at the hospital most of the time.

They didn't seem to want to waste any time talking to her. "Where is he?"

Tina tried to take care of this herself. "Please tell me what this is about."

"Look, are you going to tell us where he is, or do we come in and look for ourselves?"

Defeated, Tina let the men inside and yelled up toward the stairs. "Angie! Angie come down here right now."

Angelo emerged with a scowl on his face. "What d'ya wa—" He stopped when he saw the uniforms standing there.

"Angelo Benedetti?

"Yeah."

"We're taking you in for questioning about the assault on Mayor Steele."

⚔

Tina sat on a bench at the police station, waiting for Dominic and Angelo to be interviewed. Irene walked in out of breath wanting to know what had transpired.

"Tina, have they arrested him?"

"I don't know. They're still asking him questions."

"Where was he that night?"

"He said he went home about nine o'clock. I never saw him. Pa and I were at the hospital most of the night."

"Eva. What about her?"

"She didn't get home until after twelve. She worked the night shift." Tina sighed. "Oh, Irene. He didn't do it. He didn't know anything about it."

Dominic came down the hall with fiery eyes, and Tina ran up to him.

"What happened, Pa?"

Dominic sat on the bench next to Irene. "They're putting him in jail."

"But, Pa, you know he didn't do it."

"What I know, they don't care. Just that I wasn't home with him at ten-thirty when Steele got hit."

"How is the mayor?" Irene asked.

"They say half dead. I been wanting to kill the son of a bitch myself the last two weeks, but now I pray to God he don't die."

Tina saw a man coming out of the interrogation room. "Who's that guy, Pa?"

"Name's Goldman. He's the public defender."

Tina went up to Goldman and introduced herself. "Can I please see my brother for a few minutes before they take him?"

Goldman nodded, and Tina went into the room and wrapped her arms around Angelo without saying a word.

"I'm sorry you have to be here, Tina."

"Don't worry about that."

"I swear to God I didn't do what they said. I only said I wanted to kick the shit out of him cuz I was so mad. You gotta get me out of here."

Tina bit her lip so that she wouldn't start to cry and gave him another hug.

After they took Angelo away, Goldman came into the room. "Please sit down, Miss Benedetti. I need to ask you a few questions."

Tina sat, and Goldman continued, "Tell me about Angelo's friends. Were any of them angered by Carmen's situation enough to retaliate?"

"I know they were mad. So were my father's friends, and mine."

"Yes, but did anyone actually say they'd like to harm him?"

"I don't know. I guess so. We were all cursing him."

"Try to remember. It's important. Did you hear anyone threaten to kill him?"

Tina tried to block it out, but Tommy's words ran through her mind, "Maybe I ought to take care of him once and for all."

She raised her hand to her mouth, and shifted in her chair. "Oh, Tommy," she said, under her breath.

Goldman perked up. "Who?"

"Nothing. Nobody said anything like that."

"I understand that Tommy Capello's been spending time with your family, and particularly Carmen. He blamed Steele for his injury, didn't he?"

Tina said nothing.

Goldman wouldn't let it go. "It was him, wasn't it?"

Tina didn't want to believe it could've been Tommy, but he had been so convincing when he had told her that he would do anything for her. After all, she knew he was capable of hurting someone that badly. Maybe he did do it. She wasn't going to tell Goldman that, though, so she shook her head. "He wouldn't have done it."

"How do you know?"

"I know, that's all," she said, trying to convince herself as well as Goldman.

"Miss Benedetti, your brother could end up in reform school if we don't give them another suspect, and the most plausible candidate is Tommy Capello."

More than anything she wanted them to let her brother go, but at Tommy's expense? This was the man that she had allowed to peel back her inhibitions, that she had given herself to, and that she had professed to love. Where should her loyalties lie? She couldn't, and she wouldn't answer.

❖ ❖

Eva and Johnny's date had consisted of a movie and dinner at the bar and grill. He had been on his best behavior all night, and as far as Eva was concerned, it had been the perfect date. He then suggested that because he liked her so much, she should meet his mother. Eva was flattered and agreed to go home with him. However, after they got inside his house, she discovered that his mother wasn't there.

When Eva balked, he convinced her that his mother would be home soon and invited her to sit on the couch. After a minute of small talk, he leaned over and kissed her. "Mmm, you smell good."

Eva looked at her watch. "Where did your mother go?"

"To play bingo." He nuzzled her neck. "Have I told you how great you are?"

"A couple of times, but you can tell me again," Eva played along.

"I'd rather show it." He drew her to him and tried to kiss her again, causing her to squirm and tighten her lips.

"Yes, but I like to hear it."

"You're the most beautiful girl in town, ya know that?"

"Really?"

"Sure. And I did something really special for you the other day." His hand wandered down to her cleavage, and he began to fondle her breast.

Slapping his hand away, she tried to continue the conversation. "You did? What was it?"

"It was somethin' you've been wantin' for a while now." His hand found her breast again, and he began to massage it.

Eva pulled his hand off her. "Did you buy me something?"

"Better." He maneuvered her into a prone position and hovered over her. "I got Steele for you." With that, he unbuttoned the top button her blouse.

She pushed him back and tried to sit up. "You what?"

"I fixed him for what he did to your brother."

Eva tried to process what he had said and dropped her guard for a moment. Taking advantage of her distraction, he slammed her back down again and lifted her skirt up. "I knew you'd want to thank me."

Eva cried out, "No, Johnny."

He tugged at her panties. "None of the other guys would do somethin' like that for ya."

"Stop it!" She shoved him with all her might, and he fell backward and half off the couch.

"You ungrateful bitch! I oughta give you some of what I gave Steele." He leaped on top of her again. But she drew her leg up, kneed him in the groin, and jumped off the couch. Leaving him writhing in pain, she ran out of the house and didn't stop running until she got to her front door.

Eva spoke in breathless spurts as she described to Tina and Dominic what had just happened to her.

"Do you think he was telling the truth, or only trying to get you to go to bed with him?" Tina asked.

"Both. I know him, Tina. He meant it."

Dominic had his hat in his hand and started walking toward the door. "Let's go get Angelo out of jail."

Tina's relief over Angelo was marred by her regret over her suspicions and doubts about Tommy. A feeling of panic grew inside her. "You two go ahead. I've got to go see Tommy."

"Right now? What's wrong?"

"You don't understand. I thought he . . ." How could she explain? "Goldman was going to . . ." She ran out, leaving Dominic and Eva confused.

Despite the Benedetti family's problems, many of Tommy's regulars sat around poker tables in groups of five, drinking heavily and with one ear tuned into the announcer calling horse races on the radio. Tommy, who would rather have been with Tina and her family, instead counted money behind the cashier cage. He had a business to run, and with Steele in the hospital, he figured he should keep his distance from the jailhouse.

Suddenly the doors flew open. "All right. It's over! Everybody out." Five uniformed cops stormed the room, with a half of dozen cops in plain clothes behind them. Before the customers had time to scatter, the cops began grabbing them by their collars and yanking them out of their seats.

They pushed the men toward the door. "Let's go. Get the hell out of here, or you go to jail."

Tommy and his cousin Joe rushed toward the officers and tried to stand their ground while the cops finished clearing out the room. "What's going on?"

"You're out of business, Capello."

"You're crazy. Steele and I have an understanding."

"Not anymore. Steele's dead. We got orders from Steve Anderson, the acting mayor, and he wants your wop ass out of this town." The man looked around at the deserted place, and gave the order. "OK, take it!"

The officers went to work, flipping tables, busting chairs, pulling wires out of the wall, grabbing money out of the cash drawer, and smashing liquor bottles. Jumping him from behind, Tommy managed to flatten one guy, and then another, while Joe attempted to do the same. From behind, two guys took hold of Tommy's arms, and another one grabbed Joe and led him out.

"Matter of fact, Capello, Anderson wants you gone so much, he's willing to let you off the hook for Steele's murder."

"You're full of shit." Tommy was sure he was trying to put something over on him, and managed to pull out of their grasp. "He ain't got nothin' on me."

"Not according to the Benedetti bitch."

The words swirled around in his head, knocking him off balance just long enough for one of the cops to jab him in the mouth. Though still stunned, Tommy reacted by attempting to throw a right cross at his assailant. But the man blocked it and returned a punch to Tommy's stomach. Before he could recover from that, he felt an explosion in his right eye, and the room darkened. Now down on his knees, the last thing he heard was the sound of a boot smashing into his groin.

Tina hadn't given any thought to the time until she heard the midnight train in the distance. She also hadn't stopped to grab a sweater before leaving, even though the chilly September night air had set in. Nothing else mattered as she rushed to Tommy's place to warn him about Goldman. She needed to explain how Goldman had tried to put words in her mouth, and that whether or not Tommy was guilty, she knew Goldman would steer the cops toward him.

When Tina arrived at Tommy's, she found the door to the diner wide open. The lights were on in the back, so even though she knew that Tommy didn't like her to go back there, she walked down the hallway and right up to the open cellar door.

How strange, she thought. Tommy always kept it shut. She wanted to spot him quickly and signal him to go out front with her. Instead, she got downstairs and found the room in shambles.

"Oh my God."

She was about to turn away when she noticed what someone lying in a heap amid the rubble. As she bent for a closer look, to her horror, it was Tommy.

"Oh my God! Tommy!"

He didn't appear to be conscious, so she crouched down on her knees, lifted his limp head, and cradled it gently in her arms. Relieved to see that he was still breathing, she cried out, "Tommy, I'm so sorry."

After assuring herself that she could leave him for a few minutes, Tina dashed up the stairs and used the diner phone to call Dr. Channing. The doctor treated Tommy's lacerations and slight concussion and helped him to his apartment. Tina spent the night at his side, keeping him awake for a while to make sure he suffered no more ill effects. After a couple of hours, he told her that he wanted to sleep and that she should go home to rest, too.

The next day, while Tina slept in, the police arrested Johnny Rossini and released Angelo. She could hear Eva and Angelo joking around in the kitchen while she combed her hair upstairs, and she smiled into the mirror with relief. She wished she could feel that way about Tommy, but even though they had spent most of the night together, they had exchanged no words about her conversation with Goldman at the police station. So, after taking care of chores around the house, she went to Tommy's.

She gave his door a few short raps and waited. She had to do it again before he opened it. He was dressed but unshaven, and his injuries had deepened in color since the previous night.

"Oh, I thought maybe you were still asleep."

He motioned her inside, where she touched his black eye and leaned in to brush his swollen mouth with her lips.

He grimaced.

"I'm sorry," she said, then smiled. "You're still the best looking guy in town, ya know."

He gave her a crooked smile and motioned for her to follow him into the kitchen. She complied, and with his back still to her, she blurted out, "Tommy, you don't really think I told Goldman that you had anything to do with Steele getting beat up, do you?"

He stopped when he got to the kitchen sink, but didn't turn around. "So why did he say you did?"

"I don't know. He asked me several times, and I always told him it couldn't have been you. But he kept insisting it was."

"And why's that?"

"He thought everyone would believe that you would do something like that."

He turned to face her. "And what did you think?"

"What?"

"Did you believe it?"

"I told you that I told him I didn't."

"But you had doubts."

"No, I . . ."

"Tina, you couldn't have been very convincing, and we both know why, don't we?"

"What do you mean?"

"I mean, you weren't believable because you weren't sure it wasn't me."

Tina couldn't lie to him. She hated herself for even thinking it had been him, and now that he realized she had considered it, she couldn't deny it.

Tommy winced with pain as he sat down at the table. "You really thought I'd let Angelo take the rap for something I did?"

"No, I didn't think that, I . . ."

"You know, you talk about people like Steele, but you'll never think of me as anything but a criminal either. No matter how much you tell yourself it don't matter . . . it does."

She sat down, reached across the table, and placed her hand on his. "I'm so sorry that I doubted you. I was wrong. I'll never do it again."

He pulled his hand out from under hers. "I wish that were true, but I know how you feel about what I do."

"Tommy, I love you. I don't care about that. I only care about you." She began to well up. "Please believe me."

He got up and stood his ground. "It doesn't matter. I'm leaving today."

"What? Where are you going?"

"I told you last night that Anderson wants me out of town. I should have been gone by now."

She jumped up and threw her arms around his neck. He responded without hesitation by wrapping his arms around her, and pressing her to his sore body.

His hug reassured her that he wanted her as much as she wanted him. "If you're going, I'll go with you. Just give me time to . . ."

He pushed her away so fast that it startled her. "No, Tina."

"But why not?"

"I'm not good for you. We're no good together."

He sounded serious, and she began to get irritated. "You know that's not true. That day at the lake we . . ."

"That was wrong. I never should've . . ."

"So I had no say in that, and I have no say in this." She could feel the blood rush to her face. "Is that what you mean?"

When she could get no more than a shrug from him, she turned and walked toward the door. "You really believe that we would've made love that day if I didn't want to?"

He didn't answer.

"Well, you don't know me very well. If you think that we're not good together, and you want to go without me, go, but don't try to tell me what I should think."

"Look, this is for the best. Besides, I don't even know where I'm going." He hesitated a moment, before going to the kitchen drawer and opening it. "Tina. I want you to forget about me. Go to New York City. That's what you've always wanted to do."

"Not anymore. Now I want to stay."

He took several hundred-dollar bills out of the drawer. "Here. Take this. It's enough to get you started in New York." He tried to hand her the money, but she wouldn't take it.

"But I don't want to leave you."

He jammed the bills into her hand. "I'm finished here, Tina. Go. This is your chance."

She couldn't believe that he could let her go so easily. "You really want me to go?"

His answer was to grab her hard and long, obviously never wanting to let her go. But then he did, and stepped back.

She tried to approach him again, but he closed up. "Tommy," she cried.

He turned around.

She starred at his back for a few seconds before she wiped her eyes, threw the money on the floor, and ran out of the house.

CHAPTER EIGHT

"This was her favorite," Eva said as she pulled her mother's dress out of the wardrobe in their parents' bedroom.

"Not really," Tina corrected her while sitting on the bed next to an open antique jewelry box.

Eva held the dress in front her and looked pleased at her reflection in the cheval mirror.

"She wore it a lot," she said.

"That's because Pa liked it."

Eva picked up the picture on the dresser. "She has it on here, with her ruby pendant. Didn't she leave it to you?"

"Yes, but I'm letting Pa keep it for now."

Tina picked up a religious medal, and handed it to Eva. "She wanted you to have this."

Eva took it, and sat on the bed. "She never took this off. Are you sure she wanted me to have it?"

"Yes. She told me that she did."

"Why didn't you give it to me sooner?"

"I don't know. I wasn't sure you would've appreciated it six months ago."

"And now?"

"Now, I think you do. You've grown up this summer."

Eva squeezed the medal with one hand, and wrapped her other arm around Tina's neck. Tina threw her arms around her sister, and they wept in silence for a moment until Eva broke away suddenly, cleared her throat, and wiped her eyes.

"So you and Tommy were an item before he left town. You know, I thought you two were getting pretty chummy when he was helping us with Carmen," Eva said with raised eyebrows.

"Well, I got to know him a lot better, and"—Tina hesitated before going on—"he caught me with my guard down, and I realized that I loved him."

"It had to happen to you sooner or later."

"Well, much later would've been better. It turns out this love business isn't what it's cracked up to be."

"He's right, ya know."

"What?"

"It wouldn't have worked with you two."

"How do you know?"

"You'd have driven him crazy."

"Thanks a lot."

"Oh, not on purpose, but it's not easy to live up to your standards. I can never seem to do it."

Tina remembered her conversation with Rosie. For the first time, she understood why Eva felt that way. "I'm so sorry you think you have to," she said, her voice soft.

Eva smiled. "I don't. Besides, you can't help it; you're a hardhead, like Pa."

Tina could hear her mother's voice saying the same thing. "That's true." She smiled. "Mama always used to call him a *capa tosta*."

Somehow, hearing Eva say the words to her now made her feel closer to her sister than she had for a while. And with a hint of jealousy, she leaned over and touched Eva's hair. "And you. You're more like her."

Eva beamed. "You really think so?"

That night when all her chores had been done and everyone had gone to bed, the silent house became like an empty cavern where Tommy's words echoed through her mind. How could he leave her after they had become so close? Didn't he realize what she had given up to be with him that day at the cabin? She knew she could never go back to being an innocent, idealistic young girl again, and she wished he were lying next to her at that moment. But she would have to find a way to live without him—and do her best to forget how he made her feel like she never imagined she could.

⟫⟪ ⟫⟪

The next morning, though her heart was not in it, Tina began preparing a picnic lunch that they would take to the playground for the town's Labor Day festivities. Within minutes, Rosie was at the back door.

"Oh my God, Tina. I couldn't get over here yesterday because I had to go to my cousin's birthday party." She continued without taking a breath, "But I've heard all sorts of things about the other night. What happened?"

Tina tried to explain but was soon interrupted by Carmen needing help with his belt, and by Angelo peering into the basket to see what she had packed for lunch. She finally gave up until she finished in the kitchen and told Rosie to go outside with her to get the laundry.

"I was so mad the day that my father wouldn't sign for Carmen's surgery that I asked Tommy to drive me away from there." Tina reached up to grab a clothespin off the line. "We stopped by the lake, and started talking about ourselves. I began to see the real him, not what he pretends to be most of the time." She folded the towel and bent over to put it in the basket. "Then he . . . he kissed me."

146

Rosie's jaw dropped. "And? Did you kiss him back?"

Tina gave her a faint smile. "Yes."

Rosie sighed. "Thank goodness."

"What?"

"Well, I couldn't be sure. Knowing how you are about that stuff."

Tina turned her head away from Rosie and grinned. If Rosie only knew how she really was about "that stuff."

"So, how was it?" Rosie prodded.

Tina played dumb. "What do you mean?"

"I mean, did he make you feel wicked like Norma Shearer with Clark Gable?"

"Really, Rosie. I don't know what you're talking about."

"Oh, Tina." Rosie yanked a towel off the line without removing the clothespins. "You really are impossible."

Tina shrugged, and Rosie tried again. "So, I bet he told you that he loves you."

"Yes, and I told him that I had feelings for him, too."

"I'm glad you finally admitted that."

They took the laundry basket, and sat on the back stoop. "So what happened that made him leave town?" Rosie asked.

Tina told her about the night Angelo was arrested, Tommy's beating, and Anderson's order for him to leave town.

"Oh my God, Tina. What did you say when he told you he was leaving?"

"I told him I would go away with him."

Rosie's eyebrows went up. "You did? Would you really have gone with him?"

"Yes. But he said he thought that deep down I would always think of him as a criminal, and he couldn't stand for us to be together that way."

"Oh, Tina. That's terrible. And now he's left."

"Yes, and I don't know where he went."

"This is just like a movie I saw once."

"I wish it was a movie. If it was I could go home and forget about it. Instead, I can't stop thinking about him. I miss him already."

"This is crazy." Rosie pouted. "You're the one who didn't even want a boyfriend."

Labor Day came and went, and before Tina knew it, the first day of school had arrived. Carmen woke her up at the crack of dawn, and Angelo stayed in bed until the very last minute. To her surprise, Eva pitched in to help her with them. She grabbed a piece of toast on her way out the door to begin her senior year. "I'll get home as soon as I can after school to keep an eye on Carmen."

After Carmen's brush with death and Angelo's run-in with the law, everyone seemed to be getting along better than they had since her mother had passed. Even her father had mellowed a bit. It all certainly made her life easier as she adjusted to having found and lost Tommy within a span of only a few days.

⊶ ⊷

"Tina, will you pin up Mrs. Bello's dress, while I ring up Mrs. Kaiser's sale?" Irene said through a mouthful of pins when Tina walked through the door that morning.

"Of course," Tina replied. As she hurried to put her pocketbook and sweater on a shelf, a hush fell over the noisy room. The silence continued as she reached down to take the customer's hem out of Irene's hands.

Tina noticed that the shop seemed unusually busy for this time of day. She glanced around the room while she worked on the dress, nodding hello to familiar customers, but she also saw some new faces, women pretending to browse the racks of ready-made dresses, but not succeeding in fooling her. Instead, they seemed more interested in shooting glances at her from the corners of their eyes. *What is going on?* Tina thought, until it dawned on her.

News traveled fast in Kingsburg, and apparently, everyone had heard about Angelo's arrest.

While she thought about what she would say if they asked, she had to re-pin the hem twice before getting it right. "OK, Mrs. Bello." Tina stood up. "All done. We'll have it ready for you in a few days."

The woman climbed down from the platform, grabbed Tina's hand with both of hers, and whispered, "I'm so glad to hear that Angelo is free." She looked from side to side and added, "But what is all the talk about you and the Capello boy?"

Tina hadn't anticipated that. *So that's why they are all here this morning. They want to know the juicy details. Eva had been right about the dirty old minds in this town.*

When she recovered from the untoward question, she looked into the woman's face and scanned the room. The whole shop was waiting for her to speak. She flashed the biggest smile she could muster, and spoke in a syrupy tone, loud enough for everyone to hear.

"Thank you for your concern. Angelo is back in school today, and the real culprit is behind bars. And if all the talk about Tommy and me is that we're friends, then I'd be glad to confirm that. He helped my brother Carmen when no one else would, and I will be forever grateful to him."

With that, Tina took a deep breath, turned around and spoke to the group. "Now, who is next in line to be helped?"

When the last customer had left, Irene sat down and rubbed her head. "I'm exhausted."

Tina scurried around cleaning up the shop. "I'm sorry you had to put up with all of those nosy women because of me."

"Those old biddies should mind their own business. But you handled them fine. Have you heard from Tommy?"

"No, and I don't expect to. He left to find a new life, and he wants me to do the same in New York City. He even tried to give me money to get started there."

"Maybe you should've taken it. It's what you've always wanted."

"But after we . . . uh . . . when I realized that I loved him, I changed my mind. What I wanted was to go with him."

"Ah, young love. It makes us do silly things. I think Tommy was very wise to not let you throw your talent . . ."—Irene coughed—"away for him. He knows you better than you know yourself."

As Tina stepped out of the shop and headed for home, she shivered and wished she had brought a jacket. Most of the trees had shed their leaves, and the temperature had dropped. Normally she looked forward to the change of seasons, but this year it served only to slam the door on the summer, reminding her that she had yet to face the long dark winter without Tommy.

But apparently she was the only one who didn't think their ending was for the best. Rosie and Irene seemed to think so. But surprisingly, of all the comments she had received, Eva's had forced her to see herself most clearly, and she wondered if because of her inherited disposition she could ever change. Maybe she would never really have trusted Tommy, no matter how hard she wanted to.

═║║═

A few days later, Tina rushed into the shop dressed in a simple gray skirt, white blouse, and black sweater. "I'm sorry I'm so late, Irene."

Irene looked up from her sewing machine. "That's OK. Did you have any luck?"

"No. I went to the glove factory, two restaurants, and a bakery. Nobody's hiring."

"I'm sorry."

"I've got to find something. Eva and Angie can't work as many hours now that school has started, and I can't save anything for New York on my salary here."

"I wish I could give you more hours, but business has dropped in the past month." Irene pulled the garment out of the machine and snipped the thread. "Even the north side ladies can't afford new clothes or even alterations the way they used to."

"I guess I'll just have to keep trying. I'll do anything."

"Well, Mrs. Keller was in yesterday, complaining that she lost her housekeeper. Why don't you go up there and see her?"

"Now, here is the bathroom." Mrs. Keller, a woman of about forty-five, opened the door for Tina to look into the biggest bathroom she had ever seen.

How wonderful it must be to sit and soak in the large tub instead of having to stand in the oversized laundry basin that doubled as a tub at her house.

"On Fridays, you'll clean the toilet, sink, and tub as well as sweep, dust, and mop the floors. On Tuesdays, you'll change the bed linens, clean the kitchen, and iron."

Tina glanced around the spacious house and tried not to grimace as she imagined how long it would probably take to earn her $2.00 weekly salary. But the money would be pure profit for her and help get her to New York much sooner. She would have to keep that in mind every time she bent over to clean the Kellers' toilet and the ring around their luxurious tub.

A few weeks had passed since Tina's first day at the Kellers'. She found it took her about five hours to complete the work each day. Mrs. Keller kept an eye on her as she worked, spewing out instructions to ensure that Tina stayed on task. But Tina knew that Mrs. Keller's real concern was that Tina might tuck money, jewelry, or other valuables into her apron pockets or down her blouse. On this particular day, Mrs. Keller had a doctor's appointment and was forced to leave Tina alone until Mr. Keller arrived home from work.

"Good afternoon, Tina," he said as he entered the kitchen, where she stood at the ironing board."

"Good afternoon, Mr. Keller." She didn't realize that he even knew her name, and he had never given her more than a nod the whole time she had worked for him and his wife.

He took a drink of water and walked into the parlor with a newspaper tucked under his arm. She guessed that he didn't share his wife's qualms about her, because he left her alone to do her work. That is until she bent over to tuck in a corner of the sheet on the four-poster bed.

She heard him come into the room but didn't acknowledge him, assuming that he would get what he needed and leave. But instead of heading back to the doorway after he hung up his jacket, he took a step closer to her.

"How is your brother doing after his ordeal in the lake?"

"He's still adjusting to losing two of his toes, but otherwise he is doing fine." She moved to the foot of the bed. "It's nice of you to ask."

"You and your family caused quite a stir in town over that. I heard about your visit to City Hall."

She tucked the sheet in the last corner. "I was afraid that my brother would die."

As she picked up a pillowcase and shook it out, he crept closer to the bed. "I understand you take care of your whole family."

"Yes, my mother is dead." She grabbed the other pillow, and began to pull the case over it.

"It's a shame you have to do this kind of work outside your home."

"Times are bad right now for everyone. Work is scarce." She fluffed the pillow, and as she turned to move to the other side, she saw out of the corner of her eye that he had edged closer to the dresser next to the bed.

"Such a beautiful girl like you shouldn't have to clean toilets for anyone."

She guessed that engaging her in pleasant conversation was his way of ensuring she wouldn't steal anything, so she played along. "Thank you, but we do what we have to."

He took his pocket watch out of his pants pocket and began to wind it. "With your talents, you should have someone working for you."

She thought of her dream of success as a fashion designer. "Maybe someday . . ."

He put the watch back into his pocket and loosened his tie. "There must at least be some young fellow willing to support you. To take you away from this menial labor."

The comment was innocent enough, but somehow his tone sounded like prying, so she tried to end their conversation by moving toward the door. "No, and I'm happy to do this for my family."

She only made it a few steps before he slid in front of her and stood face to face within arm's reach. "That's very noble, but unnecessary. I would be glad to help you out; give you enough money so that you wouldn't have to work."

Close enough to smell the onions on his breath and see the beads of sweat on his brow, Tina's heart began to race at his bizarre offer. Her instincts told her that he was making a pass, but if he was only being nice, she could lose her job if she said the wrong thing. "I appreciate you saying that Mr. Keller, but I couldn't accept money from you for doing nothing."

Thinking that her answer served as an end to the unsettling conversation, she stepped around him and headed toward the door. "Please excuse me. I have to clean the kitchen now."

Before she could reach the door, his sinewy hands gripped her shoulders and spun her around. She found herself peering into his hungry face, feeling naked as he stepped back to slowly undress her with his eyes.

"You don't understand. It wouldn't be for nothing. All you would have to do is keep me company . . . say . . . once a week."

<hr />

"Thank God he didn't hurt you," Irene said when Tina told her what had happened at the Keller house.

"Yes, but I didn't know that at the time. He followed me into the kitchen, but he didn't try to touch me before I made it out the door. I guess he hadn't planned to try anything in the house, since his wife might've caught him in the act. He just hoped to make himself a nice arrangement on the side."

"So are you going back for your pay?"

"No. I never want to see him or his wife again. But now I'm out of a job."

"That's a shame. I'm sorry that I ever told you to go to that place."

"How could you have known?"

Irene rubbed her neck. "Well, would you like to work longer hours today?"

"You don't have to do that, Irene. I know you can't afford to give me more hours."

"But it would help me, because I feel bad today. I can't get rid of this chest cold. If you keep the shop open, I can go home to rest."

Tommy didn't know where he was going when he left Kingsburg that afternoon after sending Tina away. It didn't matter. He got into his roadster with as few belongings as possible and followed the Mohawk River east. By twilight, he found himself in Schenectady, where he grabbed a hamburger at the first diner he came upon, rented a room in a boarding house, and went straight to bed.

He had spent the entire ride thinking about Tina. The thoughts continued as he tossed and turned in the strange bed. How could he have pulled himself out of her arms when all he wanted to do was crawl into them and stay there forever? In the old days, he wouldn't have hesitated to take her with him—to have her by his side in his car and in his bed, without caring whether she trusted him or not. Now, he couldn't enjoy those things without having her respect, and his heart told him that he had done the right thing by letting her go.

The next morning he wasn't hungry, so he left his car parked and started out on foot down the street. He tried to concentrate on figuring out his next move, but he couldn't put Tina out of his mind. The thought that she believed even for a moment that he would be so rotten as to beat up the mayor and allow Angelo to take the rap for him made him sick to his stomach. He had tried so hard to be the kind of guy that Tina would look up to, and he ended up crapping out. It didn't seem to matter what he did.

After walking a few blocks, he thought he could eat something, so he ordered a cup of coffee and some toast at the diner a couple of doors down. When he finished, he knew where he had to go. He paid the woman behind the counter and left.

The smell of stale sweat and the sound of colliding boxing gloves took him back to the days at Hess's Gym, where he had learned to box along with most of his friends in Kingsburg. He hadn't been the best prizefighter, but he knew his way around the ring, and he figured he could make a few bucks working in this joint until something better came along. He took a few minutes to get the lay of the place, then sauntered up to a rickety old desk piled high with papers and equipment and spoke to the cigar-puffing man sitting there.

"Nice place you got here," he said.

"Yup," said the guy, who was as unkempt as his desk.

"Talent, too." Tommy pointed to the two guys dancing around in the ring.

"They ain't bad."

"Maybe this guy could use a new sparring partner. I could give him a run for his money."

"Nah, we got plenty of 'em."

Tommy couldn't hide his disappointment and looked around the room. "I'm a pretty good corner man."

⚍ ⚎

Tommy discovered that he had to work his way up to being a corner man by sweeping and mopping floors, emptying spit buckets, and folding towels. Once in a while, in a pinch, they would ask him to cover the corner for someone, and he got the opportunity to show them his ability to determine where his man was falling short and to give him specifics on correcting himself between rounds. Before long, fighters began to ask for him in their corners, and eventually they used him as their sparring partner.

He managed to survive on his salary by continuing to live in a modest room, eat diner food, and have almost no social life. He allowed himself one night out a week at the local bar and grill, where he rarely drank to excess and never made advances toward women—even when they made the first move, as they often did. This self-imposed monk-like existence worked for him for about six months, while he pined for Tina and their would-be life together.

Though sparring paid more money than corner man, it was a thankless job that could be dangerous. After all, the object was to get into the ring and be a human punching bag for a boxer. Of course, there was more to it than that. It took a good amount of skill to challenge the fighter with enough aggressive moves without going too far, and by taking enough body blows without getting thrashed. Tommy found the right balance most of the time.

Until one day he came up against an unusually cocky fighter who delighted in using him as a whipping boy. Tommy tried to pull away from him and give him some leeway, but the bruiser went after him with a vengeance. Although the trainer kept yelling at the fighter to lighten up, he battered Tommy with a series of jabs to his face.

Tommy continued his defensive stance as the pro threw a left hook into his head that knocked him into the ropes, causing his knees to buckle. Suddenly, he was back in his diner being pummeled by the cops, and he wasn't going to let that happen again for this two-bit job. He sprang off the ropes, still in defensive mode with hands in front of his face, and began to bob and weave around his opponent, looking for an opening. At the first opportunity, he threw a right cross as hard as he could and watched the guy plummet to the floor, out cold.

Tommy looked over at the manager and waited to hear him tell him he was through. Instead, the manager shook his head, stepped through the ropes into the ring, and pulled the loser to his feet. "Go get a shower, smart ass," the manager said to his fighter. He turned to squeeze Tommy's shoulder, and looked him in the eye. "You need a manager, son."

It had been years since Tommy awoke to the sound of a trainer screaming orders in his ear, and he almost belted the guy that next morning. But he had signed up for this second chance to see if he had the stuff to make a living as a boxer—the only legitimate work that he knew and cared about. There had been no promises of major matches or big money; just room and board for two months of heavy training to prove himself. That would determine whether or not Sam Gordon, his new manager, would promote him. The workout turned out to be a challenge not only to his body, but to his spirit as well.

"That's enough," Tommy panted as he handed the trainer the rope.

"No it ain't. You got two more minutes." He handed him back the rope. "When's the last time you worked out, kid?"

"Uh . . ." Tommy thought about the last few years of living on easy street; getting soft by eating too much and chasing women. "Too long, I guess. My recent line of work didn't call for it much."

"Well, it does now, so pick those legs up. Let's go, let's go."

Tommy struggled through the rest of the day. He pushed himself to the point of exhaustion to convince himself and his benefactors that he could take whatever they dished out. In reality, he went home in pain that night and spent the next couple of days with clenched teeth, in quiet agony.

Somewhere around the middle of the third week, he began to take the training in his stride. By the end of the month, his newfound strength gave him the self-confidence to push far beyond the limits he and his trainer had set for him. He slept better now, dwelling on Tina less. He could finally imagine an immediate future without her.

At the end of the two months, there was no doubt that he would fight. Sam changed his name to Tom Cole because he thought that the name Capello was too Italian. He set up a series of matches with local club fighters; guys not good enough for the big time, but respectable enough to put him in good standing. The bouts didn't pay much, only about ten dollars apiece, but he still got free room and board and a locker at the gym. He also started treating himself to more leisure time, taking advantage of celebrations after the fights with admiring men and adoring women wanting to show him a good time. He began to slip back into his old skin again, and it fit him as well as his new boxing gloves.

He knew that Tina wouldn't approve of his new lifestyle, so he tried to block her from his thoughts as much as possible. Only when he heard a voice that sounded like hers, or caught a glimpse of the back of a young woman with the shape of her neck, or felt her touch when another woman grabbed his arm, did he think of Tina. And when that happened, he could always count on seeing her in his dreams that night.

Irene's rest had turned into two weeks, but still she ran a low-grade fever and had very little energy. Finally, Tina and Dominic insisted that she be seen by Dr. Channing, who gave her a thorough examination. He held off making a diagnosis and remained optimistic while waiting for test results, saying that she had been neglecting her health and had become rundown. In the meantime, Tina tried her best to keep the shop running by working full time and cutting back store hours.

A week later Tina sat in Irene's kitchen with her as the doctor uttered the word that they had suspected, but wouldn't say out loud—tuberculosis. Irene looked engrossed as the doctor described her prognosis, and the particulars of her treatment, but Tina couldn't focus on anything, except the image of her mother lying helpless in bed and the familiar sense of doom that she carried with her throughout her illness.

"Tina, I am sorry to leave you with such a big burden, but I don't want to lose my clientele while I'm in the sanatorium." Irene sorted through a stack of papers on her work desk. "Many months or a year would be a long time to close the shop."

"I want to do this for you. I'm worried if I can do a good enough job."

"I'm not scared about that, but I will worry about Carmen without you home so much."

"Eva and Angelo will have to be there more. With the salary you'll be paying me, they won't have to work as many hours."

"That's good. I love you all for doing this for me."

Tina took Irene's hand in hers. "You've done more than this for us all of our lives. We just want you to get well as soon as possible."

"I'll try my best, but it's really in God's hands."

Irene checked into the local state sanatorium dedicated to the care of tuberculosis patients. Without a known drug to fight the highly contagious disease, this hospital provided an isolated location, along with bed rest, diet, and fresh air, which often proved to be a successful treatment. Because of the infectious nature of the disease, her shop and apartment had to be thoroughly cleaned, and the entire Benedetti family had to be tested. They spent an anxious week waiting to hear, but thanked God when they were found to be disease free.

It had only been a few days since Irene's departure, but Tina missed her already. How could she have ever been so mad at Irene that she wouldn't talk to her? She couldn't imagine doing that now . . . now that she prayed daily for Irene's complete recovery and swift return to the people who loved her.

It was lonely working in the shop by herself, so when Tina heard the bell ring over the shop door, she dropped her sewing and scurried to the counter to help the regular north side customer. "How can I help you?"

"Is Irene in?"

"No. I'm afraid that Irene is ill and won't be able to work for quite a while. She's left me in charge in the meantime. How can I help you?"

"Oh, uh . . . I need a dress, but uh . . . never mind." The woman turned toward the door. "I'll go elsewhere."

"I'm sure I could create something that . . ."

The customer mumbled, "No thank you," and slammed the door behind her.

"Brrr, it's cold out there." Rosie peeled her jacket off as she stepped into the shop and rubbed her hands together. "It smells like snow."

"Guess winter is here." Tina put the finishing touches on a jacket.

"Business getting any better?"

"Not really."

Rosie looked at an assortment of pants, shirts, and jackets hanging on a rack behind Tina. Each item had a piece of paper pinned to it, identifying the owner. "It sure looks like you've been busy."

"Sure, with mending orders, most of which are from our neighborhood. I'm not getting any orders from the snooty north siders, and we need them to survive."

"What are you going to do?"

"I don't know, but I dread telling Pa and Irene. They're going to think I'm too dumb to be on my own. And maybe they'd be right."

"That's not true," Rosie said in a no-nonsense tone. Then she sighed. "Maybe now that Roosevelt's going to be president, things will get better."

⊨⊧ ⊧⊨

Tina said goodbye to Rosie in front of her house and walked into the kitchen, where Eva stood at the stove stirring sauce.

"Did you see Carmen on your way home?" Eva said with hope in her voice.

"No, isn't he home?"

"Would I ask you if he was?"

"It's almost dark out. When's the last time you saw him?"

"Right after he got home from school. I told him to stay around the house, but I guess he took off."

"Eva you've got to watch him better," Tina chided.

Eva was on the verge of tears. "I have been, but he won't listen to me. What do you expect me to do?"

Tina moved over to the stove and patted Eva's shoulder. "OK . . . it's OK. Where's Angelo?"

"He's working."

Tina took the spoon out of Eva's hand. "I'll do this. Go to Patsy's. He's probably over there."

Eva brought Carmen home safe and sound in time for dinner. Afterward, Tina and Dominic sat him down and threatened him with corporal punishment, also known as "Pa's belt," if he didn't mind Eva from then on. By the look in his eyes as he listened to their father, Carmen knew that they meant business.

Long days at the shop meant that Tina had to do household chores before she could get ready for bed, leaving her almost no time or energy for leisure. Even though she wanted to help Irene with the shop, she found this new schedule grueling. She wouldn't mind that much if things were going well. But it hardly seemed worth spending so much time at the shop, when she had almost no orders for new dresses. How long could the shop survive with so little business?

CHAPTER NINE

Tina had a mouthful of pins when a tall stranger in a topcoat walked into the shop. She looked up from her sewing long enough to notice that she didn't recognize him. He positioned himself in front of the counter and proceeded to study the place from top to bottom.

She snatched the pins out of her mouth and moved toward him. "May I help you, sir?"

He took off his hat and flashed a broad smile. "I'm looking for Irene Janson."

"She's not here right now. I'm her assistant. Is there something I can do for you?"

"I'm from the Moore Textile Company, and I'd like to show her some new fabric samples and take her order."

"Oh . . . Where is Mr. Bergen?"

"He had a heart attack, and they've given his route to me. I'm Chet Lewis."

"I'm sorry to hear about Mr. Bergen. He's been coming here ever since I was a little girl. Is he going to be all right?"

"I imagine so, but I doubt that he'll come back to work."

"Oh. That's too bad . . . Uh . . . You'll have to wait a few minutes until I finish pinning this."

"All right, Miss . . . ?"

"Benedetti. Tina." She pointed to the cutting table. "Why don't you have a seat over there?"

When she joined him at the table, Tina looked at each sample that he showed her and one by one imagined how she would shape it into a fashion statement. When he finished, he asked her which ones she would like to order.

"I'm afraid that I'm not able to buy anything right now. With Mrs. Janson away, we don't have many orders for new garments."

"So you only alter, you don't create clothes?"

"Well . . . right now that's all that I'm doing."

"But you make them when she is here?"

"Yes."

He eyed the belted gabardine trousers she had on. "Did you make those?"

"Yes, I did." Sensing his disapproval, she looked directly into his vivid blue eyes and declared, "They're very popular with movie actresses."

"I'll bet they're much warmer in the winter than dresses."

"Oh." She hadn't expected that. "Yeah, they are."

"Do you get many requests for them from other women?"

"Some of my friends."

He nodded. "Could I see other samples of your work?"

Tina thought for a moment, then went to the dress rack and pulled the last of her originals off for him to see.

He handled the navy-blue rayon dress with a handkerchief hem and white scalloped neckline. "Not bad."

"Thank you. We've sold a couple of these."

"But you're not selling them now?"

She shook her head.

He chuckled. "They don't trust the assistant, huh?"

Tina grimaced with a shrug.

"Well, I guess I'm not going to make a sale today, so I may as well eat. Can you recommend a place?"

"I know a great restaurant, but it's across the tracks. There's a diner a couple of doors down that isn't bad."

"That sounds good. Would you like to join me?"

"Oh." She wasn't ready for that. "I don't know. I . . ."

"I have an expense account."

She was hungry and couldn't see any harm in letting his company buy her lunch. Irene had gone with Mr. Bergen more than once.

"Well, OK. Just let me close up the shop."

Their impromptu lunch turned into a four-course meal that lasted two hours, during which Chet shared some of his numerous experiences working within the clothing manufacturing business. Tina devoured every word with each bite of food, trying to glean as much as she could about her dream career in this rare and fleeting opportunity.

As good as he was at telling stories, Chet proved to also be a great listener. She responded to his disarming nature, and before long she began to share with him her passion for fashion design and her struggle to overcome the obstacles preventing her from pursuing it outside of Irene's shop.

Tina sipped her coffee. "And now that Irene isn't here to order fabric for customers, I don't even have the left-over fabric for experimenting with my own clothes."

"Business is really that bad?"

"Yes, and I don't know how long I'm going to be able to keep the shop open." Tina winced, and bowed her head. "The worst part is I feel like I'm letting Irene down."

"What have you done about it?"

"What do you mean?"

"Have you tried to advertise, offer specials, things like that?"

"Well, no. Irene never did."

"She didn't need to, but it sounds like you do."

Irene seemed to be holding her own at the sanatorium, or at least that's what she wrote in her letter. Obviously, enough time had not passed for any marked improvement, but at least her condition hadn't worsened. As the weeks pressed on, Irene began to ask more specifics about the business at the shop. Tina tried to avoid telling her the truth, by speaking in generalities and writing more about the family. She knew she couldn't keep it up forever, but it bought her more time for things to change.

This would be the first real Christmas without her mother, who had died in late November the previous year. At that time, her father had not allowed any celebration to interfere with their period of mourning. Tina wanted this Christmas to be a happy time for them. Dominic even went through the tradition of buying and soaking codfish for the Christmas Eve dinner of *baccala*. Unfortunately, trying to honor their usual customs only magnified Luciana's absence. And it didn't help that Irene was away battling a deadly disease.

Somehow they got through it and managed to give Carmen the Christmas that he deserved after a long and difficult year. Tina prayed to God that he help her maintain Irene's shop and give her the strength to keep the family going. Tina tried her best to think of the birth of the Christ Child as a new birth for her and her family, and she swore that somehow she would make it so.

⊷⊷ ⊶⊶

About a month or so after Chet Lewis had been at the shop, Tina donned her worn winter coat and hat, then yanked her rubber boots over her shoes. The slit in one of them that had begun the year before was now a gap, so she wedged a piece of cardboard between her shoe and the opening. There were so many other things she needed to do with her money; buying new boots was not on the top of the list. She would worry about that later. For now, she wrapped her scarf tighter around her neck and braced herself to meet the biting cold air as she walked onto the front porch.

It had snowed the night before, and as much as she hated the winter and all of the problems it brought, the neighborhood never looked as clean and appealing as it did carpeted in white. Somehow, the simple houses looked grander, the snow disguising the poverty that was so apparent in the hot and grimy summertime. She took a moment to admire the scene, before stepping off the porch into the snow.

Within seconds, she was airborne as the heel of her boot slid across a slate of ice that lay hidden beneath the surface. She landed squarely on her rear end with feet flailing above her. She could hear herself cry out, and was glad to see that no one was around to witness her unladylike tumble. So once on her feet, she rubbed her backside, brushed the evidence off, took a deep breath, and set out as if nothing had happened.

With the sidewalks covered in almost two feet of powder, she had to walk down the middle of the freshly plowed street. She made her way in the stillness with only the muffled sound of her boots crunching the newly fallen snow. By the time she reached the corner, the sound of her footsteps dissipated amid the rattle of car tire chains and the bustle of people starting their day. Before long, she had forgotten the gap in her boot and the encounter with the ice as she hurried to work.

While rearranging the sale sign in the small storefront window, she spotted Chet outside, grinning and holding what appeared to be fabric bolts in his arms. She had taken Chet's advice, and offered discounts on dress orders and alterations.

"How did you get here?" she asked when he got inside. "Weren't the roads blocked from the snow and ice?"

"Well, I actually got in before the storm hit last night. I've got a room across the street at the Henderson House."

"Come on in, I was about to light the stove and put some coffee on."

"I see you took my suggestions." He nodded toward her new signs. "Any takers?"

"Sure. My regulars took great advantage of the cheaper alteration prices."

"Nobody else?" He put the bolts on the cutting table and took off his coat.

"Not yet." She looked over at the table. "What's that? I didn't order anything."

"Yeah, but I got a pretty good idea of what you would've liked to order, and I got to thinking that you can't sell inventory that you don't have." He began to rip the packaging off the bolts. "I'd be willing to bet that some women won't be able to resist your work, especially if the price is better than the competition."

"But I can't afford to pay you."

"Consider it a loan. I front you the fabric, you pay me back when business picks up." He turned toward her. "What do you think?"

Tina went over to the table and caressed the cloth. She didn't know what to say.

"This isn't all of what I brought," he said. "There's more in my car."

She wanted to say, "Yes, yes, yes," but she didn't really know him. Did he have an ulterior motive? He did seem to come on to her a little at lunch the last time. Was he looking for that kind of payback?

"What if nothing sells?" she asked.

"I don't think that's going to happen, but I can always use your stuff as samples."

That seemed logical. Maybe she was wrong about the ulterior motive. She couldn't see any other reason to reject his offer, and she knew it was the only chance she had of saving the shop.

"OK." She looked up, and held out her hand. "It's a deal."

He shook it. "Great."

"It's very nice of you to do this," Tina said with a catch in her throat. "I'll get started sewing right away."

"Good. I think one of first things you should make is another pair of those trousers you had on the last time I was here."

During nearly three months on the club circuit, Tommy fought twenty fights and earned a sixteen-and-four record, receiving a number of favorable write-ups in the local paper. Thinking he'd put in his time, he asked Sam more than once to move him up to bigger bouts. But Sam hadn't done it. So after another few weeks, when Sam finally booked him into some bigger places with stronger fighters and higher stakes, Tommy was happy.

"This is what you been wantin' for a while now. So it's time to prove to me that you can do it. You got three chances to show me if you can hold your own against these guys."

"Thanks, Sam. I won't let you down. I promise."

"This means you cut out the booze, and no more runnin' around with every barfly that gives you the eye. Save your energy for the ring."

"Yes, sir."

"I signed you up as a welter-weight, so you got to watch your diet." Sam grinned. "You better lay off that heavy olive oil you dagos like to eat." He faked a punch to Tommy's gut. "*Capisce?*"

Tommy always winced when someone called him a dago so, manager or no manager, he almost punched the guy. He couldn't do it though, because Sam was his ticket to the big time, so he forced himself to look him in the eye and say, "Yeah, I understand."

Tommy sat alone in his dressing room on the night of his first fight, reflecting on how he'd gotten there. His life had changed so much in a short amount of time from his days under Steele's thumb. It also hadn't been that long since he had met Tina, fought to win her love, and then lost it in a matter of days.

How would she feel about his career as a fighter? She had always thought he should use his brains rather than his muscle to make a living. He reasoned that maybe she wouldn't mind the job since at least it was legit. That's when it dawned on him that nearly six months had passed since they'd been together, and although he had spent most of it trying to forget her, she was still the voice in his head and the throb in his heart.

"All right, shake hands and come out fighting," the referee said to Tommy and his opponent, Kempler, in the middle of the ring.

Tommy looked up at Kempler's vicious face and cringed. He had heard the expression 'if looks could kill,' but he'd never experienced something so close to the real thing. Though the guy was an ugly son of a bitch, that was nothing compared to the hate in his eyes that bore down on Tommy from the three or four inches he towered over him. Tommy prayed, when he went back to his corner, that the guy was all show and no blow. Some guys could put on an act but didn't have anything to back it up.

Kempler wasted no time dispelling that theory. He came out slugging and made contact with several jabs to Tommy's face. Thankful that he had heeded Sam's warnings to stay focused and work hard, Tommy used all the fancy footwork he had mastered in the past few weeks. He circled and sidestepped around Kempler, managing to keep him at bay through nine rounds. Then Kempler worked himself into a fit of rage, and went after Tommy with the look of a man who had decided that playtime was over.

Tommy saw the punch coming at his face, so he lifted his left arm to block it. Before Kempler had time to reposition himself, Tommy threw his formidable right cross into Kempler's eye, knocking him off his feet. When all efforts to pick himself up proved futile, the referee finished the count, and Tommy won his first major bout.

His win made him even more popular with his fans, and he went into his next fight brimming with self-confidence. As in the first bout, Tommy took a fencer's stance, bobbing and weaving through most of the early rounds to avoid his opponent's rapid fire combinations to his ribs and face. But by the tenth round, the guy showed no signs of letting up, and Tommy was losing speed. His feet moved like barbells, and with his timing off, his opponent slid inside, waging an attack of short punches. With hands in front of his face to block the blows, there was no time to throw a counterpunch. And when the fifteenth and final bell sounded, it was all he could do to make it back to his corner. Not surprisingly, the decision went to his opponent, and Tommy limped into his dressing room to face Sam.

Sam motioned for everyone else to leave, and went over to Tommy sitting on the rubdown table with his bruised head bowed.

"Well, slugger, I like the way you kept him off ya for all those rounds. You're pretty good at that, but you've yet to show me you can go the distance with a win."

Tommy could only nod.

"Ya know, I like ya kid. Ya been workin' hard. But ya got to realize that it cost me a lot to get ya here, and I ain't in the business of losing money. So I suggest you work even harder to finish on top next time, cuz one way or the other I got to get what's comin' to me."

⊫⊣ ⊢⊨

The dress shop limped along through the first month of 1933. The frigid weather did too. As usual, it played havoc with the Benedettis, who struggled to keep their drafty house warm. The toastiest place in the house was the kitchen, near the stove that burned night and day. That meant that everyone, with the exception of Carmen, had to go out into the bitter cold to chop wood when needed.

It also meant that the whole family spent most of their time in the kitchen.

One frigid Friday night, Dominic called all of them out to the small barn in the backyard to see that he had brought home a brown-and-white calf from his friend Dutch's farm. Carmen had been with him the day before, when Dutch told them that he planned to give the calf away. Even though Carmen had begged Dominic to take it home with them, Dominic had refused.

Carmen walked into the barn and let out a screech. "Oh, Pa, can we keep her? Please?"

"That's why I brought her home. We'll keep her in here. And you must remember to feed her every day and give her water."

"I will, I will."

"And when she is grown, you boys will take her to the farm to graze and milk her every day."

Angelo groaned, and Tina shook her head. It was an adorable little creature, barely able to stand up yet, but she knew that it would be one more thing that she would have to add to her list of chores.

She tousled Carmen's hair. "You'd better make sure you do."

"I want to sleep out here with her tonight. Can I, Pa?"

"No, it's too cold. I'll make her a place to sleep and give her food. Now you go to bed. You'll see her in the morning."

Tina sent Angelo out to the shed with Carmen the next morning while she cooked oatmeal on the stove. Within minutes, she heard yelling. She opened the back door, and Carmen shot inside, out of breath.

"She's frozen! She can't move!"

"What?" Tina grabbed her coat and stepped out the door.

Angelo shouted from the shed. "He's right. This cow's as frosty as a popsicle."

"Come see. Hurry!" Carmen grabbed her hand.

She let him pull her to the shed. There she found the pathetic animal unable to get up. The temperature had gone well below zero during the night, and the calf's legs had frozen.

"Oh my God. Come on, Angelo. Help me carry her into the house," Tina said.

"Are you kidding? In the house?"

"What else can we do? We can't let the poor thing die."

"You mean we can take her in the house?" Carmen screamed with excitement.

"We have no choice. Let's go."

Inside, Tina got a box, lined it with an old blanket, and placed it behind the stove. "Put her in the box."

Angelo laid the calf on the blanket, and the pitiful little animal looked up at them with soulful eyes.

Later, while Tina, Angelo, and Carmen amused themselves in the parlor, Eva washed the supper dishes. A shriek from the kitchen led them there, where they saw the calf trying to step out of the box on shaky legs. When she finally succeeded, she made her way around the room smelling everything in sight.

Carmen bounded over to her, and the calf took off in the opposite direction toward the parlor, banging into furniture and hurling things off tables.

"Come back here." Carmen chased her back into the kitchen and through Eva's legs.

Eva nearly tripped. "Carmen, get this animal out of the house!"

Angelo chimed in, contributing to the chaos by shouting and heading the frantic cow off at the pass, toward Carmen. Finally surrounded, the only thing the exhausted calf could do was stop and lie down in the middle of the kitchen floor—at which time Tina declared the calf recovered and ordered Angelo to help Carmen take it back out to the barn.

Angelo reached for the calf. "Let's go, Frosty."

⊷ ⊶

"Stop dawdling and finish your Ovaltine, Carmen," Tina said over her shoulder from the sink. "You'll be late for school."

"All right, all right. I'm done."

Tina snatched his cup off the table and dropped it into her soapy dishwater. "Good. Get your jacket on, and I'll help you with your boots."

When he was ready, Tina tightened his scarf around his neck and finished buttoning his hand-me-down jacket. Luckily, he was the youngest child, because surely that jacket wouldn't survive to see another owner.

Tina pulled his woolen hat over his ears. "Now, where's your mittens?"

"Here's one." He held out the lone glove.

"Where's the other one?"

"I don't know."

Tina sighed and threatened, "I'm going to pin them to your underwear when you get home, so you can't lose them."

Carmen knew the drill, because he ran around looking under the kitchen table, the stove, and the couch in the parlor.

"Well, sit down, and let's do your boots." She knelt down to slip his boots over his fidgety feet. How fortunate that Miss Snow had noticed his battered pair last year and brought him some new ones. If it weren't for the principal, a lot of kids wouldn't be able to go to school in the winter, because they didn't have enough warm clothing.

"OK, pull those up."

Carmen pulled one all the way up, but the other one wouldn't budge for him. "Oooh, I can't get this one up."

174

"Oh, for crying out loud." Tina bent over the problem boot. Grabbing it, she could tell something was in there, so she reached inside . . . and pulled out Carmen's other mitten. She shook her head and gave him a light tap on the back of his bare hand.

"Sorry, Tina," he said in his best pathetic voice, causing her to plant a juicy kiss on his cheek.

Now that she finally had him dressed, she walked him to the door. As she opened it, Angelo walked in shivering and caked in snow from shoveling sidewalks on the north side. She brought him a blanket and poured him a cup of Ovaltine while he hung up his soggy jacket next to the stove.

He sipped the steaming liquid and hunched over the stove. "I got to go. I'm already late for school."

"Didn't you give your homeroom teacher the note I wrote about your new job?"

"Yeah, but I've got a history test first period, and Mr. Guthrie won't let me take it if I'm late."

"All right, get your coat on." Tina poured the remainder of the Ovaltine into a canning jar. "Here, at least take this with you."

She hated watching Angelo go to school after having worked for two hours every morning. It was no wonder his grades were dropping. It couldn't be helped, though. With less income from the dress shop, she had tried, desperately to find another job.

The shirt factory had laid off a bunch of workers, so she didn't bother to go there. Then a high school acquaintance from the north side who worked at the five and ten cent store had told her about an opening there. They allowed her to fill out an application, but when she walked into the manager's office and he took one look at her Italian surname, suddenly the job was no longer available.

On top of that, the railroad had cut back during the winter months, and Dominic's salary had shrunk. Even Eva had tried to resume bussing tables at the station diner, but they had hired someone else when she left to help out with the household responsibilities. Angelo, as it turned out, was the only employable one in the family, and Dominic seemed to have no trouble securing jobs for him.

The only thing Tina could do right now was to take full advantage of the material that Chet had brought her and sew the best garments she possibly could. For that reason, she stayed at the shop well beyond closing time and sewed into the night at home. She started with the trousers, as Chet had suggested. He seemed to think they were unique enough to attract the women who had everything and wanted to emulate the movie stars.

For that reason, she took Hollywood's lead and added as much glamour to them as possible. She designed versions of what she saw in the movies: dresses and skirts cut on the bias that clung to women's hips and thighs. But she used rayon fabric as a substitute for more expensive silk. With hemlines dropping, her suit featured a mid-calf skirt that was mostly straight, but with kick-pleats below the knees, paired with a short jacket.

In the meantime, Chet stopped by often to check on her progress, and each time he praised her talent and cheered her on. It got so that she looked forward to his visits and found herself wondering what he might think of what she was doing.

"So how many items do you have finished?"

"Fifteen completed and two more almost done." She pulled the rack of garments out from the back. "Here they are."

Chet went through them one at a time, commenting on each. "Well," he said when he looked at the last one, "I think it's time to put them on sale. You've got a pretty nice line here, and I'm sure they'll sell. That is if you market them right."

"What do you mean?"

"I mean you've got to advertise somewhere besides your storefront window."

"But, where?" She couldn't think of anyplace.

"Well, you're looking for north side business, so you've got to go up there where they go."

"That's easy for you to say."

"Come on. You must frequent some of the same diners or grocers in that part of town sometimes."

Tina thought hard. "Well, there's a soda fountain all the kids go to up there. And there's the library, the post office, a couple of grocers, and a butcher shop."

"Good. We'll take advantage of spring coming." He drummed his fingers on the table. How about an ad in the local paper?"

"That would cost too much."

"Well, consider it part of the loan."

"I don't know. I'm getting into an awful lot of debt here."

"Ever hear the phrase 'it takes money to make money'?"

She sighed. "All my life. Why do you think my family is so poor?"

He looked her in the eye. "Well, here's your chance to change that."

Tina's eyes held his as she walked toward him. "Why are you doing this? What do you get out of it?"

"I get to spend time with you."

"So how do you feel about him?" Rosie asked, when Tina told her what Chet had said.

"I like him. He's a nice guy."

"He must be, to help you the way he has. But do you like him like a boyfriend?"

"I'm not sure. He's kind of growing on me."

Rosie smiled. "Like Tommy grew on you?"

Tina didn't respond to Rosie's question. Not because she didn't know, but because there was no comparison. Tommy was

Tommy. There'd been no one like him before him, and there'd be no one like him afterward. Oh, eventually there would be someone else out there for her, but it hadn't been that long since she and Tommy had been together, and she could still feel him inside of her.

CHAPTER TEN

While Tina prepared to advertise her latest designs, Chet actually got busy doing it. He had signs made up at his company that advertised the new merchandise at Irene's Dress Shop. He also used his sales skills on Main Street to convince the merchants that they should display the signs.

Chet had told her to look in the morning newspaper the next day, and when she did, she spotted the ad that he had paid them to run. You couldn't miss the quarter-page ad with a sketch of one of the outfits from her new collection. She swooned a bit upon seeing her design in the paper. Almost everyone in Kingsburg would see it.

The ad definitely brought more traffic into the shop that day, mostly neighbors stopping by to congratulate her or comment on the ad. But many stayed to examine or try on the new clothes that she had displayed in the middle of the shop, like she had seen done in the fashion magazines. Two people from the neighborhood actually placed orders, and a few of her friends, including Rosie, promised to save their pennies and order something as soon as possible.

By late morning of the next day, the foot traffic had died down, and once again she was alone in the shop. Not only had her celebrity been fleeting, it hadn't generated enough new orders to come close to what she owed Chet. How could she face him?

The figures on the balance sheet blurred amidst the tears clouding her eyes. She dropped her hands into her lap. *This will kill Irene. What do I do now?* She had lost Tommy, and all of her big dreams of being a fashion designer were going to die with this little shop.

The bell over the door rang out, so she grabbed her handkerchief and dabbed her eyes. When she looked up, she found Miss Snow standing there.

"Oh." Tina cleared her throat. "Good morning, Miss Snow. How can I help you?"

"I'm in need of three new blouses and a jacket. As you may know, Irene usually makes them for me. Is that something that you can do in her absence?"

"Yes. I've watched her do them many times, and we have the fabric and your measurements."

"Wonderful. How is Irene doing?"

"Making progress, I think."

"Good. I understand that business has been slow since she's been gone."

"Yes, Miss. I'm afraid that some people don't have any confidence in me."

"That's a very generous way of putting it, Tina. It's unfortunate that those people can't be half as charitable toward you."

<hr />

Over a week later Chet hung up his coat in the shop, and turned to Tina. "So how many have you sold?"

He looked so eager that her heart sank "Two. Only two," she mumbled.

"Oh. I . . . I'm sorry. I thought for sure there would be more."

"No one even came to look."

"Those lousy people. I was sure they would come around. I'm really surprised."

"I'm not."

Chet sighed. "You poor kid."

"Well, I guess you've got yourself some nice samples. I'm so sorry."

Chet walked over to her. "Let's not give up yet." He wrapped his arms around her. "Give it a little more time."

Tina nodded, and began to weep quietly on his shoulder.

"If you'd like, I can show your trouser design to a couple of guys I know in the manufacturing business, OK?"

"OK."

He pulled back and brushed the drops away with his fingers, then kissed her gently on the mouth.

The kiss startled her, but she gulped back her tears, and welcomed it. It wasn't Tommy's kiss, but it was soothing, and just what she needed at that moment. When she pulled back smiling at him, he leaned in again to kiss her, this time harder and with more fervor. Not sure she wanted this much, she kissed him back, but broke away quicker. He took the opportunity to nuzzle her neck moving down her V-neck sweater to her breast, where he nestled his mouth and lingered.

"Chet," she said in a warning tone.

"What?" As if he hadn't gotten the message, he slipped his hand under the bottom of her sweater and up to her bra.

Tina grabbed his arm and yanked on it until he removed his hand from underneath. "I'm not ready for this right now," she said.

"But we've known each other for months, and I thought that . . ."

"I'm sorry. I like you a lot, and you've been wonderful to me, but . . . I don't feel comfortable doing this."

"That's all right. I understand."

Tina relived that afternoon with Chet while she cleaned the kitchen that night. She still believed him to be a nice guy, as she had told Rosie. He had already done so much for her, and even understood her reluctance to allow him to make love to her. On top of that, he said he would talk to some manufacturers about her design. So, despite her disappointment in sales, she went to bed in higher spirits than she had in days.

After having tried her best to increase sales, Tina didn't know what else she could do. She had finally resigned herself to the fact that she couldn't bring in the same amount of money that Irene did, and that's the way it would be. Then in walked Mrs. Upton, and Tina dropped a stitch in surprise.

Fluffing her hair, she got up to greet her. "Hello, Mrs. Upton. May I help you?"

"Hello. Will Irene be back soon?

"I'm afraid not. They expect her recovery to take at least another three months. I'm running the shop for her."

"Oh. Well, in that case, you'll have to help me. The Ladies Club is holding a formal dinner dance in two weeks, and I need a new frock."

"Two weeks doesn't give us much time."

The woman lifted her nose toward the ceiling. "Are you saying you can't do it?"

Tina cleared her throat. "No, of course not. It's only that we might not have a fabric that you like in stock."

"What about this?" Upton pointed to one of Tina's new dresses.

Tina's heart began to race. "Yes. I have more of that fabric. What style did you have in mind?"

"Well, this one. Can you make one of these in my size?"

"I had five orders for new dresses this week," Tina said to Rosie as they walked to mass.

"Why now?"

"I'm sure it was Mrs. Upton. She looked great in her dress, and she probably told her friends where she got it. I'm finally going to be able to pay Chet back for the fabric."

"So you think you'll be able to keep the shop open?"

"Maybe. If things keep up like this."

Things did keep up like that. With the return of some of the north side business, the shop began to show a profit again. At least she didn't have to close. In fact, she was finding it difficult to get all the work done in a timely fashion all by herself. She really needed someone to help her with the alterations, so she wrote Irene a letter, asking her if she could hire someone for a few hours a week.

Irene approved, and Tina set out to find someone that could do a good job. She remembered a close friend of hers in school who used to sew lovely things for herself. Mary, whose husband had lost his job, was thrilled to get the work, and Tina was pleased to have some company in the shop.

She explained to Mary how Chet had given her the fabric to try to drum up business, and how she thought her efforts had failed, but how Chet had told her not to give up. As it turned out he was right, and she had saved enough money to pay him what she owed him. She wished she could tell him, but he hadn't been by in over a month.

Tommy's third bout proved to be worse than the second. This time, his opponent dropped him in the fifth. Sam surprised him by saying little and booking him for a fourth contest a couple of weeks later. Tommy thanked him by out-distancing the guy for twelve rounds and winning the decision.

Five more fights followed; some wins, but more losses. Still the money kept coming in. Tommy sensed that he'd found his niche and started to relax. Now somewhat successful, and a lot more homesick, he even toyed with the idea of returning to Kingsburg to visit his family.

He decided that he would go home after his upcoming fight in a city about thirty-five miles from Kingsburg. As it got closer to the date of the bout, memories of his forced departure clouded his visions of a happy homecoming. He knew that Steve Anderson had lost the election for new mayor, so he wasn't afraid of legal problems. But he had slunk out of town in shame, and maybe not enough time had passed for people to forget that. Would his success as a palooka really outshine his lousy reputation as a small-time bootlegger?

"What'll ya have?" Sam said to Tommy sitting across from him in a booth at the local speakeasy.

"Draft."

Sam walked over to the bar, and waited while the bartender filled two glasses with beer. "Here ya go." He put a glass in front of Tommy.

"Thanks."

They made some small talk while Tommy wondered why Sam had asked him there the night before the fight. He didn't make a habit of socializing with his boxers.

"So I been lookin' at your stats, and they're not showin' a lot of promise."

Tommy couldn't really defend himself. The numbers were what they were, but he'd figured that Sam was all right with that. He must have been wrong, so he braced himself for what he figured would be the axe.

"Like I said before, I like ya, kid. So I found a way to make you pay off for me, and for you too."

Tommy didn't like the sound of that. "Yeah? What's that?"

"I fixed it for you to take a dive tomorrow night."

Tommy's breathing became shallow as he rested his tight fists on the table. "I'm not taking no dive."

"I knew you would say that, so let me explain it."

"What's to explain? A dive's a dive, and I don't fight like that."

"Well, the explanation is that either you do this to pay me the money you owe, or you find some other way to pay it. You got an extra five grand layin' around somewhere?"

"Five grand?"

"Hell yes. Supporting, training, and promoting a new fighter takes a lot of dough."

Of course he didn't have the dough to settle with Sam. He'd blown all of the money he left Kingsburg with, and he'd only managed to save a few hundred dollars from his purses. He'd connived his way out of a lot of scrapes since he was a kid, but he didn't see any way out of this one. Having been on the other side of the rackets, he knew that they would come after him if he didn't pay up. Sam had played it smart by not giving him much time to consider his options before the fight, so Tommy had no choice but to agree to take the dive.

⊫⊪

Now the middle of April, snowfall finally began to change to rainfall, and Tina needed to order fabric to accommodate the change of seasons. With still no sign of Chet, she called his company, and asked for him.

"I'm sorry, but Mr. Lewis hasn't worked for us since last fall," the woman on the line told Tina when she asked for Chet. "He only took Mr. Bergen's place for a few weeks while he recuperated from having his appendix removed."

Tina's heart fluttered. "Are you sure? Mr. Bergen hasn't been around since then."

185

"Well, if I remember, Mr. Lewis told him that your shop was closed and wouldn't be needing to place any orders for several months. We were waiting to hear from you. Would you like Mr. Bergen to come by now?"

Tina didn't respond. She struggled to process what the woman had told her.

"Miss? Are you ready to place an order again?"

"Oh . . . Uh . . . yes. Please send Mr. Bergen out soon. And . . . uh . . . did Mr. Lewis leave a forwarding address or phone number?"

"I'm afraid not, miss. Is there anything else we can do for you?"

"No. No, thank you very much."

Tina dropped the phone receiver. Chet had lied to her. But why would he do that? He'd given her all that fabric for free. Why? He must have lied so that he could keep on seeing her.

But he could've told me the truth. I liked him enough to stay friends with him, especially after he helped me so much.

And why did he finally just drop out of sight? Maybe she'd been right in the beginning. He was only after sexual favors. Well, he didn't get what he worked so hard for. On the other hand, maybe he would still come back to get his money for the fabric, or maybe he was still waiting to interest a manufacturer in the trousers, before coming back.

Oh my God. He has my sketch!

———

Tina called the fabric company back and asked to talk to a manager. He had no forwarding contact information for Chet and said that he hadn't seen or heard from him since he had finished his job with the company. If he had stolen her design, she'd never see him again, and if his intentions had been honorable, he would eventually show up. Her only alternative was to wait and see what happened.

In the meantime, she and her assistant had their hands full with alterations and dressmaking. Before long, spring had moved on, and summer had arrived, stirring up memories of the heartbreak of the previous year. As usual, time brought some changes. Mrs. Farina finally put her black dress away, although the pain of Tony's passing still showed on her face. Carmen had mastered walking without two of his toes, and Angelo was happy to have received his promotion to the next grade in school, despite all the hours of working three jobs. She and Eva had settled into a routine with managing the household and their jobs, and Dominic actually appeared to appreciate their work, and helped with the cooking.

The family's biggest concern was Irene. They had awaited the doctor's report with apprehension because his last report showed that her progress hadn't been as good as he had hoped. The next month, their prayers were answered when Irene was released. Since no active TB had shown in the x-rays, the sanatorium doctor felt that she could go home to complete her recovery.

Tina placed a bell on the table next to Irene's bed. "Ring this bell if you need something."

Irene grabbed her hand. "You're such a dear."

Tina patted Irene's hand, smoothed the sheets, and walked out of the bedroom. Her family had gathered in the shop for Irene's homecoming.

"She's still very weak and will need someone with her at all times for a while," Tina said. "I arranged for Mrs. Szaminski to stay with her during the night, just as she asked, but you will need to take turns coming by throughout the day."

⚬━⟨ ⟩━⚬

Tommy's stomach churned as he sat in his dressing room, rubbed down and taped. The thought of what he was going to do brought on waves of nausea, until he finally had to run into the toilet to vomit. He didn't know how to fight to lose, and he wasn't even sure he could make it look real.

Tommy looked out over the audience in the arena, full of people who didn't know that they would be cheated that night. He did a double-take when he saw a young woman seated in the stands with a face the shape of Tina's. Of course it wasn't her. It never was, even though he had seen her in every crowd and around every street corner, only to watch her disappear with the blink of his eyes.

Tonight was no different, except that while in the ring, he actually imagined she was in the audience. He went through the introductions sensing her eyes on him, and when the bell signaled the beginning of the first round, he had to rely on his instincts to jump to his feet. Suddenly without warning, he saw the two of them together at the cabin, and as he danced around his opponent, blocking jabs and upper cuts, he relived the night they had spent together. How could he go through with Sam's plan, knowing how she would feel about it? She was everything that was good in his life, and no matter how hard he tried, he could never be the person he was before he met her. Once again, he was torn between her standards and his livelihood. Why hadn't he had enough guts to tell Sam to go to hell?

So, distracted by his dilemma, he managed to avoid his opponent's blows through the third and designated knockout round.

"What the hell are you doing?" his corner man said as he handed him water. "Sam's pissed."

Tommy ignored him and the signals Sam continued to give him throughout the rest of the bout. The decision went to his opponent on points, and he knew that he had just ended his boxing career. That wouldn't be all that would be over if he didn't get out of town fast enough. The look on Sam's face told him that Sam would stop at nothing to get his money.

There was no sign of Sam or his pals in the dressing room when he got there after the fight. It didn't surprise him, because he knew that they wouldn't come after him in there. He did figure, however, that they'd be waiting for him outside to follow him to a secluded place. After the others left the room, he grabbed his clothes, went into the bathroom, and locked the door behind him. He washed the sweat off his upper body and threw his clothes on. He climbed on top of the sink, pushed the window open, and shimmied out of it.

Once outside, he found himself around the corner from the building entrance. He saw his car parked across the street and knew that he'd stick out like a sore thumb if he drove it off, so he stood there and looked at. Boy, he loved that car, but it was part of his old life, and after tonight, he knew he was through with that. What the hell, he might as well leave it for Sam. He owed him a pretty penny, and the car was worth about a grand. If Sam took it, at least he would have paid off part of his debt.

Tommy took one last look at the roadster and ran toward Main Street, where he could blend in with the crowd.

He figured that when they didn't find him in his room, they would check the train station and bus terminal. To avoid that, he slipped into a movie theater to get out of sight. He sat through a movie, the cartoon, and the newsreel before venturing out. It was after midnight, and the local buses had stopped running.

The out-of-town bus was in front of an all-night diner so that the passengers could get something to eat. He talked the driver into letting him on by handing him a five-dollar bill. He hadn't bothered to check where the bus was headed because he didn't care, but he soon found out that he was on his way to Syracuse with a stop in Kingsburg.

Wherever he ended up, he would have to find a job. He only had about seventy-five dollars on him, because he had left about four hundred in his room at the boarding house. He was sure that dough would be found by Sam's guys when they rifled through his stuff to search for clues to his whereabouts. Too bad Sam would never get the money to put toward Tommy's debt, because those guys would pocket it themselves. He hated to admit that he had done that plenty of times himself when he made collections.

Anyway, he'd need to work and would just be one of the thousands of poor slobs his age looking for a job and a place to flop. He was only about an hour away from Kingsburg, but how could he go home now, no better off than when he left? Maybe even worse off. Now he was on the lam from Sam and his goons, who might even show up in the town that had run him out last year. Boy, he'd really screwed himself up this time.

Still, the thought of the one person that he'd always been able to trust and rely on for help continued to creep back into his head, in spite of how hard he tried to push it out. Maybe it was because he dreaded seeing the disapproval in her eyes, even though he deserved it, and more.

When the driver called the Kingsburg stop, Tommy looked out the window and saw the familiar signs for Bush's Drugs and Henley's Soda Fountain. He flashed on the many pleasant hours he had spent in both places, but at that moment anxiety overtook his nostalgia, so he pulled the brim of his hat down over his eyes and followed a couple of passengers off the bus.

He made his way to her house and hid behind some bushes until Miss Snow opened the door and walked down the steps. He knew that she would be on her way to school, and he wanted to catch her before she left.

He emerged from the bush. "Miss Snow?" he said in a low voice.

She turned to face him. "Tomas, what are you doing here?"

After hearing that he was in trouble, she told him to meet her behind the school at five o'clock. When he did, she let him in, and they sat in her office while he explained his situation.

"I'm proud of you for not giving into those thugs, but you do have a problem; two of them actually. I won't give money to a man who insisted that you commit a crime for his gain."

"I never expected you to give me the money, Miss Snow." He dropped his head. "I hoped that maybe you knew somebody in another town who could give me a job."

"I assume that you'll stay at your parents' house while you're here."

"For a day or two, anyway."

"About that job. I have an idea, but I'll need a few days to look into it."

Tommy's mother cried with joy when she saw him, but his father seemed cool toward him.

"All this time, and you don't tell us where you are. You make mama sick with worry, and then you come strolling in, for a couple of days, you say."

"I can't stay here too long, Pa. Those guys, they'll find me here."

For the next few days, he laid low and told his whole family that they couldn't tell anybody that he was in town, because it could be dangerous. He also didn't want his buddies or his old customers to know, and especially Tina. She couldn't about know the jam that he'd gotten into this time.

⚔ ⚔

After a couple of weeks of bed rest, and another two weeks of taking it easy, Irene returned to work part-time in the shop. Not only did this arrangement give Tina more time at home, it also allowed more time for working on new designs. The whole time that Irene had been gone, Tina had kept her sights on going to New York City. She had managed to save enough money to go, but with Irene still not up to par, she would have to put her trip on hold once again. She began to question whether or not her dream would ever come true.

Tina couldn't wait to get off work that afternoon because she knew that the September issue of *Vogue* magazine, the year's

191

biggest, would be waiting for her at the newsstand. She only had enough time to flip through it when she got home before she had to begin her chores. Later, in her bedroom she savored every page, critiquing each dress and every outfit. She only made it through a quarter of the publication before she had to turn the light out.

The next morning, she took the magazine with her to the shop and began to share it with Irene.

"Look at this. The designer obviously only cares about making a statement with his design, not whether or not the dress flatters the woman wearing it." Tina lifted the page up for Irene and Mary to look at. "One of these days I'm going to"—Tina turned to the next page—"show them how to . . ." Tina stopped, and studied the next picture. "Oh my God. No, no," she cried.

Irene's head popped up. "What's the matter?"

"That rotten, miserable snake. He did it. He sold my design!"

CHAPTER ELEVEN

Tina spent the next few days trying to discover the manufacturer of the trousers she saw in the magazine. She couldn't let Chet or the manufacturer get away with stealing her property. Finally, she tracked them down—a company located on Seventh Avenue in New York City. She called but couldn't get through the receptionist.

"You don't have any choice, Tina. You've got to go to New York to talk to the owners of the company." Rosie paced up and down in Tina's bedroom.

"You're right. I have to, but that would mean leaving my family and Irene alone."

"They'll just have to get along without you for a while. Besides, this is good practice for everybody for when you move there."

"That's true. I won't stay long. Just long enough to get what they owe me."

"Good. Want some company on the train?"

The train pulled into Grand Central Station about two o'clock in the afternoon. Tina placed one hand over her racing heart and grabbed Rosie's hand with the other while they both looked out the window to watch their approach. It didn't seem real until the porter walked through their car announcing, "Grand Central." Then she knew she had made it to New York City at last.

When they walked out of the station onto the busy street, Tina flinched at the sights and sounds of the bustling city and stood in awe at the crowds of people pushing her as they hurried by. They asked a policeman for directions to Seventh Street in the Garment District, and somehow proceeded to get lost in the daunting city anyway. They had to be close, because the biggest clothing rack Tina had ever seen barely missed mowing them down.

"That kid didn't even say excuse me." Rosie wiped her brow. "God, I'm soaked. It's a lot more humid here than at home."

After brushing themselves off, they looked up, and the eight-story building of the Hinklestein's Dress Company dwarfed them. Tina's stomach turned over. She suddenly wanted to run back to Irene's shop. This had sounded like such a good idea at home. Did she really think they would let her talk to the owner or manager of the company, and if they did, what would she say?

"Jeez, this is a big company, Tina."

Tina took a deep breath, and exhaled a little bit at a time. "I know. I wasn't expecting it to be so big."

"Well, let's go in."

"I don't know . . ."

"You've got to. We came all this way. Remember how mad you were when you saw that ad?"

Tina nodded.

"Good. Now's your chance to tell them what you think."

They walked inside. Tina pointed to a chair in the reception room, and Rosie took a seat. Tina went up to the receptionist. "Hello, my name is Tina Benedetti, and I would like to speak to your manager."

"Do you have an appointment?" the woman said with a thick Brooklyn accent.

"No."

"Well, he's pretty busy today. I don't think—"

"I really need to talk to him about this." Tina held out the picture from *Vogue* that she had brought with her.

"What about it?"

"I designed those trousers."

The woman looked at the pair of trousers that Tina had on. "Uh, all right. Just a minute."

Mr. Rubin took his feet down off his desk and scooted his chair up as Tina and Rosie walked into the office, "Now . . . Miss Benedetti, is it?"

"Yes. And this is my friend, Rosie.

He tightened his tie. "What can I do for you?"

"Well, I'm a dress designer from Kingsburg, and last year I designed these trousers." She tugged at the material on the pants she was wearing. "And a few days ago I picked up *Vogue* and saw this."

He looked at the picture, then at her pants. "Really? For all I know, you copied the design and showed up here."

"Well, I didn't."

"Can you prove it? Do you have your original sketch?"

"No. I gave it to someone."

"Well then, I'm a busy man," he said in a patronizing tone.

"I have some other sketches with me."

He gestured to her to stop. "I'm not looking at those. You'll probably try to accuse me of stealing them, too."

Tina put the magazine picture under his nose on the desk. "Do you see the design on the pockets?" She pointed to a small emblem on each one.

He squinted to see it. "Yeah?"

"That's my emblem. It is on this pair of pants that I sewed, and if you'd glance at these sketches you would see it on every one of them. I put it on everything I sketch and sew. See? It's CB. My initials. Constantina Benedetti."

Rubin rolled his eyes and rose. "Wait here," he said, and left the office.

He returned with a file folder in his hand. "Well, I checked and found out that Mr. Chester Lewis offered this design as payment for three thousand dollars that he owed us. I assume that you hadn't given him the right to do that."

"Of course not," she said. "I gave it to him so that he could try to find a buyer for me!"

"I'm sorry, but as far as we're concerned we paid for the rights legally, and I'm afraid you have no grounds for suing us for any more money." He continued in a parent's tone. "This should teach you not trust anyone with your designs in the future."

Tina knew it had been her own fault, and she couldn't decide if she was more angry at herself or more disappointed that she would not get credit for the trousers. Either way, she felt foolish and embarrassed. She couldn't wait to get out of there, so she stood up to leave.

"You know," Mr. Rubin said before she could get to the door, "I couldn't help noticing your swell figure and how good you wear clothes. We can always use pretty, young models to show off our line to the buyers. How'd ya like a job?"

"But I didn't come here to model someone else's clothes," Tina said to Rosie on the subway toward the Little Italy section of the city.

Rosie gave her arm a light slap. "I know, but my God Tina, a model. You've got to do it."

Tina clutched the piece of paper containing the address of Mrs. Farina's distant relatives living in New York's Italian neighborhood.

Arrangements had been made for the family to put Tina and Rosie up for the few days they would be there. After disembarking from the subway car, they walked a couple of blocks and looked around at the tall rows of nearly identical houses, tightly lined up on both sides of the crowded street.

The heat had driven the residents to their open windows, and the familiar scent of garlic and tomatoes made Tina picture her kitchen at home. She and Rosie nodded to many of the neighbors sitting on their stoops as they neared their destination. Before going up the steps, Tina stopped and stared straight ahead. "You're right, I do have to stay." She turned to her friend. "Maybe if I do, I can find someone to buy my designs. But how do I tell my father and Irene?"

⊷⊶

Tina sent a telegram to her father and Irene to let them know of her plans. She told her father how much she would be making but told him she would be sewing in a factory. His brief reply told her he wasn't happy, but he didn't tell her to come home. She told Irene the truth, and as expected, she was delighted with Tina's new prospects. Tina apologized for leaving the shop in the lurch, but Irene assured her that she and Mary could handle things.

Having gotten their blessing, Tina went back to Seventh Street to accept Mr. Rubin's offer. He told her that he wouldn't need her for another week, so she and Rosie used the time to find her a more permanent residence. Over the next week, Rosie helped Tina get acclimated to her new city. They took in as many sights as they could on their next-to-nothing budget, and people-watched the rest of the time. Tina found everything about New Yorkers fascinating, from their accents and manners to their attitudes and fast-paced lives. *Where are they always rushing off to?*

Before Tina knew it, the time had come for her to start work and for Rosie to return to Kingsburg. Tina had gotten used to having Rosie with her. How she would make it on her own in a place that still seemed so strange, so intimidating? She found that out on Monday, after leaving Rosie at the train station.

She had an hour to kill before reporting to Hinklestein's Dress Company, so she treated herself to a doughnut and a cup of coffee at the automat. Sitting there by herself, amid the clamor and throng of faceless people, she shrank further and further into the chair. Never had she felt so alone.

Her nervous stomach would only accept a bite or two of the doughnut, so she wrapped the rest up in a napkin and put it in her pocketbook for later. She took a deep breath and set off for work. Why she had taken the job? Her only modeling experience consisted of a few turns in the dress shop for one of Irene's clients, and she wished she were on the train headed back there with Rosie at that very moment.

Hinklestein's seemed like a different place that day. The place buzzed with people, all of them running in different directions. The middle-aged receptionist was busy talking to a young man clutching a tall cart with packages and dresses. Tina finally got her attention and introduced herself as a new model.

The woman looked her up and down. "Oh yeah? Nobody told me to expect ya."

"I was here last week, and Mr. Rubin offered me a job."

"Oh, all right, honey. If you say so. They never tell me anything around here." She shrugged. "Come on. I'll take you back."

Tina followed her down a long hallway, past a room the size of Kingsburg High School gymnasium. But this one was decorated with heavy velvet draperies and stuffed sofas. They came to a door off to the side, and the woman opened it. "Here ya are, honey. Go on in."

Tina looked around the cramped room, where three young women were in various stages of undress.

"Uh, excuse me. My name is Tina, and I'm supposed to start work today. Do you know where I can find Mr. Rubin?"

A blonde girl finished pulling a dress over her head. "Hi. He's probably with a buyer. He told me to give you this list of numbers."

Tina took the slip of paper, and looked at it. "I don't understand. What are these numbers for?"

"You never did this before?"

"No, I haven't."

"Well, the numbers are the model numbers of the dresses that we're trying to sell to the buyers. Those are the ones that you'll be modeling today."

"Oh, where are the dresses?"

"Come on. I'll show you."

Tina wiggled into number 854, a pale blue belted shirtwaist with two breast pockets and a tight skirt. It fit her pretty well, but she thought that the stitching around the pockets accentuated her bosom too much. The color flattered her though, so she smoothed her hair, applied some lipstick, and stepped out into the showroom with a smile on her face.

She took her place behind the other models, but panic soon overtook her confidence, and she struggled to maintain that smile. Though too scared to move, she willed her feet to mimic the girls cycling around the room. She turned, twirled, and stood in front of each buyer sitting on the sofas and chairs. At the same time, she could hear the company's salesmen flirting with the women buyers and joking with the men as they coaxed them to order large quantities of their $10.95 dresses. Tina didn't know which made her more uncomfortable, the women in their designer suits and fur wraps looking down their noses at her or the bald-headed men shooting her provocative glances.

"Tina."

She looked up at the sound of her name and saw one of the salesmen directing her over with the crook of his index finger, so she walked up to him and the cigar-smoking buyer at his side.

"Mr. Gelding would like to get a closer look at the dress."

Tina edged closer to the client and flinched a little when he reached out to touch the dress.

Mr. Gelding tugged on the sleeve. "Ve-e-ry nice," he said, as he rubbed the fabric between his fingers and stared at her chest.

Tina wanted to pull out of his grasp, but she saw the salesman sneering at her, so she hesitated before making a move.

"Oh, yes it is." She smiled, and took a step back to show off the dress. "And very comfortable. I'm sure your customers would love it."

The salesman waited for Mr. Gelding to agree before giving Tina an approving glance.

The rest of the day continued in much the same way: the flurry to get the dresses on, then the rush out to face the buyers while the salesmen cajoled them with their fast-talk. Tina went home exhausted and dreading another day of it. Over a supper of fettucine and marinara sauce, prepared on her hotplate in her boarding house room, she longed for her family. How were her brothers and sister doing, particularly Carmen? She hated leaving him and carried constant guilt for having done so. Could this belittling modeling job be worth abandoning her siblings? Of course not, but the possibility of getting the opportunity to earn a living designing clothes kept her going back to Hinklestein's every day.

⊷⊹ ⊹⊶

Summer melted into fall, bringing welcome relief from the heat and the realization that as with most things, Tina had become more comfortable with her job. She found she was even getting satisfaction when the buyers placed a considerable order for the dresses she modeled. Some of the salesmen gave her small tips when that happened. But they soon made it known that the bigger tips were given to the models that helped to wine and dine the male buyers, so she often agreed to meet them at Schrafft's and other restaurants for lunches and dinners.

She learned to flirt with them just enough to help secure the sale, but drew the line when the buyers insisted on more attention. She grew adept at squirming out of lecherous embraces and evading roving hands. The salesmen knew her standards and usually didn't press her for more, but it was common knowledge that if a girl showed signs that she would be agreeable to accompanying a man to his room, the salesman would show his appreciation by upping her tip considerably. Tina couldn't imagine needing the money that badly.

She believed that women buyers were more critical, so she balked when one of them spoke to her after a showing.

"What's your name?" the head buyer at a large department store said.

"Tina."

"You're quite lovely, and you look good in everything you show."

"Thank you. It's nice of you to say that."

"Have you lived in New York City all of your life?"

"Oh, no. Only a couple of months. I'm from upstate."

"Oh, so you came here to be a model."

"No. I'm a designer, but modeling is a living for now."

The woman smiled and nodded as if she'd heard that story before.

"Well, we could use a first-rate model for our winter fashion show. Would you like to help us out? The money's not bad, and you won't have to put up with sleazy buyers like him." She nodded toward her cigar-smoking colleague across the room.

The extra modeling job went well, and helped Tina to see that the biggest department store market was the $10.95-priced dresses.

She saw that many of her designs didn't fit in with that rate and began thinking of ways to alter them. The cutting room was not far from the models' dressing room. She had looked through the door many times, but hadn't ventured inside.

Hyman Steiner was the head cutter or "factory man." A slight, balding man with a wiry gray mustache, he was never without a tape measure around his neck. He had only ever nodded at her a few times when they passed in the hallway, so she didn't know if he would talk to her if she wandered into his work area. She decided to give it try before going home one afternoon while he was rolling out a bolt of material.

Tina stuck her head in the doorway. "Hello."

The man turned toward her. "Yes?"

She slipped inside. "Do you mind if I watch you for a few minutes?"

"If you like." Steiner said with a shrug.

Tina watched him cut out three dresses while she told him about herself and her design experience. He seemed interested and agreed to look at her work and let her know what he thought.

Mr. Steiner found two of Tina's designs good enough to be included in their upcoming line. Bursting with excitement, she splurged on a phone call to Irene to share her news.

"He said if they sell, he'll give me credit next time."

"How wonderful. I'm sure they will sell," Irene said. "I'm so happy for you."

Tina was happy, too, and gaining confidence every day. By winter, she had learned the ropes of the modeling business and had made friends with a couple of the girls. They even invited her to move in with them when they lost their roommate. Tina jumped at the chance to live in Greenwich Village, which was closer to the factory. That would mean less rent and travel time for her. It really helped, since the winter winds blowing from the ocean onto the streets of Manhattan could seem ten times as bitter as the cold in Kingsburg, and without a flake of snow on the ground.

Sharing an apartment meant also sharing good news like the repeal of Prohibition on December 5th, 1933, which would leave scores of bootleggers looking for a new livelihood. Tina found herself and her young roommates joining thousands of other New Yorkers at bars around the city, toasting each other as they took their first legal alcoholic drinks ever. The moment was bittersweet for Tina, because she remembered Tommy and the disagreements they had had over his involvement with illegal booze.

Luckily, with the comings and goings of the other girls, she had less time alone to think about Tommy. Wherever he was, or what he was doing, she assumed that he didn't lack female companionship, and she experienced a twinge each time she thought of him doing and saying the things he had done with her. Although she avoided sharing her feelings in her letters to Rosie, she had no trouble confiding in her new friends, and that helped.

⊨⊰⊹⊱⊨

Miss Snow came through for Tommy again. She had called in a favor from a government colleague who pulled some strings and got Tommy a job with the newly formed Civil Works Administration (CWA). One of the first job creation programs of Roosevelt's New Deal, the organization was charged with the construction and repair of buildings and roads nationwide. The workers were chosen from a list of thousands of unemployed men who had applied.

Tommy jumped at the chance to earn an honest living, despite the mostly backbreaking work and crude living conditions. The jobs took them from Central New York and north to the Canadian border. Over the next few months, he dug a number of trenches and laid thousands of feet of sewer pipe. It was the kind of work he had gone to extreme lengths to avoid since quitting school. Yet it became his salvation in his quest to free himself from his old life.

To his surprise, he found the work satisfying and tried to learn more advanced skills whenever he could. His newfound interest did not go unnoticed by his boss, who began to take Tommy under his wing and teach him how to cut, bend and weld the various kinds of metal pipe. Pipefitters were well respected among the trades as being indispensable to the infrastructure of all buildings.

For that reason, when the CWA disbanded in March of 1934, Tommy accepted his boss's offer to continue on as his apprentice in Rochester. After a few months there, although not yet eligible to work as a union journeyman, he had gained most of the knowledge necessary and had earned enough money to support himself while saving a few bucks.

Once again, he owed it all to Miss Snow, and he wished he could thank her in person. Instead, he had to settle for a long letter, to which she replied with her approval, praising him for his success. He looked forward to the day that he could return to Kingsburg, walk into the Southside School with head up, and present a bouquet of flowers to the woman he had both feared and revered.

⊷⊷ ⊷⊶

"But, Mr. Steiner, you told me if my designs sold, you would give me credit for the next ones," Tina said on an early spring day after hearing the bad news.

The man threw up his hands. "I don't make the rules. Talk to Mr. Rubin."

Tina did. Rubin listened to her state her case, but spoke without emotion. "I hired you as a model, and you're a good one. I can't afford another designer. Times are bad, haven't you heard?"

"But my dresses sold. That's more money in your pocket."

"Two dresses do not make a line."

"Well, at least give me the credit."

"Credit means I gotta pay ya, and like I said, times are—"

"Yeah, I know. Times are bad," she said with all the sarcasm she could muster.

Her roommates sympathized with her after she spilled out her disappointment to them over dinner, but they had come to New York to be models and were happy to have the opportunity at Hinklestein's.

"Just be glad that you have rent money," one of them advised. "A lot of people don't even have that these days."

Of course she knew that, but modeling was not why she was in New York City.

OK, she had tried her best at Hinklestein's and failed. She'd have to use all the contacts she had made to get what she wanted. There had to be somebody willing to give her a chance.

A few months later, Tina believed that she had found that somebody in Max Heller. He knew the business, and she appreciated everything he had taught her, even though he had an ulterior motive.

"Tina, I've been thinking, and I'm pretty sure I can sell your dresses," Max said, while saying goodbye after a date.

"That's wonderful." Tina gave the middle-aged salesman a firm kiss on the lips. "So will you put them in your next show with my name on them?"

"Well, I'll do better than that. I'm going to a manufacturers' convention next week in Albany, and I want you to come with me." He nibbled her neck. "While we're there we can introduce you and your line."

"I don't know . . ."

"You don't know if you want me to introduce you, or if you want to share a room with me?"

She pulled back, but remained in his arms. "Of course I want to meet potential buyers, but I . . ."

"Look Tina, you've put me off long enough. A guy can only get strung along for so long."

"But, you know that I . . ."

He broke out of her embrace. "This coy act was all right in the beginning, but I'm not buying it now. Either you go with me next week, or we're done."

Tina awoke that Saturday morning still thinking about Max's ultimatum the night before. *Why can't I shake this? I'm not actually considering going with him, am I?* But Max knew a lot of people in this business, and the thought of having the opportunity to become a paid designer kept gnawing at her. So she did what she always did in a major crisis. She went to church to light a candle.

Just the fragrance of the burning candles in the rack below the Blessed Mother calmed her. She lit the punk, then the candle, and watched it burn for a moment before kneeling to pray. She was a little embarrassed to bring this problem to church, but she had had many heartfelt talks with the Blessed Mother about her dreams and asked nothing of her today except the strength to live with whatever decision she would make.

After church, she walked several blocks out of her way, considering the choice before her. Finally, when she arrived home, still unsure of what she would do, she was met by what she interpreted as a sign from above standing in front of her door.

"Pa, what are you doing here?" she cried, wrapping her arms around Dominic with both surprise and fear in her voice. "Are the kids all right?"

"Yes, they are OK."

Tina unlocked the door and pushed it open. "Oh, good," she said with relief, but confusion. "Well, come inside."

He stepped in, looking around at the tiny place, and Tina took his hat out of his hand.

"Sit down." She pointed to the couch across the room.

Dominic sat on the edge of it and examined his daughter. "You look skinny. Don't that job of yours pay enough to eat?"

Tina smiled. "I'm eating plenty, Pa. But models can't be too fat, you know?"

"Women look better with more meat on their bones. I should have come sooner."

"So is that why you came, Pa? To make sure I was eating enough?"

"No, I came to bring you home."

"But, I thought you said that the kids are all right?"

"It's Irene."

Dominic explained that Irene's TB had come back, and she would have to return to the sanatorium.

"She needs you to run the shop for her like you did before."

Tina hadn't been ready for this. Just minutes ago, having been so wrapped up in her own dilemma, Irene and her family had been the farthest thing from her mind. A wave of guilt washed over her, but she remembered that Irene had wanted her to find her own life.

"Did she send you here?"

"No. She told me not to come." He went on to explain that Irene had begged him not to tell Tina. She preferred to go on relief and become a ward of the state rather than interfere with Tina's chances for success. But if that happened, the shop would close, and Irene's belongings would be sold off for whatever profit the state could make.

Tina gave Hinklestein's two weeks' notice. Then, before boarding the train, she said goodbye to her roommates, to the now familiar sites that she had come to appreciate, and her hopes of selling her designs to Max or any other company. Watching the skyline fade from sight was like seeing her dreams dissolve into the clouds. She yearned to reach out and pull the city to her in one last attempt to cling to its promise. But of course, she couldn't, so she turned around in her seat to face a future that she feared would be no different than her past.

CHAPTER TWELVE

Rosie stood in the dress shop chatting with Mary while she waited for Tina to finish with a customer.

"I'm sorry, Ro," Tina said as the door closed behind the woman. "She dropped in to place an order, and I had to take her measurements."

"That's OK. I was talking to Mary about my wedding plans, and she was telling me how business has picked up in the last couple of weeks."

"Yes. Can you believe it? I've never seen it like this," Mary said. "It's because Irene told everyone she knows that Tina has been designing for a big manufacturing company in New York City. And those people told their friends."

"Yeah, now I have to try to live up to that reputation," Tina added with a doubtful expression.

"I don't know if I can afford such a big-shot designer to make my wedding gown," Rosie said with a touch of sarcasm. "Do you even have time today?"

Tina smirked and waved her over to a chair. "Are you kidding? I'd kill you if you didn't let me design your dress."

Rosie had arrived home from New York City to a marriage proposal from long-time boyfriend Frankie. She told Tina that absence had made his heart grow fonder when he worried that he had lost Rosie to the lure of the big-city lights. But in fact, when she returned to Kingsburg without Tina, she realized that Frankie held the key to what she truly wanted: a home and a family of her own. Her decision had not surprised Tina; for all Rosie's worldly talk, Tina had always known that she would wind up being Frankie's wife.

Hearing Rosie's wedding plans reminded her that she had been ready to marry Tommy in spite of her career ambitions. Would she really have been happy to give it all up for him? She had to admit that having a shot at fame and fortune in New York City made her realize that Tommy had been right to leave her behind to follow her dream. But now that she was back, living her former life among family and friends, she began to wonder where she really belonged.

A few weeks after taking over the dress shop, she found she had little time to ponder the meaning of her life. When a grateful Irene had given her twenty-five per cent of the proceeds, Tina developed a renewed interest in making the shop a success. She became flooded with orders for new clothes and mending.

To keep up, she increased Mary's hours and often worked late into the night herself. Eva sent Angelo with dinner on those days, and on some days, Tina had ended up spending the night on Irene's couch.

She began to realize that moving into Irene's apartment would allow her more time for work, and for sleep. When she broached the subject to her father, he would hear nothing of it, saying that a single girl should not be living alone. She reminded him that she had lived on her own in New York City, but he argued that it wasn't done in Kingsburg, and what would the neighbors say?

After a particularly busy day, Tina put her scissors down, answered the knock at the locked door, and found Dominic holding a plate of food covered with waxed paper.

"Pa, what are you doing here?"

He handed her the plate. "You got to eat."

"Where's Angelo?

"Home."

"Then why are . . . ?"

He hesitated before speaking. "You work so hard."

"Yes, I do, but I'm making a lot of money for Irene, and for us too."

He rubbed his chin. "I know you didn't want to come back."

"No, I didn't want to, but I had to."

"You're a good girl." He stroked her hair. "Mama would be proud of you."

Tina stared into his weary face with appreciation.

"I want you to move your things into Irene's apartment," Dominic continued. "Angelo will help you this weekend."

The Depression continued to drag on into June of 1934. Roosevelt's New Deal had put many more people back to work, but not nearly all of them. Like Irene's shop, the businesses that managed to stay afloat did so with skeleton crews. Tina and Dominic were grateful to keep a roof over the family's head and food on the table. Living in Irene's apartment made it so much easier for Tina to put in the hours she needed to, but she missed seeing her family every day. She tried to make up for her absence by cooking dinner for them every Sunday and helping out with Carmen when she could.

This weekend would be taken up with Rosie's wedding. In addition to creating Rosie's dress, Tina was maid of honor. She had held Rosie's bridal shower the previous Sunday and sewn and sold bridesmaid dresses to the wedding party at cost. The 9:00 A.M. mass would be followed by a breakfast reception at Eduardo's, the best man's Italian restaurant.

Eddie Pecora was Frankie's older cousin and owned the largest restaurant on the south side. Tina had dated him with Rosie and Frankie a couple of times during high school, but he'd been a boisterous joker and she'd found him irritating. Luckily he had mellowed a bit and matured into a nice guy with a quick wit, because their wedding duties had thrown them together, and she'd helped Eddie plan the rehearsal dinner, also at his restaurant.

After the wedding reception, when the last piece of cake had been eaten and the bride and groom had left for their honeymoon, Tina stuck around the restaurant to help clean up the remnants of the celebration.

"You know, I'm kind of sorry it's all over," Eddie said as he lifted some glasses off a table.

Tina picked up some matchbooks left behind. "I know. Things are going to be different now that Rosie's married."

"Oh yeah, I suppose so. But I meant that now you and I won't be seeing each other anymore."

"True. We won't have a reason to."

Eddie placed a hand on her arm. "Do we really need a reason?"

Tina couldn't come up with one, so she continued to see Eddie in between their busy schedules. Their dates consisted of quick lunches and an occasional movie, even though Eddie made it clear that he would be happy to find more time for her. She enjoyed his company because it added some gaiety to her rather somber life. But with so many demands on her, she had no more energy to give to the relationship.

Her hard work proved to be a shrewd decision. News of Tina's experience in NYC, coupled with her stylish women's fashions, spread from the neighboring villages to Syracuse. Women of means came to order the closest thing to haute couture that they had available, but they also took advantage of Tina's everyday line of dresses. She was forced to hire another seamstress to do the mending work in order to allow Mary to help her fill the over- whelming demand.

Tina rushed into the diner as if she'd run all the way. "I'll have a hamburger and a cup of coffee," she told the waitress, and slipped into the seat opposite Eddie.

"How about some home fries?" he said.

Tina looked at the pies sitting behind the counter. "No, thanks. But I will have a piece of that blueberry pie."

Eddie smiled. "Sweets for the sweet."

"More like sweets for my sweet tooth. Sorry I'm late."

"I don't mind, but I hate how your work keeps you on the run all the time."

"That's because business is good, and that's a good thing."

"You know that my offer to take you away from all of that still goes."

"I know, but I love my work."

Eddie looked doubtful. "Are you sure it's not still Capello?"

"No. He's out of my life."

"Then what is it?"

"Eddie, I told you that I don't want you to have to take care of me and my family."

"Jeez, Tina, it's not as if I wouldn't be getting a beautiful wife."

Although Eddie was the only guy she would even consider marrying since Tommy, she continued to turn him down. The business was going so well, and with her continued opportunity to create and sell her designs, she couldn't give it all up to be Eddie's wife. Besides, she still had an obligation to Irene. Who would watch out for Irene's interest the way she did?

As fall approached, the demand for Tina's designs continued to increase. Sometimes women had to wait weeks for their orders, or Tina had to turn down their business. She hated doing that, so she hired another part-time seamstress.

⊷✛✚⊶

Tommy wasted no time that fall before writing Miss Snow with his news. He had purchased a business license under the name of Capello Building and begun doing side jobs in between working for his boss. His goal was to become a general contractor, so he accepted work in all phases of construction. Miss Snow wrote back praising him for his accomplishments and encouraging his ambition. He began to see that it was time to pay her and his family a visit.

He looked forward to his trip to Kingsburg, set for the end of October, when business would slow down. Now, in early October, he was busy finishing up three projects, so he took one more gulp of hot coffee before putting the cup in the sink and heading for the door to begin his day.

When he opened the door, he stood face to face with a Western Union boy. He had been anticipating a response from a bid he had sent out a couple of weeks ago for a big job, and he grinned at the kid holding up the telegram.

"You Tom Capello?"

"Yes," Tommy said, reaching for the wire.

He tipped the boy and tore open the envelope. It took a few seconds for him to absorb the fact that it wasn't from the customer, but from Kingsburg. His eagerness turned to sorrow as he read, "Sorry to tell you Miss Snow died yesterday. Funeral next Friday. Hope you can make it. Joey."

The butterflies that had been fluttering in Tommy's stomach for the past twenty miles worsened as the familiar sights of Kingsburg appeared out the window of the train. He saw door after door of houses and businesses swathed in black wreaths. The gray skies above added to the deep pall blanketing the town. He still couldn't believe that she was gone.

He had called his parents and learned that the south side had been in shock since the news of Miss Snow's sudden death from a stroke. Schools, government agencies, and businesses had dimmed their lights in her honor for two minutes the evening she died.

The viewing and a prayer service was to take place that evening in the school gymnasium. The funeral would take place at the south side Protestant church tomorrow morning, with a reception to follow in the gymnasium. Tommy had dreamed of returning home to a smiling Miss Snow beaming with approval when hearing of his recent accomplishments. He had planned to shower her with gratitude for her diligence in seeing that he did not become one of the "lost boys" from the south side. Instead he shuddered to think that now all he could do was be there to show his respect along with all of her other admirers.

"Hey, Tom. How are ya?" Joey grinned and shook Tommy's hand on the platform.

"I'm OK. How about you?"

"Glad that you could make it home."

"Me, too."

They walked toward the terminal. "It's sure good to see ya, but too bad it's because Miss Snow died. She's all everybody's talkin' about."

"She helped a lot of us kids."

"I guess."

Joey stopped and looked Tommy over. "Hey, you look a little different." He studied Tommy's face. "I know," he said, pointing to Tommy's clean upper lip. "You got rid of the 'stache. How come?"

"I shaved it when I was boxing and just kept shaving after that."

"Hey, uh, by the way, I'm sorry I never got to see one of your bouts, but I . . ."

"Don't worry about it. It was only something I did so I could eat."

Joey led Tommy to his car and opened the passenger door for him.

"Like my wheels?"

"No kidding. You got your own car?"

"Sure. I'm working over to the quarry," Joey boasted as they both hopped in.

"Well, good for you," Tommy said, but he couldn't help feeling bad that Joey had settled for working that dead-end job.

Joey started the car. "Hey, Tom, I know you gotta spend some time with the family, but the guys are anxious to see ya. I told 'em I'd bring you buy the roadhouse later on tonight."

Tommy took a deep breath. "I don't know . . . We'll see."

Tommy watched from the back of the room as the line of familiar mourners proceeded past the casket. He saw both friends and enemies, but overcome with grief at seeing Miss Snow lying small and lifeless, he found himself barely affected by their presence—that is, until he recognized a wisp of auburn hair framing a delicate face. He wiped his misty eyes, and the figure he had longed to touch all those months materialized. This was not the figment of his imagination that he'd seen so many times over the past year. It was Tina. His heart began to race, and he shifted from one foot to another, then back again, not knowing what he should do.

Before he could decide, the minister called for everyone's attention to begin the prayer service. Try as he might, Tommy could barely recite the prayers. Instead, he succumbed to the thoughts of Tina swirling round his mind, and tried to catch another glimpse of her whenever possible. Should he try to talk to her tonight? What would he say to her, and would she even listen to him? At the end of the service he felt guilty that he had cheated Miss Snow of her well-deserved devotional, but he had decided not to approach Tina. Frustrated and ashamed, he snuck out the back door and never made it to the roadhouse with Joey that night.

The next morning, Tommy sat with his family in a back pew as a group of students from the boys' band processed up the aisle playing a dirge. Directly behind them eight pallbearers struggled to carry Miss Snow to the front of the church altar. They were a variety of ages, and Tommy knew most of them. He wished he could've been among them. Knowing his reputation, there was no way that he would've been chosen, but he had bought himself a conservative black suit to show his respect to her.

As the service continued with prayers, music, and eulogies, Tommy spent the entire time engaged in his own silent tribute, reliving his tumultuous boyhood and Miss Snow's part in it. He had trouble remembering every one of his offenses, but he recalled every instance when Miss Snow had stepped in to save him from being tossed aside as an incorrigible with no redeeming value. She had done that for many, but he never quite understood what she had seen in him. The fact remained that she offered him help, and for the most part he had been smart enough to take it. He gave himself credit for that much.

⊨⊣⊢⊨

"You know, you're going to have to see him at the reception," Eva warned Tina as they readied themselves to leave for the funeral that morning.

"Well, he's going to have to see me, too. After all, he's the one that left me. Besides, I've gotten over him, and I'm sure he's over me."

"You don't fool me. I know you're nervous about it."

Tina wouldn't admit her apprehension to herself, let alone Eva. "Eva, don't worry about it."

Eva shook her head. "OK, whatever you say."

Tina's family had paid their respects at the reception following the funeral, and gone home. She stayed behind to wait for Eddie, who had volunteered to provide the food for the buffet from his restaurant. He had been so busy that he only had time to stop and talk with her between tasks. She had just begun to think she should go ahead and leave without him when she heard a familiar voice.

"I used to love weddings and funerals when I was a kid. All that food, and . . ."

Tina looked up, saw Tommy standing there, and couldn't help smiling. "Oh, hello."

"Hi. Been waiting to get to talk to you."

She thought that she wouldn't have to see him. "I heard you were in town."

"I had to come for Miss Snow. If it wasn't for her I'd . . ." Tommy took a breath, and pursed his lips. "She helped me a lot, and I'll never forget her."

"I know."

Tommy smoothed his tie. "You look great. You make that dress?"

"Of course. And you look well." He looked more than well. He looked wonderful. Even better without the mustache.

"I'm doin' all right. Thanks to Miss Snow."

"That's good."

"Hey, they tell me you went to New York City for a while. Didn't you like it?"

"I did, and I wanted to stay, but Irene needed me to run the shop."

"My mother said that you've turned it into some big business."

"We're pretty busy." She shifted her feet. "How about you? What are you doing?"

"Construction."

"And you like that?"

"Believe it or not, I do. Enough to start my own business."

"Well, that's great. I'm happy for you." Her eyes searched the room for Eddie. She spotted him wiping a table while glaring at her and Tommy. "Look, I'm sorry, I've got to—"

He glanced Eddie's way and smiled. "I was watching you with Pecora. How long's that been going on?"

"About six months."

"No ring, though, I see."

She shook her head. "How about you? Anybody special in . . . , where is it?"

"Rochester. Nope."

That didn't surprise her. He always liked to play the field. "Well, I've really got to get going."

"Sure. Uh, all right. Maybe I'll see ya around. I'll be here a few more days."

Tommy went by Tina's shop that Monday morning before leaving on the noon train. He stood across the street as rain drizzled over him and watched her walk up to the door and go inside. He wanted to run to her and throw his arms around her before she could disappear, but he couldn't bring himself to do it. What if she rejected him? After all, she was Eddie's girl now. Eddie had a spotless reputation as a successful businessman. How could he compete with that? He boarded the train that day more despondent than when he had arrived.

Rosie burst into the shop later that morning and didn't bother to say hello. "So how was it to see Tommy again?"

Tina's back went up as she sat at the sewing machine. She had already been through this third degree with Eva and Mary. She tried showing the same lack of interest with Rosie, but she was finding it difficult to keep up the act.

"It was all right; very harmless. Like a couple of school chums meeting at a reunion."

"After what you two went through together? I don't believe it."

"Rosie, we were there for a funeral. What did you think would happen?"

"I don't know. Nothing, I guess. But didn't you get those old feelings back a little?"

"Of course I did. I'm human. But what am I supposed to do with those feelings now that he's gone again?"

⋯⋯

By the beginning of 1935, the town had still not fully recovered from Miss Snow's passing. The mood of south side residents slumped under the weight of grief. Students and teachers continued to muddle through the winter without their beloved principal and advocate. There seemed to be no way for her admirers to lift the shroud her death had cast over their lives.

Tina also wasn't satisfied with her growing business, even though she and her staff were not hurting for work. She hadn't been able to suppress her desire to reach a wider audience with her designs. But even if she could reach more customers, she and her small staff could never handle an increase in volume. Expanding the shop would take a lot of money, and she had no capital for that. She needed another way to get her designs out there.

She got off the bus in Barnstall, and made her way down the city street toward a red brick building that took up the entire block. Dunbar Sportswear had been one of only three dress manufacturers within twenty-five miles of Kingsburg willing to meet with her. The two closest to Kingsburg turned down her offer to give them her designs for a percentage of the profits. They couldn't risk putting their resources into an unproven commodity. Tina knew that her options had dwindled, so she arrived at Dunbar's with a different plan.

"Thank you for seeing me today, Mr. Klein," she said as she extended her hand to the manager.

"Well, Miss Benedetti, most women with your, uh, background apply to us for seamstress jobs. I had some time on my calendar and couldn't resist hearing what you could possibly have to say."

So that was the only reason he had asked her to come. She had had to take time away from her shop, ride three buses, and walk a mile to get here, simply for this man's amusement.

"Well, I brought a resume with me. Why don't you take a look at it before we get to the entertainment?"

Klein gave her a half-smile, and took the paper from her hand. He scanned it, confirming each entry with "Mmm-hmm."

He looked up. "You were having some success in New York. Why did you leave?"

"Family obligations. As you can see, I've continued designing and have made a name for myself in Kingsburg and surrounding areas with dresses like this." Tina rose from her chair and modeled her dress as she would have when working at Hinklestein's.

Klein seemed impressed. "And what do you want from us?"

"I'd like you to produce a small line of my designs with my label in them and sell them to your clients."

"And why would I do that?"

"Because they will make you a lot of money and give me more recognition than I can get by just selling out of my shop."

Dunbar Sportswear had agreed to contract with Tina for ten designs, contingent on their approval. She already had six designs on paper, so she set out to create four more within their allotted timeframe. That meant more time spent on her designs, and less time on orders in the shop. But she was determined to make it work.

This day seemed no different than any others until Mary came into work. "Tina, look at this." Mary spread the morning's newspaper in front of her. Across the front page was a banner headline: MISS ABIGAIL SNOW LEAVES MAJORITY OF HER FAMILY INHERITANCE TO SOUTHSIDE SCHOOL. NEW ADDITION TO BE BUILT ON ADJACENT LOT.

Tina leaned over the paper. "I knew she had some family money, but I'd never dreamed it would be enough for a building."

A month later, Eddie took Tina to a lovely out-of-town restaurant to celebrate the completion of her designs. She welcomed the leisurely dinner after the frenetic schedule she had imposed upon herself to get the designs to Dunbar on time.

"This was a great idea, Eddie. I really needed to get away to relax."

"It's my celebration, too, after a long month of hardly seeing you at all."

"I know." Tina lifted her wine glass to him. "Thanks for being so patient."

He touched her glass with his. "You're worth the wait."

After they both enjoyed roast duck for a main course and cherries jubilee for dessert, Eddie began to tap his foot under the table, and Tina noticed sweat on his upper lip.

"Are you all right, Ed?"

"Sure, why?"

"I don't know; you look kind of funny."

He reached into his jacket pocket. "I hope you don't mind if I combine your celebration with this . . ." He pulled out a diamond ring, and held it up.

Tina gulped a sip of wine.

"Tina, please say that you'll marry me. It doesn't have to be right away, but I want everyone to know that you're spoken for."

<hr />

"Oh my God, oh my God!" Rosie danced around her kitchen waving a dishtowel in celebration after Tina showed her the ring. "I can't believe you finally did it."

"Well, I did."

"Frankie told me that Eddie had bought the ring, but I didn't think you'd take it."

"You mean you knew, and you didn't warn me? Some friend."

"I didn't want to ruin it for Eddie. He really wanted to surprise you."

"Well, OK."

"I'm so glad you said yes. He's so much better for you than Tommy." When Tina shrugged, Rosie added with a smile, "Well, at least nobody is trying to run him out of town."

"Oh?" Tina replied. "I seem to remember that you drooled over Tommy because you thought he was a gangster."

Rosie snapped the dishtowel at Tina. "I was just a kid then. Anyway, now it's time to start planning your wedding."

"Whoa, hold on, "Tina protested. "We haven't even set a date."

Tina pushed her dinner dish away from her. The Benedettis had gathered to have an engagement dinner for Tina and Eddie. The boys had poured the wine, and Dominic had given a toast. "Wow, Eva," Tina said, "that was delicious. You're really becoming a good cook."

"Yeah, I could use you in my restaurant." Eddie said.

"Thanks for the compliment, but I wouldn't want to spend all day cooking. I only do it when I have to."

"Hey, Eddie, maybe you need somebody to wash dishes." Dominic looked over at Angelo. "Angelo could help you on the weekends."

"I might have some work for him. Angelo, you come by the restaurant next Saturday."

"OK, sure," Angelo said.

"Hey, Eddie." Carmen held up a deck of cards. "You said you'd show me some card tricks after supper."

"OK, kid." Eddie tousled Carmen's hair and took the cards. "Come on in the parlor. You're gonna love these."

After Eddie had left and the dishes were done, Dominic stopped on his way to bed, and put his hand on Tina's shoulder. "You make me happy, Tina. Eduardo's a good boy, and now I don't have to worry about you no more."

Tina squeezed his hand. "I'm glad, Pa."

"I don't know if you knew, but when you were little, Mama started to save her extra pennies to put toward your wedding."

"No. I didn't know that."

"I've kept what she saved in a special place for you. It's not much, and I don't have much to add to it, but I know she would be happy to know that you will be able to use it for your wedding like she planned."

Tina wiped her moist eyes and hugged his neck. "Thank you, Pa."

Eva, who had overheard her father, looked over at Tina. "It seems that your plans to marry Eddie have made everybody very happy. But what about you, are you happy?"

CHAPTER THIRTEEN

March brought the winter thaw. Though trees remained bare, the melted white snow on sidewalks and roads had turned into a dirty slush that spattered everywhere as pedestrians and cars made their way through town. But with the mess came the promise of another spring, summer clothing, and rolling hills in green.

For Tina, it also brought the news that Dunbar would be manufacturing her line in the near future. The news made all of the mundane tasks she had to do around the shop more tolerable. Just knowing that her clothes would be reaching women all over the country expanded her own horizons.

Tina didn't want to be late for dinner at Rosie and Frankie's, so she made her way to the back of the shop to see if she could help the two remaining customers huddled among the dress racks.

She turned the corner and overheard the murmur of one woman bragging to her friend. "They could've picked any of the other local contractors for Miss Snow's building, but they gave it to Henry's company."

"No kidding?"

"Well, Henry is the best. And there was no way they were going to give it to that guy that Miss Snow put in her will. He doesn't even live around here anymore. I hear they ran him out of town a few years back."

Tina's jaw dropped, and she attempted to digest what they had said. Then with a deep breath, she walked up to them. "Uh, the shop is closing now. Can I ring something up for you?"

Later that evening, even though Rosie put on a lovely dinner party, Tina couldn't even concentrate on the food and company, let alone enjoy them. She kept hearing that woman's catty voice in her head. The more she thought about it, the more it made sense that the guy Miss Snow had wanted to build her building was Tommy.

⇥ ⇤

Tina had never been to Albany before, so once again she walked the streets of a strange city. She savored it. The fast pace of the big-city atmosphere reminded her of New York and all of its possibilities.

She pulled open the heavy door of the Law Offices of Masters and Langley and made her way to the receptionist's desk. She had located the firm's name in the newspaper article about Miss Snow's building.

"Hello, I have an appointment with Mr. Spaulding."

"And you are?"

"Tina Benedetti."

"Oh." The woman cocked her head and hesitated. "Uh, please have a seat. I'll let him know you're here."

Tina sat down in a soft leather chair grounded by an unusual oriental rug and surrounded by masculine shelving that displayed a variety of award plaques and trophies. She had been afraid they wouldn't give her an appointment when she had called. It must have been the mention of Miss Snow that had given her credibility when she told them she needed an estate attorney.

Within a few minutes, the buzzer on the reception desk sounded, and the woman signaled Tina to follow her into the adjoining office. With the formalities out of the way, the lawyer leaned back in his chair and began their session.

"Now, I understand that you were referred by Abigail Snow. A fine woman. May I ask how you knew her?"

"She was the principal of my school."

"Oh. So you live in . . . Kingsburg."

"Yes. The south side."

Spaulding winced, sat up and looked at his file. "It says here you came about estate planning." He cleared his throat. "A little young for those concerns aren't you?"

"Yes. I didn't come to talk about my estate, sir. I'm here to talk about Miss Snow's."

"I don't understand. Miss Snow's affairs are confidential. I can't share anything about her estate with you. So, I don't know how I can . . ."

"I'm actually here to share something with you."

Tina went on to explain what she had overheard in her shop about the building contract, and how apparently Tommy had been overlooked for the job.

"Isn't it a lawyer's responsibility to see that his client's wishes are carried out?"

"Well, yes, but how those wishes will be executed depends on how the will was drawn up."

"Well, you should know, you drew up the will." She cleared her throat. "Is it stated that Tommy shall be appointed contractor or not?"

"Well, yes."

"Then what happened?"

Spaulding sat back and folded his arms across his chest. "I was told by the school board that Mr. Capello had left town a few years ago and he couldn't be located."

"And you took their word for it?"

"I had no reason to doubt them."

"Obviously you don't know much about small towns, Mr. Spaulding."

Tina hadn't given serious thought to what would follow after her trip to Albany. Her anger at the ever-present discrimination in Kingsburg is what had what spurred her on. *How could they disregard a legal document in order to satisfy their own bigotry?*

Now that Tina had confirmed that Masters and Langley did exist and were in fact representing Miss Snow, it was time to contact Tommy. She knew he lived in Rochester, but she had no address. She didn't want to involve his family, so she got hold of Joey. She couldn't tell him what it was about, and he was leery about giving her Tommy's address. He offered to send Tina's letter to him instead.

She sat down to write the letter. Then she tore it up. She started again. Then tore it up again. This was harder than she had figured. As waves of memories and the feelings associated with them came flooding up inside her, how could she say what she needed to say without sounding emotional? She still resented Tommy's abandonment of her, despite having reconciled it with the career success she had experienced in his absence. Their uncomfortable meeting at the funeral had made it easier for her to close the book on their relationship and accept Eddie's proposal. But if she was over Tommy, why was she experiencing pangs of guilt for lying to Eddie about the reason for her trip to Albany and for this letter she was finding so hard to write?

—‹‹+ +››—

When Tommy had returned to Rochester, he went back to work devoid of purpose. With Miss Snow gone and Tina out of his reach, he had to dig deep to stay on the path he had mapped out for himself. They had both instilled a desire in him to succeed, and now he had to find that desire from within.

Tommy's hands shook as he fumbled with the envelope and unfolded the letter from Tina. He couldn't imagine why she had sent it. After reading a few sentences, he staggered to a kitchen chair, pulled it to him, and sat down. When he finished, he reread it more slowly. Now convinced that he'd read it right, he smiled with pride at Miss Snow's confidence in him. Soon his smile turned to anger, and he cursed at the school board and anyone in Kingsburg who had ever tried to keep him down because of being Italian. *Well, not this time, you sons of bitches. This time I'm going to get what's coming to me."*

＊━◁┼ ┼▷━＊

Tina tried to be nonchalant as she took one last look around the platform before stepping onto the train bound for Albany. Her eyes swept the seats as she strode down the aisle of the crowded car. Satisfied that she saw no one she knew, she dropped into the nearest empty spot. She knew that Tommy had boarded the train in Rochester, but she could not be seen with him. She fidgeted and wished the train would leave before someone boarding could recognize her.

She didn't want to have to make small talk or lie about why she was on that train. Although it seemed an eternity, only a few minutes passed before the car finally jerked her forward and snapped her back in her seat. When the wheels began to rotate beneath her, she breathed easier and tried her best to relax.

Since she had travelled by bus to Albany the last time, she knew nothing about the Albany train station. After disembarking, she looked for signs to Gate 7, but didn't see any, so she went back to ask the porter. As she turned around, she spotted Tommy coming toward her. With his hair less slicked back, it was lighter, and with no mustache, he looked much younger than his twenty-five years. His muscular arms, tanned from working outdoors, reminded her of how they had felt around her that rainy day in the cabin. *Oh, maybe meeting him in Albany was a mistake.*

"Tommy, there you are. I was looking for Gate 7."

"I was in the next car and got off ahead of you. How was your trip?"

"Uneventful."

"Good. Thank you for coming."

"I had to."

Spaulding kept them waiting for almost an hour. When he finally let them into his office, he seemed distracted and pressed for time.

Tina offered her hand. "Good to see you again, Mr. Spaulding."

Ignoring her gesture, the attorney straightened some papers on his desk and glanced over at Tommy. "What brings you back to Albany, Miss Benedetti?"

Tommy jumped in. "She thought that you and I should meet. I'm Tommaso Capello, and I understand that Miss Abigail Snow mentioned me in her will."

When they left the law firm, Spaulding had agreed to draft a cease and desist letter to the Kingsburg school board, stating that all building construction would be on hold until Tommaso Capello could take his rightful position as general contractor for the school's new Abigail Snow Wing.

Tina and Tommy beamed with delight for their victory over the school board. But Tommy wasn't naive enough to think that it would be that simple. "That was the easy part," he said as they parted at the train station. "Facing the school board members is another story."

"You heard the lawyer; they have to give you the job." Tina flashed a smile at him.

It was a smile he'd thought he'd never see again.

"This all happened because of you. Thank you."

He had a lot to thank Tina for. She could've easily overlooked what she had heard in her shop that day and gone about her own life—which, as it turned out, now included being officially engaged to Eddie. Instead, she had put her work on hold and made two trips to Albany. He didn't quite know what to make of that, except that he knew she felt that his triumph over the school board was a win for the south side. He couldn't deny that her long-awaited approval filled him with pride.

⚓

Despite her delight over their success in Albany, when Tina returned home she never let on that she knew anything about Tommy's contract, or her part in it. She went about her work in silent satisfaction and waited for word to get out and spread through the town. She didn't have long to wait.

"Can you imagine? Miss Snow wanted Tommy Capello to build her school," Mrs. Sarducci exclaimed while bagging Tina's groceries.

"Where did you hear that?" Tina asked.

"Three customers told me the same thing today."

The next day, at a funeral in the Benedetti neighborhood, the mourners whispered among themselves.

"Why would she pick him for such an important job?" said one mourner. "What does he know about building? He was a bootlegger."

"Yeah," another replied, "my husband says he was only out for number one at our expense."

Rosie leaned into Tina. "I guess a lot of people don't know that he's a contractor. They only remember that he was a crook, and in cahoots with the mayor."

Tina said nothing for fear that anything she said might let on that she knew something about Tommy and his business.

"What do you think about all of this?" Rosie asked Tina.

"If he's capable, I'm happy for him, and I think it's a great chance to show the town that he can do something worthwhile."

"And how do you feel about having him back in town?"

"I guess Kingsburg is big enough for both of us. I'll just have to get used it."

⟫₊ ₊⟪

After a month had passed, Tommy received a letter inviting him to meet with the Kingsburg school board. He arrived in Kingsburg the night before his board appointment and checked into a motor court outside of town. He had very little chance of running into any of his friends or family there. He went to bed early, so he would be sharp when he met with the board members. They would do their best to put him in his place.

The next morning, Tommy walked into the room, and faced the seven members of the board with their backs straight up against their chairs and their chins in the air. Suddenly the violent criminals in his former business and the desperate boxers he had faced in the ring paled beside these men who held his future in their hands. A wave of nausea came over him as he took a seat. These guys with the education and business savvy that he lacked would use that to try to intimidate him.

"So, Mr. Capello, what makes someone like you, with your, let's say, questionable background, think that you qualify to oversee a multi-thousand dollar project?"

"I admit it will be my biggest job so far, but I'm sure I can do it."

"Yes, well, we will be checking on your state license and your business practices. And we'll require a list of references from you before you leave here today."

"I'm sure you've already looked into those things and couldn't come up with anything negative. Otherwise we wouldn't be here talking."

231

"Yes, uh . . . well, rest assured we will be appointing a member from this committee to oversee your work during the project."

"You do all of those things if it makes you feel better, but we all know that your hands are tied. You've been ordered to hire me by Miss Snow's attorney. And like Miss Snow, her will speaks loud and clear and won't take no for an answer."

⋙⋘

When Tina heard that Tommy had gotten the project and would be coming back to Kingsburg to live, reality set in. The thought of running into him around town sent her into a panic, because even though she had acted nonchalant in front of Rosie, she knew that seeing Tommy on a regular basis would be awkward. Well, actually more than that. It would be painful.

Luckily, Tommy remained in Rochester for three months while the architectural drawings were being completed. During that time, Tina tried hard to focus on her own work. She began working on a new line of designs for Dunbar. Although they hadn't offered her another formal contract, she wanted to be ready when they did.

She had also started making time to see Eddie two nights a week. This particular night, Eddie needed to stop at his restaurant to check on something on their way to a dance. While he was gone she waited in the car. What would her life be like, married to him?

"I just realized," she said to him when he got back in the car, "that Eduardo's will be my restaurant, too, when we get married."

He put his arms around her. "Of course. By the way, any idea yet when that might be?"

"What are you doing August 1ˢᵗ of next year?"

He sat back and grinned. "Really? Are you kidding?"

She looked directly into his eyes and shook her head.

"Well, you've got a date."

His lips found hers and delivered the deepest and longest kiss he had ever given her.

They booked the church for a nine o'clock Saturday morning mass, and Eddie noted the wedding on his restaurant calendar, to make sure no one else would be able to book the room on their date. Tina then announced it to her family at Sunday dinner and began telling as many friends and customers as she could in the next few days.

Everyone was pleased for her, but nobody was happier than Rosie.

"Finally. Poor Eddie was trying to be patient, but he loves you so much, Tina, and all he wants is to marry you."

⟻⟼

In September 1935, Irene was released from the sanatorium and returned to her home behind the shop. Tina stayed with her, sleeping on the couch, to help her to adjust to being home. Irene was much stronger than she had been after her first hospital stay and was only down for a couple of weeks before she began to work part-time. It was time for Tina to move back home.

"It's so great having you back working with me again," Tina told Irene.

"It's good to be home and not be an invalid anymore."

"I prayed for the day when you could come home to us."

Irene touched Tina's face. "God bless you," she said, and looked around the room at all the new sewing machines and furniture. "You've done wonderful things with the shop. It's so different, I hardly know it."

"But it's still Irene's Dress Shop."

"I want to talk to you about that. I've decided that it should have your name on it."

"No, that's not—"

"I did lots of thinking in the hospital," Irene said with a smile. "There wasn't much else to do. And now that I'm home, I see that my thoughts were right. The customers come for you, not me. You've worked very hard to support both of us for a long time now, and I'm grateful."

"I know, but—"

"I can't work like I used to. But that's OK, because I don't need much. Just room and board. I can earn my keep by sewing a few hours a day."

"Irene, that's not right. I'll—"

"I've talked to a lawyer, Tina, and I want to sign the business over to you."

Tina, although delighted and proud that Irene wanted to give her the shop, didn't feel comfortable accepting it. Irene had worked so hard all of her adult life to build the business into a decent livelihood, and Tina couldn't snatch it from her, and make her a boarder in her own home and shop.

"Irene, would you consider just splitting the business with me? That would help you, and still give me time to create and sell my designs to a manufacturer."

Irene turned quiet. "OK, Tina. That may be the best way to do it after all."

＝＜＋ ＋＞＝

Tommy had moved into a boarding house in town late that summer and began work on the building plans and lining up subcontractors for the job. With the winter months fast approaching, the intention was to put off breaking ground until the spring, but a late onset of frost and snow allowed for digging the foundation. Once construction ceased, Tommy used the time to finalize the hiring of the subs and brush up on the state's school construction codes.

In March 1936, operation resumed, and Tommy came under fire from some resentful workers who felt he didn't deserve the job. They also didn't want to take orders from "the dago." It took all of the strength he could muster not to haul off and flatten the guys who made no bones about how they felt. When he came close to breaking, he thought about Miss Snow and what she would think if he let those guys ruin his chance to build the building she had wanted the school kids to have.

Tommy also tried to remember how he had reacted to his boss in Rochester when he first started working for him on the CPA. Although he had been glad to have the job, the first days of his boss standing by as he performed the backbreaking manual labor had put a chip on his shoulder. But before long, the boss was pitching in while supporting and leading him and the other guys to complete their jobs with pride.

That's the kind of boss he tried to be on this job, and it seemed to pay off. By May, the project was well underway, and Tommy had won over many of the guys by showing them that he respected their talents. He complimented them when they deserved it, but at the same time, called them on it when he felt they weren't doing their best work.

A guy named Jim Rafferty began to show an interest in Tommy's knowledge of heating and pipefitting. Jim, too, had tried his hand in the boxing ring but had hated the business, so they often shared stories over drinks at the nearby bar and grill after work.

"I'd much rather work with my hands than my fists," Tommy said after downing a gulp of beer. "At least ya don't get the shit knocked out of you by a left hook ya never saw comin."

"I know what ya mean. Three broken noses is enough."

"Pipes, I know. I can make 'em do whatever I want them to. When I'm finished with a job, those pipes and the system sing."

Tina's decision to accept only a fifty-fifty partnership with Irene proved wise, as her success at Dunbar had given her leverage with Benchley's, the first local dress company she had approached the previous year. When they ordered a winter line from her, Tina was able to spend the spring designing and submit her products to Benchley's owners in June.

It didn't take Tina long to figure out that she had taken on too much work again when she had agreed to create the line for Benchley. On top of that responsibility, she was spending more time looking after the family now that she had moved back home. Even though she had tried not to, she had soon fallen back into her "mother" role to the boys.

Eva's job, though bringing in money, wasn't helping Tina's problem. Eva worked every other day at the glove factory and still tried to maintain an active social life. Mrs. Farina had stepped in to help them out, but she had her own kids to take care of. Luckily, Irene had insisted on sewing Tina's wedding gown, because Tina simply had no time to complete it for the upcoming wedding.

At the shop one day, Irene put the finishing touches on the blouse she was mending and looked over at Tina, sketching at her easel. "You've been working so hard on those designs the past couple of months. Your shower on Sunday will give you a nice break."

"I guess so, but I barely have the time for it."

"You'll make time. Rosie has planned such a beautiful party."

"I know, and I'm sure I'll enjoy it. But I'm worried about making my deadline in two weeks." Tina looked up from her easel. "In fact, I wondered if you could be at the house when Carmen gets home tomorrow. Eddie wants me to go with him to his grandmother's because she's been sick, and I told Eva I would be home to watch Carmen."

"Yes, of course I will."

"I don't know why I need to go with Eddie."

"He loves you, and he wants his family to love you, too."

"I guess, but he knows how busy I am."

"Tina, you'll be married to him in a couple of months. You had better get used to giving him a lot more of your time."

"I don't know how I'm going to be able to do that."

Irene leaned over from her sewing machine and placed her hand on Tina's shoulder. "Is it that you won't be able to do it," she asked as she searched Tina's face, "or that you won't really want to do it?"

It surprised Tina to learn how obvious it was that she didn't put Eddie at the top of her list of priorities. Eddie seemed all right with it most of the time, and it hadn't really occurred to her that things might have to change after they got married. Would she be acting this way if it were Tommy she was marrying? She hadn't seen much of him since he'd been back to supervise the school building project. That was a good thing.

⊷⊷

Tommy got to the worksite well in advance of the state inspector, who was scheduled to show up that day. He took care of some paperwork, then paced around waiting for the head electrician to show up. He had faith in the company he had chosen, since they came recommended by his former boss. What he had seen so far confirmed that he had selected the right men for that job.

Even so, today would be the first inspection of the building's ground wiring. He had passed many inspections in the past. However, he had never been subjected to a state-appointed inspector, there to ensure that he had followed the strict guidelines set by the New York State Department of Education. In order to avoid problems, he had studied the regulations and talked to electrician friends to make sure his sub got it right.

Normally the biggest fear of not passing an inspection was the loss of time and money to resolve the issue. But he knew he had more at stake this time. As promised, the board's representative had been close on his tail, waiting to have something that would give the board an excuse to fire him from the project. So as he introduced himself and his electrician to the inspector, perspiration drenched his forehead and armpits.

After a thorough going over of the ground wiring, the inspector wasted no time in telling Tommy that he had found serious problems with the wiring and connections. "Mr. Capello, this system, as is, could easily catch fire and subject children to a horrible death. This inspection is over."

Eva slammed the back door and dropped her handbag on the kitchen table. "Tina, did you hear that the school board is meeting tomorrow night to talk about firing Tommy?"

The word had gotten out that Tommy and his electrician had not passed the inspection. Tina looked up from her work at the table. "It doesn't surprise me. They never wanted him in the first place."

Tina couldn't let on to Eva, but the news about Tommy incensed her. After all she had done to get him the job, this couldn't happen. She had to talk to him. *But how to do it without being seen?* Once again, she contacted Joey with a message for Tommy to meet her that night at a roadhouse on the outskirts of town.

Tina drove the station wagon to the roadhouse, but when she arrived, she didn't see Tommy's truck. So she pulled over to the side of the parking lot to wait for him. With the flashing neon sign lighting her up like a spotlight, she slid down in the seat to hide. When Tommy arrived, she waved him over to get into the wagon. After he got in next to her, she drove down the road and found an inconspicuous place to pull over.

Tina turned the engine off. "I'm sorry that we have to be secretive about this, but nobody knows I've been helping you."

"It's all right."

Tina turned to him. "So, what went wrong with the job, Tommy?"

"I don't know. Galecki, the electrician, swears everything was good when he left it the night before the inspection."

"Do you trust him?"

He continued to stare straight ahead. "I don't know. I did."

"Could someone have gotten in there afterward to mess things up?"

"That's what Galecki says happened."

"Will he fight them?"

Tommy shrugged. "He said he would. His reputation is on the line."

"Well, if he does, it could help you, too."

"It wouldn't do any good. They would only find something else to nail me with."

"But what about your reputation as a contractor?"

"The best thing for that is to get out of this town as soon as possible."

"There must be something we can do to help Galecki find—"

"Tina, I know you're getting married in August. You must have enough to take up your time."

She nodded. "Too much, in fact. But they can't get away with this."

Tommy shook his head. "You never give up, do you?"

"Well, I—"

"Look, I had my chance to come back as a big man, and I flopped."

"But, I think we should—"

"Tina, if this was happening to some other schmuck, would you be sneaking around, wasting your time with him?"

She smiled. "But you're not some other schmuck."

Tommy took her hand and squeezed it. "No, I'm the guy who pushed you out of his life toward a better one, and you found it." He cleared his throat. "Go live it. It's what you deserve."

CHAPTER FOURTEEN

Tina had no choice but to give up on making things right for Tommy. If he wasn't willing to stick around and fight for his reputation, there wasn't much she could do. She heard he'd gone back to Rochester, and she forced herself to tuck away her pent-up feelings for him, allowing herself to become immersed in submitting her designs to Benchley and finalizing wedding plans.

It wasn't hard to do and, with her friends and family making such a fuss over her at her shower, she couldn't help but get swept up in the excitement of what was to take place over the next three weeks. She became the giddy bride she never thought she could be.

With the wedding the next day, Carmen watched Tina fold a sweater and pack it in the suitcase on her bed. "Gee, Tina, we just got used to having you living here again, and now you're gonna move."

She reached for a blouse. "I know, Carmie, but that's what happens when you get married."

"I'm gonna miss ya."

"I'll miss you, too, but I won't be that far away. You know where Eddie lives, above his restaurant, just a few blocks from here."

"I know," he whined, "but I won't be your special boy anymore."

"Of course you will. Why wouldn't you?"

"Patsy's sister got married and got a new baby. Now she loves him better than Patsy."

Tina scooped him up in her arms. "Carmie, no matter how many babies I have, you will always be my first one, and very special to me."

It felt strange to be talking about having babies. Let alone to Carmen. She and Eddie had only talked about it in passing, and she had never given much thought to the reality of it. She wasn't quite sure how she would prevent it from happening. All she knew was she had to put it off as long as possible—as long as it would take to be a successful fashion designer. If she did turn up pregnant before that, she would find a way to continue working no matter what.

Eva stuck her head into the room. "Tina, I got off work as soon as I could."

"Good. Take the station wagon and go pick up your dress and Rosie's at the shop. Rosie's going to dress here with us tomorrow."

"OK."

"Oh, and please make sure the boys are on time for rehearsal tonight, will you?"

Eva bumped into Rosie as she turned to leave and smiled. "I'll try, but you better tell Angelo, too. Where's Pa?"

"He went to get a haircut."

"Did I hear my name?" Rosie walked into the bedroom.

"Yes. I told her to pick up your dress with hers and bring them here."

Rosie pushed a skirt aside so she could sit on the bed, strewn with Tina's clothes. "Taking all of this to Niagara Falls?"

"No, but I thought I'd better get organized for the move to Eddie's."

"Looking at this room, you'd never know there's a depression going on. Your wardrobe looks like the fine clothes rack at Macy's Department Store."

"I'm pretty lucky."

"And not just because of the clothes. Eddie's a great catch."

"I know."

"You don't sound too pleased. Nervous about your wedding night?"

"Yes, that's it."

"I was, too."

"Really? The way you always talked I figured you and Frankie had already, you know . . . "

Rosie shook her head. "Are you kidding? I talked a big game, but I always knew I would wait."

"And was it worth the wait?"

Rosie patted Tina's arm. "Don't worry, kiddo. It's a little scary at first, but you might even be surprised that you kind of like it."

Tina did like it. With Tommy. She had no idea how she would feel when Eddie touched her in that way. She loved him, but she knew her physical response to him would never quite match the one she had to Tommy. And what about Eddie? He thought he was marrying a virgin. Could she recreate the innocence of her first time and not give her secret away?

Maybe this marriage was a mistake . . . but was it this marriage, or marriage to anyone other than Tommy?

━┥┝━

Tina slipped the lavender A-line dress over her head, put her arms through the armholes, and shimmied it down around her hips. She had made the sleeveless dress with a matching short jacket especially for the wedding rehearsal at the church and the dinner following it at Eddie's restaurant. She stepped in front of the mirror to adjust and admire it. *Yes, the perfect choice for the occasion.* She barely had time to check her make-up and fluff her hair before she heard Eddie talking to Dominic downstairs.

Eddie whistled when she walked into the kitchen, and she curtsied.

"A vision of loveliness. Maybe I should marry her." He winked at Dominic. "What do you think, Pa?"

"You're a lucky man. Remember that." Dominic shook his finger at Eddie, but his mouth curled into a smile.

"Are you ready to go, Pa?" Tina said. "Eva's bringing the boys."

"I'm ready. Let's go. Irene will be waiting for us."

The wedding party was small for an Italian wedding. Eva would be the maid of honor and partner with Eddie's brother as best man. Rosie and Frankie were bridesmaid and groomsman, and Eddie's teenage sister would be the other bridesmaid and walk with Angelo. The rehearsal took less than an hour, and everyone, including Father Milano, all headed back to the restaurant for the festivities.

Eddie's staff was waiting for them. They had arranged the tables in horseshoe fashion in order to accommodate the party of twenty-five. Tina, Eddie, Frankie, and Rosie took their seats at the head table, and the others filled in the tables on the sides.

As the waiters brought out the antipasto, the group began the introductions. In addition to Eddie's parents and grandmother, his married sister and her husband had come, along with his three other siblings. Rosie and Frankie's parents were introduced, along with Mrs. Farina and her oldest boy, and Mary and her husband. When they finished, Eddie's father rose and lifted his glass of zinfandel.

"Welcome, everyone, to this special occasion on the eve of the marriage of my son Eduardo Pecora to Tina Benedetti. His mother and I could not be happier that they have found each other and have chosen to spend the rest of their lives together. May God bless you both. *Salute.*"

Eddie drew Tina to him, brushing her face with his lips as his father spoke. She knew that though Mr. Pecora's sentiments were sincere, his words gave the impression that he was the host. In reality, Eddie was paying for the dinner, since his father had very little to contribute. But that would be the case for the wedding reception, too, because her mother and father's money couldn't come close to covering the cost of that.

When they had all toasted, he added, "Before we begin the wonderful meal my son has prepared, Father Milano will give a blessing."

The priest stood, began with the sign of the cross, and bowed his head before blessing the food before them. When he finished, Eddie's father stood again, and instructed the group, *"Mangia, mangia!"*

To abide by the Friday fast, the meatless dinner began with an antipasto of fried calamari, provolone cheese, marinated roasted red peppers, pickled vegetables, and Italian black and green olives. A hearty minestrone soup led into the main dish of linguine and clam sauce, followed by a green salad of iceberg and romaine lettuce with assorted vegetables in a vinegar, oil, and oregano dressing. It was all accompanied by loaves of crusty Italian bread.

Before moving on to the dessert, Eddie's younger brother started his best man speech. "I want to congratulate my big brother on snagging one of the most beautiful and talented girls in town. It doesn't surprise me, though, because he's a great guy who has always been there for me and our family. He's smart and well-respected in his business." He smiled. "Truly a hard act for a kid brother to follow. Even so, he deserves the best there is, and Tina is it." He raised his glass. *"Salute!"*

When the waiters brought out cannoli for dessert, with espresso in small demitasse cups and bottles of anisette liqueur to pour into them, Frankie stood up to speak.

"When Eddie and I were kids, he stayed out of trouble and was always trying to get me to do the same. I have him to thank for keeping me out of reform school." Frankie looked over at Eddie. "But I think he would agree that I paid him back in full when my wife Rosie and I encouraged Tina to go out with him. And tomorrow he will have one of the two best-looking women in Kingsburg for his wife."

Eddie threw out his chest and raised his glass high. "Here, here."

Tina hugged him when he sat back. With family and friends surrounding them, praising them, and championing their marriage, her eyes became moist with tears of joy. Her doubts and fears about Eddie drifted from her mind, replaced by the certainty that she was making the right choice. She was suddenly anxious to begin their life together.

Soon afterward, Eddie thanked everyone for their love and support. He said that he and Tina looked forward to seeing everyone at the wedding and wished them all a good evening. The group got up from their seats but remained in the room chatting among themselves. Then they formed a line in front of the soon-to-be bride and groom awaiting a hug from them.

Only a few guests had left when a man in a business suit entered, accompanied by two uniformed state troopers. The suited man shouted from the back of the room. "Eduardo Pecora?"

Eddie looked up at the sound of his name. "Yes?"

Tina broke out of her future mother-in-law's embrace and turned to follow Eddie toward the three men. She halted as one of the troopers said, "Mr. Pecora, we have a warrant for your arrest on a charge of felony vandalism of the Southside School building."

Tina ran forward. "What are you talking about?"

"Who are you?" the trooper asked.

"I'm his fiancée. We're getting married tomorrow."

"Not unless someone posts his bail before then."

"But I don't understand. What do you think he did?"

"He paid off one of the electricians on the new building project to rig the system to fail."

⊨⊢ ⊣⊨

After the police had taken Eddie away in handcuffs, his friends and family stood together in shock. Eddie's father tried his best to comfort his sobbing wife. "They must be wrong," she cried. "My Eddie is a good boy,"

Eddie's kid brother chimed in. "She's right. My brother wouldn't do something like that."

"Yeah, why would he?" his sister said.

A million thoughts spun around in Tina's head. *Could Eddie have actually done this terrible thing?* Carmen startled her by grabbing her hand to get her attention. "Tina, why did they take Eddie away?"

She looked down at him. "I'm not sure yet, honey, but everything will be all right. Come on." She walked Carmen over to Eva, Angelo, Irene, and her father. "You'd better take Carmen home."

Eva nodded, and Irene squeezed her arm and asked, "Do you want me to stay with you?"

Tina gave her a hug. "No, you go on home, too. I'll stop by later if it's not too late."

After her family had left, she walked over to Rosie and Frankie, waiting at the side of the room, and whispered to Frankie. "Did you know anything about this?"

"No, and I don't believe them. They're always looking to pin stuff on one of us. You know that."

Of course she knew he was right. "Will you take me to the police station? I've got to try to talk to Eddie."

When they got to the station, they found that Eddie had already been booked and placed in a cell. A lawyer had been called and was on his way, but bail could not be posted until Eddie could go before a judge. That wouldn't be until the next morning. The wedding would have to be postponed, and it would probably not be possible to get the word out to all of the guests.

"Thanks for bringing me," Tina said to Frankie and Rosie. "Please go to the church, and then try to contact as many people as possible tonight."

Rosie gave her a hug. "Oh, Tina, of course we will. This is such a shame."

"You should go home, Tina," Frankie said. "There's nothing you can do here."

Tina shook her head. "I'm not leaving until I talk to Eddie."

Despite her anger and frustration, Tina tried to be as polite as possible when she asked to see Eddie.

"I'm sorry, ma'am, but it's against the rules to let him see anyone until his lawyer gets here."

"Won't you please make an exception?" Tina pleaded. "We were supposed to be married tomorrow morning, and now . . ."

"Well . . . that was a pretty raw deal for you." The officer took a deep breath. " OK, I'll give ya ten minutes. Follow me."

Tina walked past a cell holding what sounded like a couple of drunks; they whistled as she went by. Then she passed a cell with four teenagers inside that she was pretty sure were from the south side, and another housing a sleazy character she would never want to meet in a dark alley. At the end of the row, Eddie sat with his back to the cell door. The officer unlocked it, and Tina walked into the dark room.

"Eddie, are you all right?"

He turned toward her, but kept his head down. "I guess so."

Tina went to him, and stroked his hair. "What makes them think that you did this?"

Eddie took her hand and pressed a kiss into her palm. "They said someone told them I did."

"But who would say such a thing?"

"The police aren't saying much. They're waiting to give the details to my lawyer before he talks to me."

"Do you know who he is?"

"I think they said Klein."

"Oh . . . is he supposed to be good?"

"I guess so."

"You know, Frankie thinks they're just looking to hang it on somebody from the south side. Nobody on the school board wanted Tommy to be general contractor for the building, and more than likely it was one of them."

"Tina, thank you for not asking me if I did what they said."

"I admit that as they were taking you away I wondered if you did it, but I realized you would never do something like that, and you had no reason to anyway."

"Didn't I?"

His remark startled her, but he went on. "I knew from the beginning that you had been hung up on Capello, but I was persistent, and eventually you seemed to care for me, and you let me get closer to you. But only so close. There was always something that kept you from giving all of yourself to me: your family, your work. Especially your work. I know how important that is to you and didn't mind the competition from it. In fact, I liked that you were so talented, and becoming successful. But I knew that with Capello around he would always be between us, and I had to get rid of him."

Tina took a few moments to absorb his remarks. Then she twisted the diamond ring off her finger and placed it on the cot next to Eddie.

"Officer," she said, "I'm finished."

⊶ ⊷

Tommy was summoned back to Kingsburg and resumed work on the building. He fumed about what Eddie had done to him, and he avoided Tina whenever possible. She did the same during the months of the building completion because she couldn't face him. Somehow, she felt ashamed.

She tried to occupy her mind by continuing to design for Benchley while working for Irene. But still Tommy inched into her thoughts despite her best efforts. When this happened, she told herself that he wanted no more to do with a woman who he believed would never accept his past.

The following April brought the official opening of the new building, and a dedication ceremony took place in the new auditorium. In addition to students, teachers, and parents, the school board and some state dignitaries spoke. Though Tommy was still not the board members' favorite person, they had to admit that he had done a good job and realized that he was entitled to a few minutes at the podium. Tina went with Irene, and they took seats in the back of the room. She had to be there for Tommy's victorious moment, which turned out to be last on the agenda.

"Every speaker here today has spoken of their gratitude for the generosity of one woman, Miss Abigail Snow," Tommy began. "And I couldn't agree with them more. But my gratitude is on a more personal level, because if it hadn't been for her, I would never have had the opportunity to be the general contractor for this project. In fact, if it hadn't been for her persistence and support during my youth, and later, I would have remained the juvenile delinquent and criminal that I had become.

"But I'd also like to take the opportunity to thank another important woman in my life, who in spite of her high standards has overlooked my faults, sided with me, and fought for my right to do this job."

Tommy twisted his neck to make eye contact with Tina. "Tina Benedetti, will you please come up here?"

Tina's face turned crimson, but Irene nudged her toward the platform, so she walked up to stand next to Tommy.

He took her hand and continued, "Though I've wanted to do this for a long time, it wasn't until today, as I stood up here having proven my ability to bring Miss Snow's dream to reality that I finally feel worthy enough to ask you. Tina, will you marry me?"

The room went silent as the audience waited for her response and remained that way until she said in a loud whisper, "Yes, Tommy," and leaned in to meet his kiss.

CHAPTER FIFTEEN

Carly smiled. "I knew they would end up together. So, Tommy Capello is my great grandfather.

Grandma nodded.

"Do you have a picture of him here?"

"Come with me."

Upstairs, her grandma led her into a bedroom and pointed to Tina and Tommy's wedding picture.

"He was a cutie," Carly said. "No wonder she wouldn't give him up so easy." She turned to her grandmother. "So they lived happily ever after?"

"Oh, they had their share of problems like everyone does; some illness, a miscarriage, and money, of course. Even after his success with the school, it still took Tommy a good amount of time to build his business."

"And did Tina ever become a famous designer?"

"Well, eventually she became the head designer for a chain of department stores around central New York. Her clothes were very popular, and she managed to raise us kids at the same time. That wasn't very easy in those days."

"I'm glad."

"Between the two of them, they did quite well during the war years and in the fifties. By then the discrimination lines had blurred. They bought a big home on the north side of town." Grandma looked around the property, and smiled. "And this place was always very special to them. They even became one of the prominent business couples in town. Not bad for two kids from the wrong side of the tracks, eh?"

"Pretty amazing, actually," Carly said.

Grandma jumped up. "Come on. We've got a few more things to do for the party."

Carly moaned. "Oh, I almost forgot about the party."

Carly would have preferred to stay in the background and let Brooke greet the party guests as they arrived, but Grandma insisted on introducing each one to Carly. Nearly one hundred guests attended: friends of Brooke and her parents and, of course, relatives . . . relatives who two days ago would have meant nothing to her, but she now found cool.

Ninety-year old Carmen arrived with his son, Patsy. Angelo's son and grandson came, as did Eva's great-granddaughter, and Tina's son Tommy Jr.'s great-granddaughter. They all made a big fuss over Carly, and since she felt as if she knew them, she spoke to each one of them. But she soon tired of the same old questions. Needing a break, she slipped out a side door to find an isolated spot on the steps. But someone was already there.

"Oh," she said to Brooke, "I didn't know you were here."

"They won't miss me. They're more interested in you."

"Yeah, I'm sorry about that. It's your graduation party."

"Sure you are."

"Believe it or not, I can only stand answering the same questions for so long before it makes me crazy. That's why I came out here."

"All my mother wants to do is brag about me being in the beauty contest. I didn't even want to enter it."

"Why not? I thought it was a pretty big deal around here."

"Not with my friends. And I hate the dress she bought me to wear. It makes me look about thirty years old."

"That's lousy. She wouldn't even let you pick out your own dress?"

"You may have noticed. My mother is a control freak."

"Yeah, I can see that. My mother can be one, too. That's why I'm here. I didn't want to leave my friends to stay with a bunch of strangers, but she made me."

Brooke nodded. "Speaking of mothers, mine is probably looking for us. We'd better get inside."

"Hey, I'd like to see your dress sometime," Carly said, as she followed her cousin into the house.

The next day, Aunt Maria drove to Brooke's house to pick up the sweater she had left at the lake, and Carly went along. On the way, Carly chatted happily with her aunt. Now that the party was over she would be going home to her mother, friends, and her own car. She didn't even mind having to see Brooke since they had found some common ground at the party.

"So, Carly," Aunt Sandra said when they arrived, "did you have a good time at the party?"

"Yes it was OK." Carly turned to hug her grandmother. "I especially liked meeting all those other relatives."

Grandma winked at Carly. "Christina is upstairs with Brooke. Why don't you go say hello?"

Carly thought Christina was cool, so she didn't hesitate to go up.

"Hi guys," she said as she walked into the room.

"Hey, Carly." Christina gave her a quick hug. "I didn't get to see much of you yesterday. I bet you're anxious to get back home."

Before Carly could respond, Brooke dangled a pair of high-heeled strappy shoes in front of her face. "Don't you love these? I got them for the contest."

Carly had to admit that they were great shoes. Definitely something she would wear. "Oh, yeah. Very sexy. So where's your dress?"

"Wait a minute. I'll try it on with the shoes."

While Brooke changed, Carly and Christina made small talk, mostly about Carly's return home and the upcoming school year. They were interrupted when Brooke came out, whining.

"Well, this is it. Look, you can't even see my cool shoes. I hate this long dress."

Carly understood. She didn't like the dress either. The teal color wasn't bad, but the style was all wrong for somebody Brooke's age. *What had Aunt Sandra been thinking?*

"Well, maybe you can get it hemmed so you can see the shoes better." Christina looked over at Carly. "Don't you think, Carly?"

"Sure."

"In fact, you just told me that sewing is your thing. Maybe you can hem it for Brooke."

"Uh, I don't know . . ."

"Me, either." Brooke said. "She might mess it up worse than it is. Then my mother would kill me."

"I doubt that. What do you say, Carly?"

Carly rolled her eyes at Christina and took a deep breath. "Hemming is no big deal. I've done it plenty of times."

Brooke looked at Christina, then at Carly. "OK. Let's do it."

They had decided that Brooke would sneak the dress over to Aunt Maria's house, to hide what they were doing from Aunt Sandra. Christina told Aunt Maria and convinced her to not tell Brooke's mother or their grandmother. So when Brooke arrived the next morning, Aunt Maria had lemonade and jelly donuts waiting for them in her sewing room.

Aunt Maria took a few minutes to show Carly her sewing box and where to find things. "I like having you girls here, but God forbid that Brooke's mother finds out."

The girls had already considered the consequences of that, so as soon as Aunt Maria left the room they went to work.

"OK, Brooke, put your dress on and stand on this stool."

The girls didn't speak much, as Carly experimented with lengths that would show off the new heels.

"How's this?" Carly stood back to take a better look.

Brooke examined the hem, and said, "OK, I guess. At least you can see my shoes."

Carly continued to study the dress.

"Carly? Don't you agree?"

"Sure, but . . ."

"But what?"

"Ya know . . . this dress would be a lot cuter if it were short."

A smile came over Brooke's face. "Oh my God. You're right!"

"I can do that, and take off these goofy sleeves, to make it sleeveless."

"Could you really?"

"Yeah, but what about your mom? I'm leaving soon, but you've got to live with her afterward."

With only five days left until the contest, Carly had to work fast to finish the alterations. Brooke spent a part of every day with Carly and her dress. When Carly needed a break, the two would take off in Brooke's birthday car, a new Ford Focus. They would go get something to eat or hit the mall.

"Look, Brooke." Carly pulled a rhinestone necklace off the hook at the accessory shop. "This necklace would be great with your dress."

Brooke took it and held it to her neck. "You think so? It's really pretty."

"Absolutely."

After the mall, Carly accompanied Brooke to the registrar's office of the local community college to turn in some paperwork for the upcoming semester.

"I plan to transfer to Colgate University to major in computer science after two years here," Brooke explained, "because Colgate is really expensive for four years, and I'm not ready to leave home yet."

"That's what I want to do, but my mother is pushing me to go right to fashion school."

Their secret to alter the dress had been their only bond, but Carly noticed that the closer she got to finishing it, the more they found they had in common. Apparently, Brooke felt that way, too, because she invited Carly on a double date.

"C.J. and I are going to a club tonight. Do you want to go?"

"Oh, he won't want me tagging along."

"Our friend, Dylan, is going, too. You know, you saw him at the party."

"I did?"

"Well, he saw you and wants to meet you."

"Really?"

"Why are you surprised? All my friends think you're cool because you're from California."

Carly heard the horn and hurried out of the house.

"Hop in." Dylan, a tall, muscular guy, stood holding a door to the backseat open.

Carly looked up at his welcoming face. "Oh, thank you."

She slid into the backseat, and he got in from the other side.

Brooke turned around in her seat. "Carly, this is Dylan. Dylan, Carly."

The two strangers nodded and said hello. Brooke rambled on about the county fair. But Carly's mind was on Dylan's smile and the way he'd opened the door for her. Ryan hadn't done that for her even on prom night. He also differed from Ryan physically. Where Ryan had a smaller frame, lean body, and long, sun-bleached hair, Dylan had broad shoulders and short, dark hair.

"So what's it like in L.A.?" he asked her.

"I don't live that close to L.A. I live over a hundred miles away, near San Diego."

"Oh yeah, the Padres and Petco Park. Do you go to many games?"

"Uh, no. I went once with my class."

"I'd love to see a game there. I heard the weather's great, too."

"It's nice. Not as humid as here in the summer."

Despite the usual questions about California, Carly enjoyed her evening with Dylan. He was smart and funny, but also attentive. Nothing like Ryan.

⊷⊶

Now that the dress was exactly the way that Carly had envisioned it, she knew they had to reveal it to Aunt Sandra and Grandma. Aunt Maria thought it would be best if she invited everyone for lunch at her house for the unveiling. The kids agreed that they needed the moral support.

During lunch, they hinted that Carly had made a few adjustments to the dress, so everyone sat with anxious trepidation while Brooke changed into it. Brooke soon entered, strutting her new outfit, which included the new necklace and a trendy new belt. In fear of their reaction, Carly skulked behind her. She watched as her aunt's and grandmother's mouths dropped open.

"Oh my God. What happened to the dress I bought?" Brooke's mother whispered.

"Oh, Sandra, it's beautiful," Grandma cried.

Brooke stood in front of her mother. "I love it, Mom. Don't you? I can't wait to wear it."

Sandra looked over at Carly. "Was this your idea?"

"Well, yes. Brooke wanted to be able to show off her new shoes, and I thought this would be the best way to do it. I'm sorry that you don't like it."

"Don't like it?" Sandra touched the hem of Brooke's dress. "I think it's amazing!"

The next morning Carly sat alone with Aunt Maria at the breakfast table.

"Well, your time with us is growing short," her aunt said. "But I'm so glad you came. You've brought new life to our family."

"You guys have been great, too."

"It's a shame, though, that you won't be here to see Brooke wear her dress in the contest."

Carly was almost sorry herself. "I know. Especially after working so hard on it."

"I'm sure Aunt Sandra will send you the video.

"I guess so."

Aunt Maria started clearing the table, so Carly helped.

"Ya know," Carly said, "there really isn't any reason why I can't stay a few more days. If it's all right with you."

"Well, of course it's all right. But isn't your birthday coming up soon?"

"Yes."

"Your mother probably has plans for it."

"Nothing special. Just dinner at my favorite restaurant."

"Well, you better check with her right now."

Carly called Amanda to ask her if she would change her flight plans, and her mother said yes. They agreed to have their own celebration when she got back home.

The New York family decided to spend the day at the lake and throw a party fit for an eighteenth birthday. Even Brooke pitched in to help, and Carly had to admit that it might have been her best birthday ever.

The fairgrounds sat in a valley surrounded by emerald-green hills. Though much smaller than the great San Diego County fair near Carly's home, it made up for its small size by overflowing with quaintness. There were many of the same activities and events, only with a homier feel.

Carly had bought a new outfit for the occasion, and with her hair and makeup done by Brooke's stylists, she thought she looked pretty good. *Ryan, eat your heart out.* The contest was almost as important to her as it was for Brooke. Her work would be on display and could make or break Brooke's chances. Normally, it would've thrown her into a panic, but she was enjoying herself too much.

After the contest had concluded, friends, family, and townspeople clustered around the two girls. Carly lapped up their compliments on the dress and beamed as they bestowed kudos on Brooke for winning first runner-up. With all the pictures and formalities of the contest over, they celebrated with Brooke's friends by taking advantage of the junk food and games around them.

Later that night, Brooke took her aside. "Carly," she said, "I can't thank you enough for helping me win tonight. I wish we had more time to spend together now that we understand each other better."

Carly gave her a hug, "Me, too."

Carly tossed and turned all that night. She kept thinking about Brooke's suggestion that she stay in Kingsburg and go to school with her for a year. *How could it be that only three weeks ago, I didn't even want to come here, and now I'm considering staying here?* For some reason, she felt more comfortable around Brooke and her friends than she did with her own.

⊷ ⊶

The next evening, Carly phoned her mom. She told her all about the contest and her part in it. "Things are much better between me and Brooke. In fact, we're kind of friends now."

"I'm glad. You don't want to leave there on a sour note. Maybe she can come and visit us onc of these days."

"Well . . . actually, Mom, I've been thinking about maybe staying here and going to Brooke's college with her. It's very close by, and they have courses in fashion design."

Carly couldn't tell how her mother felt about her proposal because she ended their conversation so fast. She did receive a text from her the next day saying that she would arrive in Albany tomorrow about four-thirty, would rent a car, and see her a couple of hours later. Carly wasn't quite sure what to expect.

With light left in the sky, she spotted her mom's car coming up Aunt Maria's drive around seven o'clock. She rushed to it, and her mother signaled her to get in. It felt so good to have her mother's arms around her again, but the mood was broken when Amanda sat back and said, "So what's going on, Carly? Tell me you're not serious about staying here."

"Mom, no one's more surprised than me. I hated it when I first got here. But that was before I got to know everybody. They're all so nice to me, and treat me like they've known me all my life."

"Well, of course they do. I'm sure they're very nice, but that doesn't mean—"

"Mom, it's cool being part of a big family. I love you, but we don't have any relatives nearby. Grandma's in Phoenix and Uncle Brian is in Oregon."

"I know, honey, but we can visit them more if you like."

"It's not just that. I've met some nice kids." Carly lowered her voice. "And I'm kinda popular here."

"But what about your friends at home? Won't you miss them?"

"Sure, but—"

"Carly, I don't think you've thought this through. This is a big decision to make in . . ."

Before she could finish, Aunt Maria appeared at the car window. "Hello, Amanda. I'm Carly's Aunt Maria. Please, come inside. It's starting to get dark."

Carly introduced her mother to Uncle Joey, and they chatted over coffee and cookies for more than an hour. By the time her mother got settled into Carly's room, both were exhausted, and Amanda agreed to continue their discussion the following day.

Carly spent the next morning showing her mother around the farm. In the afternoon, Brooke arrived with her mother and Grandma for lunch. Carly noticed that her mother didn't bring up the subject of Carly's staying. She seemed more interested in learning about her daughter's new family.

After a couple of hours, Aunt Sandra and Brooke had to leave to do errands, but Grandma stayed to continue her visit. Aunt Maria went in to clean up the kitchen, leaving Carly and her mother with Grandma. It was the first time her mother had spoken at length to her father's mother. With both women praising him, there was no animosity between the two. Carly found it weird to hear them speak so candidly about her father.

Her grandma explained, "He received his degree in architecture after he came back from California. He never spoke about what had happened there, but somehow he seemed different. Eventually he decided that his best prospects for work would be in New York City. He was right. He joined a company there and did quite well."

"I'm happy to hear that," Amanda said.

"After a while, he met a young woman in his field. They lived together for many years, but never married. Of course, his father

261

and I were disappointed that there were no grandchildren. But after a while, we resigned ourselves to the fact that he was happy with his life, and we were happy for him. And then, the unthinkable happened. I never knew that he was sick until I got that horrible phone call."

"I'm sure," Amanda said. "I was so sorry to get that call from your sister, too. It had seemed that he and I had been together in another life, but the news brought it to the forefront again."

"I know things couldn't have been easy for you, raising a child on your own."

"That was my choice, not his. I want you to know that. He was ready to marry me. I was young and self-centered. I didn't realize that denying him his daughter would hurt him so much."

"Thank you for telling me that. And did you ever marry?"

"No. Guess it took me too long to realize that I'd had the best, because I've never found anyone better."

Carly found her mother's comments about her father bizarre. Her mother had never said she was sorry she didn't marry her dad. This was a side of her Carly had never seen.

Her mom continued, "Carly tells me that your mother was quite the independent woman herself. And quite successful as a result."

"Oh, yes. We're all very proud of her legacy." Grandma looked at Carly. "It so happens that Maria is storing a trunk full of my mother's mementos in her attic. Would you both like to see them?"

Up in the attic, her mother and grandmother watched as Carly touched each keepsake with reverence.

"Here's that picture of Tina that I told you about." Carly handed her mother the photo.

"That's incredible. You were right. There's definitely a resemblance."

"Oh, look. Here are some of her sketches. Oh, and newspaper ads of her fashions. Mom, here's the ad for her pants that she saw in *Vogue* that that guy stole from her."

"No kidding. That's terrific."

"And"—Grandma unzipped a vinyl bag—"here are the original pants she sewed for herself."

"Oh my God, they're cool. And there are her initials, C.B. Constantina Benedetti. She sewed them into everything she made."

Grandma handed her a letter on yellowed stationary.

"What's this?"

"It's the letter she wrote to your great-grandfather, Tommy, to tell him he was in Miss Snow's will."

"Unbelievable. He kept it, and she saved it."

"I heard that was some love story," Amanda said.

"Oh, it was, Mom. I'll tell you the whole story one of these days."

"Oh dear," Grandma said. "It's time for me to help Aunt Maria make dinner. We're losing the light, anyway. You can come back up with Aunt Maria tomorrow morning. That's the best light."

"Oh yes, Carly," her mother prompted, "we should all go help with dinner."

"One thing before we go." Grandma pulled a metal box out of the trunk. "There are some interesting sewing what-nots in here."

Carly took the box from her, lifted the lid, and thumbed through it. "Oh, cool. Pins, needles, thread puller, and wow." Carly pulled out a gold thimble. "Look at this."

"That was my grandmother Luciana's thimble that she brought with her from the old country. Mama used it many years, and then for fear of losing it, she stored it safely away."

"That's amazing." Carly put it on her finger. It was like holding hands with Tina.

"So you like it, honey?" Grandma placed her hand on Carly's shoulder.

"Oh, yes."

"Well, it's yours."

<hr />

That night in their room, Amanda pulled the covers back, sat down on the bed, and patted it. "So sit down and tell me more about your plan to stay here and go to school."

Carly knew it had to come up, but the matter-of-fact way her mother said it took Carly by surprise. "Well, I kind of like it here. It's different."

"It is very pretty, but I understand that it snows a lot."

Carly sat down. "I know. I like snow. It was fun in Colorado that time."

"Of course it was. We were on vacation at a resort, but you've never lived in it. It's not so easy to drive in, either."

"It can't be that bad. I'm a good driver."

"And what do you plan on driving? Your Mustang is in the garage in Encinitas."

"That's true."

"Carly, why do you really want to stay here?"

"I told you. I like being with my father's relatives. They're kind of cool. Different than anyone I've known."

"How?"

Carly thought a moment. "They have history. They know who they are."

"And my family doesn't?"

"Sure, I guess they do."

"Mmm. So you're saying that you want to go to school here, so you can spend a year with them?"

"Yes."

"And then what? You'll come home and go to design school? Or is it that you don't want to be a fashion designer anymore?"

"Of course I do. Even more than before. Now I know I was meant to do it. Like my great-grandmother. If she could do what she did with so many odds against her, I have no excuse."

"And you expect to do that at a small junior college here?"

"No, I want to apply to a design school in New York City, so I can be in the heart of the fashion industry. It's too late for this year, but I could start next fall."

Her mother stood and walked to the other side of the room. Without turning to face Carly, she said, "Well, you really have thought this through. It didn't take you very long."

"I know. I think I knew that second day, when grandma told me the story about Tina."

Silence filled the air. "Come on. It's late. Let's get some sleep." Amanda sat on the edge of the bed and checked her phone for messages. "We'll talk more about this tomorrow."

The next morning, Carly awoke to an empty room. She threw on her shorts and t-shirt and galloped downstairs.

"Good morning, Aunt Maria. Have you seen my mom?"

"Well, good morning, sleepyhead. She took her coffee outside."

Carly stepped out and breathed deeply. She had learned to appreciate the crisp fragrant mornings on the farm. She wiped some dew off the rocking chair and sat down next to her mother. "The seasons must be changing," Carly said. "Even that big oak's leaves are turning brown."

"I bet it'll be gorgeous here in a few weeks."

"What do you say? Will I be around here to see it?"

"I don't know, Carly. I've been up most of the night thinking about it. There's a lot to consider, and you'll be so far away."

"I know, Mom. I know I'll miss you. That's going to be the hardest part."

"That's true, but that's not all. What would you do for a car in Kingsburg? It would be way too expensive to get the Mustang out here, and we'd have to sell it to buy you some used car to drive until you go to the city. Besides, you would have to pay out-of-state tuition for a year, and that would cut into your college savings account."

Amanda took a sip of coffee. "I'm guessing the tuition would be about the same at the school in New York City as it would be in San Diego. But your living expenses would be over the top. The rents are outrageous. The great thing about FIDM San Diego is that you can live at home. You certainly couldn't afford a car in New York, so you'd have to take public transportation all the time. And all that is not counting the airfare back and forth to San Diego for you and me, and you know we'd want to do that whenever we could."

"Jeez, I guess I didn't think about all that stuff."

"Sweetie, I want you to follow your dream, but just because you don't go to a New York design school doesn't mean you can't go there to work later. I'm afraid you'll have to go to school at home as planned."

⊷⊶

Carly spent the rest of the day alone, walking through the countryside and into town. She passed by the house where Tommy and Tina had raised their family, and she sat on a bench in the park where Miss Snow had ordered the mayor to build the pool. She and her mother were leaving the next day, and she wanted to feel close to the people so long ago who were responsible for her existence.

That night, the whole family gathered at Aunt Sandra's house for a farewell dinner. As usual, the food tasted wonderful, and the evening was spent reminiscing and sharing family stories that dated back to Italy. As the evening wound down, Carly called everyone to attention.

"As you all know, I didn't really want to come here. I fought my hardest to talk my mom out of it, but it was a losing battle. Now, I'm glad, though. I'm sorry for the way I acted when I first got here. Luckily, I was smart enough to appreciate all of the love and kindness that you all showed me anyway." She looked over at Brooke and grinned. "Well, with the exception of Brooke."

Brooke shrugged and mouthed, "Sorry."

"Getting to know my dad, through his family, was a dream come true—one I didn't even know I had. So thank you all very much."

The group responded with like comments until Carly spoke out again.

"By the way, you probably know that I was hoping to come back here for a year of college and then go to New York City for design school. Well, Mom arrived and informed me that there's not enough money in our budget to do that. So, it's back to San Diego for school. But she promised me that I can spend next summer here. And maybe"—Carly looked at Aunt Sandra—"we can even get Brooke's parents to send her to our house for spring break."

Aunt Sandra smiled. "Well, that can probably be arranged."

Everyone was pitching in to clean up the kitchen when Grandma waved Carly and Amanda toward her bedroom and told them to sit.

"There is something that you need to know. It's about your father. It's something that he did for you a long time ago. After he left California and went back to graduate school here, he took out a life insurance policy with Carly as the beneficiary."

Amanda's hand flew to her mouth. "Oh my God, he did?"

"Obviously, since he'd never told us about you, we learned about it from his attorney, after he passed."

"I don't believe it," Carly said. "What does that mean?"

With watery eyes, Grandma handed her a certificate and some other papers. "It means that because he cared so much about you"—she glanced at Amanda—"that even though he couldn't have you in his life, he wanted you to know that he was thinking of you."

"And, Mom, you never knew?"

Amanda shook her head, and reached for a tissue on the nightstand.

"Apparently he started with ten dollars a month and increased it over the years. As a result, the total cash value is $75,000."

Carly couldn't speak, but Amanda threw her arms around Theresa. "Oh, Michael," she sobbed.

After they had all regained their composure, Grandma spoke directly to Carly.

"Well, sweetheart, with this and your college fund, you probably have enough to go to whatever school you want. But if you'll take some advice from your wise old grandma, you will go back home to your college for at least a year. You have a lot to learn about the fashion business, and I understand that it's a pretty good school for that.

"If at any point you feel you're ready for New York, you can go. You're a very lucky girl. You have two loving parents who have provided well for you, given you options. You also have an extended family, past and present, from which to grow. But always remember that you are your own person. You will succeed or fail by your own strengths and ambitions."